THE OCEAN IS ON FIRE!

"GOOD EVENING. A NEWS FLASH HAS JUST REACHED THE NETWORK, REPORTING AN INTERNATIONAL DISASTER OF UNPRECEDENTED PROPORTIONS. SHORTLY AFTER DAWN THIS MORNING TWO MILLION-TON TANKERS COLLIDED OFF SOUTHERN ALASKA IN HEAVY FOG. BOTH SHIPS WERE FULLY LOADED: THE AMERICAN, THE *KODIAK,* WITH CRUDE; THE RUSSIAN, THE *SAKHALIN,* WITH A CARGO OF HIGH OCTANE . . . AN OCEAN AREA OF ALMOST TWO THOUSAND SQUARE MILES CAUGHT FIRE EARLY THIS MORNING AND IS NOW BURNING FIERCELY OFF THE NORTH AMERICAN CONTINENT . . . TOTALLY OUT OF CONTROL."

FIRESPILL

A novel about the fire of the century

FIRESPILL
IAN SLATER

BANTAM BOOKS
TORONTO
NEW YORK
LONDON

FIRESPILL

A Bantam Book / published by arrangement with
McClelland and Stewart Limited
Bantam edition / September 1977

ISBN 0-553-10890-5

Bantam Books are published by Bantam Books, Inc. Its trademark, consisting of the words "Bantam Books" and the portrayal of a bantam, is registered in the United States Patent Office and in other countries. Marca Registrada. Bantam Books, Inc., 666 Fifth Avenue, New York, New York 10019.

PRINTED IN THE UNITED STATES OF AMERICA

For MARIAN

ACKNOWLEDGMENTS

I would like to thank the following for their help in the preparation of this book:

At the University of British Columbia, my gratitude is extended to Robert Macdonald, an old oceanographic shipmate of mine in the Department of Geology, and in particular Dr. K. L. Pinder of the Chemical Engineering Department.

I am grateful for the information and courtesy given me by both the United States Air Force and the Canadian Armed Forces, specifically by Major D. M. Ryan and Captain W. R. Aikman of the Department of National Defence's Office of Information, Esquimalt, British Columbia; and submarine Sub-Lieutenant M. A. Dunne, also of Esquimalt. Special thanks must go to submariner Lieutenant Gary Davis, Canadian Armed Forces (Navy), for his patience and expertise.

Most of all I am indebted to my wife, Marian, whose typing and grammatical skills have augmented her invaluable support to me in my work.

Ian Slater
Vancouver, B.C.

ONE

June 22

"I do think they could have given you a bit more notice."

Captain James Kyle, a short, robust fifty-three-year-old with a cherubic smile and thinning white hair, moved slightly in his kitchen chair to face the bedroom where his wife was hurriedly packing his seabag. "Phil Limet hardly knew he had a heart attack coming, Sarah."

"Oh, I suppose not." Sarah maneuvered a bulging toilet kit into the seabag and checked his socks for the third time. "I just want to have you at home, that's all. I'm sorry for Mr. Limet, and I hope he recovers. I didn't mean to be unfeeling, love."

"I never believed otherwise." Kyle turned back to the big kitchen window. It was almost time to go, but he lingered over his coffee, taking a last look at their garden, his eyes straying beyond to the ships in Esquimalt Harbor, lying like toys on the wide gray slate that stretched out from the southern tip of Vancouver Island. It was the beginning of a long, hot summer on Canada's west coast, and they had told him he would not be back before the fall. By then the black-red blossoms of the Nocturne roses might be finished.

Picking up the binoculars that he always kept by the kitchen's picture window, Kyle focused on a huge, black, rectangular form in the distance. Looking like a skyscraper floating on its side, it slowly made its way through the Strait of Juan de Fuca. It was the MV *Kodiak,* one of the giant American supratankers. No moral problem there, he thought, apprehensive about his own cruise. Three months boxed up in a submarine with a crew of raw recruits. For a moment, he envied the officers aboard the million-tonner, which now began cranking out its side fins and opening its bulbous nose to take in water in order to brake its 190,000 horse power, seventeen-knot push into the waters of Georgia Strait towards the refinery and shore leave at Cherry Point, Washington. Their pay was better than his, and even if life wasn't varied on a "floating armada," as each of the tankers was called, he imagined that it might be a pleasant change—at least for a time. Tricky work, steering these monsters through the treacherous reef- and island-peppered coastline all the way down from Alaska's ice-free port of Valdez past Sitka in the Alexander Archipelago to Point Conception in California nineteen hundred miles away or to Puget Sound in Washington State. But the idea of a twelve-day return journey in place of the three months ahead of him now was singularly appealing.

But as it always did, the idea went cold. He reminded himself that he hated the smell of the hydrocarbon vapors that escaped whenever the crude was pumped out from the forty cavernous hundred-and-twenty-foot-deep tanks that each held twenty-five thousand tons of oil. He didn't mind the smell of diesel, even in the confined space of a submarine that would look like a slug next to a whale alongside the *Kodiak,* but he hated the smell of the unrefined crude. He sympathized with the fight that the California Air Resources Board had put up—and lost—in trying to stop the tankers from coming down the West Coast. Every time one of them unloaded in California or near the Canadian border in Washington State, it pumped at least a hundred and sixty tons of hydrocarbon vapors into the air—as much as would come from the exhaust fumes of twelve million automobiles in twenty-four hours. But the discovery of oil on the Alaskan North Slope in the Beaufort Sea and the desperate need for fuel during the Arab embargoes of the seventies had finally defeated the environmentalists. Soon project "Skinny City," the eight-hundred-mile, four-foot-diameter steel pipe that carried one point two million barrels a day across Alaska from the Beaufort Sea to the North Pacific, was feeding the supratankers. From Valdez the high-sulphur crude made its way southward via tanker to the long-established, ever-expanding refineries of the U.S. West Coast. These refineries complemented Alaska's own relatively small refining facility. As far as Kyle was concerned it was utterly insane, but nonetheless the Alaskan refinery also supplied Russia with high octane as part of a massive Russian grain deal with the United States.

Still thinking about the price his lungs might have to pay on the supratankers—gas masks or not—Kyle decided that he didn't want any part of their run after all, no matter how fantastic he'd heard the scenery around Sitka was, no matter how high the pay or how high the "hazard" bonus, which everyone knew was really a "poison" bonus. He'd stick with the navy. Putting the MV *Kodiak* out of his mind, he lowered the binoculars and sipped his coffee.

Sarah, glancing down the bungalow's small corridor to make sure James was still in the kitchen, quickly scribbled a message on a thin slip of paper and tucked it into a pair of socks. "Your things are all packed," she called.

Kyle didn't answer. He was thinking, somewhat guiltily, about how he had told Sarah that "orders were orders" even though he knew that because of his age he could have refused and they probably wouldn't have pressed him. He was both reluctant and eager to go. Reluctant because it meant leaving Sarah alone, now that the three children were grown up and gone, but eager because he had never lost the thrill of going to sea. When he had unexpectedly received his orders, he had experienced the same excitement he had known over thirty years before when he had first joined the navy. Of course he knew he was just a fill-in on short notice, but that didn't make him any less enthusiastic.

Swordfish's previous commander, Phil Limet, had

suffered the coronary barely four hours before, and Kyle had been ordered by Maritime Command in Halifax to take charge of the sub immediately.

"Couldn't they postpone the patrol?" Sarah had asked.

"The preparations are too far advanced, hon. The politicians wanted to stop money for patrols. But the Old Man put up quite a stink—said that the only way Canada could insist on a two-hundred-mile fishing zone and a twelve-mile mineral zone was to show the flag, otherwise we'd lose the grab-as-grab-can game between the other Pacific Rim countries. That got Ottawa off its butt and got us the money."

"I thought it was to train new recruits?"

"That too. That's the other thing the Old Man drove home. Said how the hell can we have an active core of submariners—let alone a reserve—if we don't train them? Ottawa couldn't disagree."

Kyle knew full well that in the near future he would be referred to by the admiral as a case in point. At fifty-three he would normally have been considered far too old for command of a submarine. Actually he was several years older than his record showed, having enlisted when the recruiters of a volunteer navy weren't too concerned about birth certificates. Soon after the war he had become one of the youngest sub commanders in the Canadian Navy.

Now ex-sub captains were being transferred in their late thirties, at the latest in their forties, to the kind of desk job that Kyle had endured for the past seven years in SOAMCP—Submarine Operating Authority for Maritime Command (Pacific). But the navy was so short of experienced men due to the long-range effects of postwar cutbacks that Kyle had been the only logical short-notice choice. It was what an old sub commander tied to the dull grind of a nine-to-five office job dreamed of—a chance to flee the files and get back to the real job of the navy.

Still, he was anxious and Sarah knew it. She knew that it wasn't only that he'd miss her, as she would him. There was something else. It couldn't be that he hadn't been to sea for so long; he'd kept up with all the refresher courses. And *Swordfish,* after all, was a conventional Ranger class sub, and he knew well enough how to handle one of those. She began massaging his shoulders. "What's wrong?" she asked gently.

"Oh, nothing," he replied unconvincingly.

"Tell me."

He moved uncomfortably, almost angrily, in his chair. "Oh, it's all this damned 'democratization' business they're pushing through now. The 'new breed' of sailor that I'll be in charge of." He almost spat the words out. "It's no longer a navy where you do what you're told." He half turned towards her. "Can you believe that under the new rules the men can elect—*elect,* for God's sake—representatives to air grievances directly with commanding officers almost at will? What a way to run a navy!"

"But you've been doing all right. It hasn't bothered you before—has it? At least not this much."

Kyle grunted. "Of course it has. But ashore, behind a desk, I can walk away from it at the end of the day, come home to you and forget all about it. At sea you have to live with it twenty-four hours a day—every day till the end of the patrol."

Sarah could feel the tension in his back muscles increasing as his voice rose. "Christ, in my day you kept your mouth shut, did your job and helped win a war." He turned suddenly in his chair. "I was saying the same thing to Phil Limet only last week. I don't know why in hell these bastards who aren't prepared to obey orders join the submarine service in the first place. I don't know why they join anything, to tell you the truth."

Sarah didn't like him to use obscenities, but she knew better than to interject. She hadn't seen him so angry since she couldn't remember when. She forced her fingers deep into the muscle, but it was like pushing into taut leather.

"Christ," continued Kyle. "Look sometime at the stupid bloody posters they're putting up all over the place. 'Join the new breed,' they say. Before their precious new breed will obey an order, they have to cross-examine it." He turned to look at Sarah. "They might get hurt, you see. Couldn't risk that—might even get their hands dirty."

Sarah smiled faintly.

"I'm not kidding you, Sarah. You should hear them. And can you believe they're allowed to wear civvies on sub duty? Civvies! Looks like a bloody Los Angeles street. Next they'll be assigning a crew's lawyer aboard."

"But they can't all be that way, can they?" suggested Sarah hesitantly.

She felt his muscles relax a little. He rubbed his eyes and ran his fingers through his thinning hair. He spoke more quietly now. "No. Course you're right. Guess I'm just keyed up. Been bugging me for months."

"Feel better now?"

Kyle forced a smile. "Yes, love. Thanks for listening."

"That's all right. I'll put it on your bill."

He patted her hand, calmer now he'd vented his anxiety.

After a few more minutes of rubbing his back, Sarah's fingers grew tired and weak, but she kept forcing them deeper into his shoulder muscles.

"Hm, that's good," he murmured appreciatively, willing her to keep going. In the reflection of the kitchen window Kyle saw that the last traces of youth had deserted his wife's deep brown eyes. This morning, dressed in a well-worn tweed suit, she looked much older than her fifty-two years, the worry lines creasing her forehead as she worked hard on his shoulders.

"I didn't go looking to leave you, Sare. I don't want to leave you. Never did."

She felt tears starting again, so she rubbed a little harder and laughed. "Oh why don't you admit it, Jim Kyle—you just wanted to leave me with all the weeding."

"Well, it won't be long, sweetheart."

She punched him good-humoredly on the shoulder. "Not long? Not long, he says. Three *months!* I'd hate to know what you call a long time."

"Well, the nuclear boys in the States are sometimes out for six."

"Oh, lovely," said Sarah.

"Three months is better than six."

"Hmm—I suppose. Will you be stopping off anywhere?"

"No. Haven't seen the written orders yet, but the usual drill for these long training runs is to go right through."

"Oh. I was hoping you'd be able to write."

"I'll do better than that. I'll think of you every day."

Suddenly Sarah started to cry. Kyle got up, knocking over his cup and spilling the remainder of the coffee on his newly pressed uniform. Sarah reached for a tea cloth and began wiping his trousers. He gently took the cloth away from her and put his arm about her. "Sare—" She buried her head against his chest as his other arm enveloped her. "Sare, honey, I'm not going to war, baby. It's just a patrol."

"I know," she sobbed. "But everybody's—"

"Everybody's what?" he asked softly.

"Everybody's so—so dangerous nowadays. Everybody's trying to kill one another."

"Sare, honey, this is just a routine training run. Out towards Japan, up north and back to Vancouver Island. It's a milk run. No trouble out there—just fish."

"Oh, I know," she said, pushing herself away and wiping her eyes. "I know. Good Lord," she added, admonishing herself gently, "it isn't as if you'd never gone before. But you're not as young as you used to be."

He smiled at her, bent to lift his seabag, and stopped for a moment. "No, I'm not. You're right, Sare—I am older. But I love you."

She said nothing, but put her head against his shoulder and walked hand in hand with him to the car as if they were still courting. It had always been their custom for her to drive him to and from the base whenever he had gone to sea. As Sarah drove the VW Rabbit out along the dirt track through the firs to the highway, Kyle gazed proudly over the garden's brilliant profusion of flowers and shrubs, from the cherry red roses to the deep royal blue of the lobelia borders sloping down towards the bottle green fir woods. But of everything in the garden he liked the dark Nocturne roses best, because he and Sarah had planted them together. As they drove past the old cedar gate, he watched a fat bumblebee taking nectar from the heart of a rose, and momentarily he envied it its freedom. Right now there was nothing he would like better than to putter round the garden all summer with Sarah.

On the way to the base they didn't talk very much, except for a few words about the roses, which were just as special to Sarah, and about how the tomatoes would probably ripen earlier this year. It was a hazy Vancouver Island day, warm but not too hot, with a gentle breeze coming in from the sea.

From the summit of a high hill they could see a long trail of log booms being dragged by an ant-sized tug across Juan de Fuca Strait. In front of them a huge semitrailer, coughing black clouds of smoke, roared as it topped the peak of the oil-stained grade. Kyle wound up the window to keep out the diesel smell of the truck. He would be breathing enough of that for the next ninety days. Sarah tried to pull out around the truck but dropped back at the last moment, afraid to pass. She hated the monstrous machines; they frightened her in the same way that submarines did.

When they reached Esquimalt Base, Sarah pulled the car over beside the main gate. She had never wanted to see the ships he sailed on, having been brought up to believe that anything that floated was unsafe and that submarines were therefore the unsafest of all. She had never forgotten hearing a junior officer at their home explaining to the children why so many doors were closed on a sub during emergencies. He had described the conventional sub as "not much more than nine hollow steel balls welded together with one or two on top, with a streamlined casing that makes the boat look much stronger than it really is." Sarah harbored the same idea about machines that many have about the sick—that if you avoid them you'll be spared their fate. She did not subscribe to the theory that the more you know about them the less frightened you are of them. She believed that if she knew all the things that could go wrong with a car, she'd never drive one. Besides, it was enough strain to wave your husband good-bye; knowing the details, all the terrible possibilities, only made it worse.

As Kyle leaned over to get his seabag from the trunk, Sarah noticed once again how his movements betrayed the fact that he was a man well beyond his prime, a man too old for submarine duty.

Seeing the armed guard at the gate, she was reminded of all the times they had parted during the war. Suddenly she felt the chill of old farewells flooding back. She kissed him gently but quickly on the cheek. He hugged her, and she said in a choking whisper, "Now mind the cold," fidgeting momentarily with his collar as if it were crooked. He squeezed her hand and walked through the gate.

The world around was at peace. The waters of Juan de Fuca Strait were only faintly rippled, the sun had brightened, and the sky was empty of clouds. But Sarah did not feel at peace. She felt the same as she had thirty-six years ago, before they were married, when she had seen him off from the other side of the country to the war in the Atlantic.

The guard saluted her and smiled. She said hello, not recognizing the man, and turned to the car before she lost her composure.

Leading Seaman Lambrecker's farewell in a downtown Victoria apartment had been much shorter. His face, dominated by pale blue, deep-set eyes, was long and thin like the rest of his body, and for a man of barely thirty-five he had a hungry, tired look. He had been awake since five that morning, lying still in the darkness of the bedroom, his creased face illuminated now and then by the glow of a cigarette as he tried endlessly to unravel the tangle of lies and frustrations threatening to strangle what remained of his two-year-old marriage.

Before going to bed he and Frances had been arguing again. They had been shouting louder than usual. "You're a monk," she had yelled. "You always want to stay in. Jesus Christ—hanging around that tub of yours all the goddamn time, you'd think when you had a chance you'd want to break out. I'm *twenty*-seven, not fifty-seven! I want some fun. Christ, I don't know—why can't you let your hair down like normal people do instead of locking yourself up like a monk?"

"Like Morgan, you mean," he had replied acidly.

"Yeah, like Morgan," she answered, her jaw moving up and down on her wad of gum. "At least he knows how to enjoy himself."

"Son of a bitch is too dumb to do anything else."

Fran pouted her lips as if addressing a petulant child. "Tch, tch. That a fact? Well, he's not too dumb to be a lieutenant, is he now?"

It was then that Lambrecker had lost his temper and grabbed her by the arm. For months Morgan—his half brother, a lieutenant in air force stores—had come between them, ever since the day he arrived from back east with that damned imitation French Canadian accent of his that sent Fran into gales of laughter.

A hundred times Lambrecker had wanted to smash Morgan's face in, but instead he kept hoping that Fran would get tired of him. Besides, he knew that if he ever laid a hand on Morgan, it would be an enlisted man's word against an officer's.

Still, whenever he thought of all the times he had come home from Esquimalt Base to find Morgan lounging nonchalantly in the kitchen, his feet up on the window ledge, laughing and drinking with Fran,

Lambrecker wanted to kill him. His grip had tightened on Fran's arm.

She had screamed. "Let go of me, you idiot!"

Lambrecker had pushed her away roughly before he could hurt her.

"Oh dear me," she taunted, straightening the transparent blouse that looked like a second skin. "Look at his wittle eyes—they all bulging out. Poor wittle him."

"Jesus Christ!" he had yelled, sweeping the kitchen table clean with his fists, sending a pile of sticky sauce bottles, plastic plates, and spent beer cans crashing to the floor. Fran surveyed the debris scattered about the cheap linoleum. She flushed with anger, but then smiled sweetly. "Oh—wittle man's gone all crazy again. Poor, poor wittle man."

They hadn't spoken since. It was a repetition of what had happened a hundred times before—the unbearably long silence that he knew he would break though he'd vowed not to.

He didn't know whether Morgan was sleeping with her yet. But underneath it all, beneath the hatred he had for his half brother, he still loved Fran. He couldn't explain why and he didn't even try to. He only knew that while he was a loner, a man who did not need friends like others, he did need at least one person who needed him, and that person, he still believed, was Fran. It never occurred to him that she might be staying with him only for simple financial security.

He drew heavily on another cigarette. It wasn't sex that had been the cause of it all—at least that hadn't been the trouble at the beginning. Now, of course, they never made love. But he recalled that even when that part of their life had been all right, she had started acting strangely—yelling and screaming at him over trivialities each time he had come home.

It was only then, that morning as he lay silently smoking beside her, that it occurred to him that it was possible she'd been sleeping with someone before Morgan had even arrived on the scene, that she was just using Morgan as an excuse after the fact. Her remark about his half brother's being a lieutenant came back to Lambrecker as he lay staring out at the pale wash of dawn. The other man must be an officer. It would have to be some son of a bitch impressing her with his rank, he thought. She loved to imagine herself always moving up in society, refused to settle for what she had.

Lambrecker turned towards his wife. His eyes followed the contour of her body from her hip to her neck. He could see nothing else. She took care nowadays to wrap her shapely figure in uninviting nightdresses obviously designed to dissuade him from making any advance. He put his cigarette out, pushed it so hard that the still burning butt scorched his finger. He turned back to look at her. Who was it? For a moment he had the impulse to slap her awake and beat her until she told him, put his hands around her neck and choke the life out of her. Instead, he quickly got up and dressed, then gulped some cereal and shaved.

After a while he returned to the bedroom and stood motionless in the doorway, watching. She moved a little in her sleep and the blanket slid off her shoulders, revealing the gentle rise and fall of her breasts beneath the pink nylon as she breathed.

He thought her more beautiful than when he had married her. He knew women were supposed to become less attractive more rapidly than men, but to him she had improved with age. There was now a fullness about her figure that made her seem even more sensuous. He remembered when he had first seen her; she had reminded him of Lauren Bacall. She still did. Gradually, after the realization that he would not see her for three months had struck him full force, his anger started to ebb. He bent down to kiss her forehead. Suddenly her hands shot out from beneath the covers and pulled the blankets over her head. Aware now that she had known he'd been watching her—desiring her—Lambrecker felt humiliated. He grabbed viciously at his seabag, stamped into the kitchen, and rang for a cab. The dispatcher, bothered by static, asked him to repeat the address. He shouted it this time and slammed down the receiver. Taking care to bang the door, he walked out into the gray, crushed-stone parking lot where the sun never came, and waited in the early morning chill.

He was beginning to hate the coming patrol—more than he had any other. It would take him, not for a rest, but away from the chance to fix what was wrong. For some men such a cruise would have meant an escape. For Lambrecker it would be torture. The only possible explanation for Fran's behavior was that she had taken a lover even before Morgan. He tried not to think who the other man might be. He wanted to lock out the thought until he returned from sea, until he could do something about it. But the more he tried not to think about it, the more it filled his mind, until it was the only thought he had. For a moment he contemplated going AWOL; then he dismissed the idea, not because he thought it was wrong, but because it would not help him solve anything if the MPs were hunting him.

His wife's comment about Morgan's being a lieutenant kept haunting him, and the more he thought of the other man, the more certain he became that it was an officer. "And what," he thought as the cab drove down towards the taverns on Esquimalt Road, "can you do against an officer?"

The executive officer of H.M.C.S. *Swordfish* gave Kyle a brisk salute. "Welcome aboard, sir."

"Thank you. Bud O'Brien, isn't it?"

"Yes, sir."

"Pleased to meet you." They shook hands. O'Brien, a tall, deeply tanned man in his early thirties, nodded appreciatively.

"Same here, sir," he said, his heavy eyebrows not moving as he took care not to register surprise at Kyle's age. Kyle didn't notice; he was too busy looking at the boat. From the moment he had stepped aboard the long, black sub, resting in the water like a harbor seal, he had felt the old sense of security afforded by the various symbols and the familiar routine, from the Canadian flag at the stern to the officer on watch. Doubtless first impressions were often wrong, but O'Brien immediately added to Kyle's general sense of well-being. The sub's black, slatted decking was spotless, the flag lanyard taut, and though the bridge surface had been recently painted, the small night-running light set aft of it at the base of the metal sail was clear of even a speck of paint. They were small things, but they told Kyle a lot about the first officer. O'Brien might be much younger, but he obviously wasn't a paid-up member of the "new breed." He did things right.

Of course the sub's performance and endurance had been updated. She had been fitted out with large Exide-Tarpon batteries that greatly reduced recharging time, and a streamlined hull that now gave her a submerged speed of eighteen knots. Even so, for a moment Kyle felt as if he had just stepped back in time and said good-bye to Sarah before going on yet another Arctic convoy run. Some things would be unfamiliar, but from the refresher courses he knew that things had not changed so much that all the old ways had been abandoned. Before he unpacked his seabag he asked to see his engineering, electrical, navigating, and weapons officers in the control room, immediately below the conning tower. With such a short time remaining before sailing, he had no time for a more informal gathering with his officers. His first job was to ascertain the state of the sub's readiness.

"Enginecring Officer?"

"Sir?"

"Diesels fully charged?"

"Yes, sir, and all air banks fully charged."

Kyle grinned slightly. "Good, but never volunteer additional information." The others laughed, and the moment of tension when a new commander first meets his officers was over. Kyle went on. "But seeing as you're so keen, Chief, how about the compressors? All operational?"

"A-1, sir."

"Good. Navigating Officer?"

O'Brien stepped forward. "I'm doubling up for that, sir."

"Right. How about our charts?"

"Everything we need, sir."

"Sea of Japan?"

O'Brien was impressed. The Old Man might look like a museum piece, but he was certainly up to date. "Yes, sir, I know it's just been revised. It came down this morning."

Kyle nodded. "Fine. Weapons Officer?"

O'Brien spoke again. "He's been held up in traffic, sir." Kyle glanced disapprovingly at his watch. "Hm. Well, he'd better hurry it up. Can you tell me what fish we're carrying?"

O'Brien opened his tunic pocket and flipped over some pages of his notebook. "Six war shots and eight exercise, sir."

Kyle nodded. "Right, carry on. I'll discuss our course with you later, Mr. O'Brien."

"Yes, sir."

After O'Brien showed the captain to his tiny cabin, the two men went up to the bridge so that Kyle could inspect the new compass mounting. They were just in time to see a crewman coming down the gangplank. Pretending not to see them, the sailor raised his hand in a particularly sloppy salute to the Canadian flag astern instead of to O'Brien as officer of the watch. O'Brien called out angrily to him. "Lambrecker!"

Lambrecker wheeled a little unsteadily and walked up to the bridge without answering, openly scowling at the first officer.

"Lambrecker, why didn't you salute the officer of the watch?"

Lambrecker stared ahead. "Didn't see you. Sir."

Kyle had noticed something odd in the way Lambrecker had swung about in response to O'Brien's call. He stepped forward. "Are you ill?"

Lambrecker stared ahead.

Kyle's face flushed. "I asked you if you're ill."

"No."

"No *sir!*" bellowed O'Brien.

"No, sir," answered Lambrecker sourly, still staring ahead. Kyle turned to O'Brien, who by now knew as well as the captain what was the matter. "This man's drunk. Put him on a charge."

"Yes, sir. Lambrecker, follow me."

Applying extraordinary concentration to his walk, Lambrecker endeavored to walk a straight line behind O'Brien. As he disappeared down the conning tower he shot a defiant glare at Kyle. The captain shouted after him, "Come back up here, you!"

Lambrecker hesitated for a second, then crawled up. As regulations dictated, he stood at attention; but his slovenly demeanor plainly teetered on the brink of insolence.

Kyle's face was purple. Nothing enraged him more than this kind of unspoken insubordination. He came across it daily on shore. The "democratization" of the navy. Well, "democratization" or not, the only way to deal with old-fashioned insubordination was by the old-fashioned method—let the smartasses know that you weren't going to tolerate it.

"Stand up straight, man," Kyle snapped.

"I am. Sir."

"You listen to me, sailor. You look at me like that again and there'll be trouble. Understand?"

Lambrecker looked down at O'Brien as if utterly confounded, then turned back to face Kyle. "How are we supposed to look? Sir?"

Kyle ignored the baiting tone. "You're supposed to look respectful."

"Of what? Sir."

O'Brien glanced first at the deck, then out to sea. Jesus, he thought, what a start to a three-month cruise, and a training one at that.

"Respectful of rank, sailor—that's what," answered Kyle.

"Oh," began Lambrecker, and belched, issuing another cloud of spirit fumes. "Oh, now I remember, sir," he said facetiously. "It's not the man we salute; it's the rank, isn't it?"

Kyle had not known such anger since the war. The veins in his temples bulged and he clung desperately to his self-control. "Get below!" he snapped. "Long voyage or not, sailor, you ever turn up in this condition again and you'll be more than on the charge sheet. You'll be in front of a court-martial. Now get yourself sober before we cast off."

Lambrecker saluted and descended the conning tower for a second time, grinning smugly to himself.

O'Brien climbed to the bridge again. Quite unreasonably, he somehow felt responsible for the crewman's condition. "Sorry about that, sir," he said apologetically.

Kyle, by now somewhat cooler, waved it aside. "Not your fault. Is that his usual style? Or is he a newcomer?"

"No, he's one of the old hands," answered O'Brien, looking puzzled. "Matter of fact, I don't recall him ever being drunk before. He's a bit moody at times, but he's not normally the drinking type—or I didn't think he was."

Kyle raised his eyes from the new compass mounting. "Hmm. He did at least salute the ship. But it's his attitude that I mind. I've seen that bitter look before, and it's poison, especially among new recruits. How's he get on with the rest of the old crew?"

O'Brien shrugged. "He's quiet—very quiet. But I've had no complaints."

"We'll keep an eye on Mr. Lambrecker just the same. Don't want any of the new lot bothered by him."

"No, sir."

"Then again," added Kyle, "maybe I shouldn't have chewed him up so much, but dammit, you can't let that kind of thing pass."

"No, sir, I agree."

There was a long silence. Then Kyle said hopefully, "'Course, he was probably working off a head of steam. No doubt he'll be a new man when he sobers up."

"I expect so, sir."

Kyle looked at his Rolex Oyster. "We cast off at 1500, Number One. Call me at ETD minus five."

"Aye, aye, sir."

In crew's quarters Lambrecker, having arrived earlier than most of the men on shore leave, tossed his seabag onto the lower bunk, which he considered his by right of long service. His eyes didn't seem to be focusing properly, so he didn't see another seabag whose owner had chosen the same sleeping space. Before the double occupancy registered, a young, fresh-faced seaman, obviously a newcomer, rushed to apologize. "Sorry, sir."

Lambrecker scowled. "Don't call me sir."

"No, sir. I mean no. Sorry."

Lambrecker swayed a little, steadied himself against the upper bunk, lit another cigarette, then stuck out a callused hand. "Name's Lambrecker."

"Nairn," said the newcomer quickly, only too anxious to make friends.

Quite apart from Lambrecker's drunkenness, there was something about the way his pale blue eyes seemed to look right past you as he was talking which immediately put the youngster on his guard.

"You want the bottom slab?" grunted Lambrecker in the friendliest tone he could manage.

"Oh, doesn't matter. I just tossed my kit there," answered Nairn. "Not much room, is there?"

"It's yours," said Lambrecker, throwing his seabag onto the top bunk.

"I don't mind really—" began Nairn.

Lambrecker cut him short. "It's yours," he said, dragging out his tin of homemade cigarettes and offering it to Nairn.

"No thanks. I don't smoke, but thanks for the bunk."

Lambrecker didn't answer. He pulled down a few things from his bag and stuffed them into a small drawer in the dull scratched aluminum locker. Nairn, not sure what to do, tried to think of something to say. He lifted up the leaves of a small wall calendar hanging on the side of the locker. Each month's leaf had a British Columbia mountain scene on it, and as he flicked up June to see what July's mountain was, he said lightly, "Going to be a long one."

Lambrecker dragged himself laboriously up to the top bunk, wanting to get some sleep before the sub got under way and he was required on station. Thinking that Lambrecker hadn't heard him, Nairn spoke again. "They normally this long? The patrols, I mean."

"All fucking long," answered Lambrecker, dragging a blanket up to his shoulders.

Nairn nodded slightly. "Ah, would you like some coffee? I managed to find the galley." There was no reply.

When he returned from the mess, Nairn sat down on the bunk and drank the lukewarm liquid. It was the worst coffee he'd had for weeks, but he drank it all, partly from habit, partly for something to do. It wasn't until he got up to wash out the sandy dregs from his cup that he noticed three leaves missing from the calendar. June, July, and August had been torn off and lay crumpled on the honeycomb decking. He glanced up at Lambrecker, who now lay smoking and staring at the metal deckhead no more than two or three inches from his nose. The steel plate that seemed to be pressing down on Lambrecker reminded Nairn of stories he had heard at training school about men going claustro, raving mad in close confinement. The thought made him feel uneasy. He looked at the calendar again—at September—and then up at the top bunk. He wondered what would happen when Lambrecker's hangover had passed.

As the *Swordfish* sailed out of Esquimalt Harbor and Kyle slowly began to unpack his seabag, he found Sarah's note stuck in the socks. He drew the green curtain across his cabin door and sat down on the bunk's edge. After all these years, he thought, and felt a deep yearning to hold her, to tell her he would be home soon, that he would never leave her again. He unfolded the note and read, "With you always, My love, Sarah." He put the piece of paper in one of his tunic pockets. As was his custom, he would not look at the note again until they neared the end of the long patrol. In September.

TWO

September 21

It was an unusually mild morning as Elaine Horton, whom Kyle and Lambrecker, like so many others, had often seen but never met, walked down one of the wide streets on the outskirts of Sitka in Alaska's Alexander Archipelago. On either side of the roadway, Colonial-style bungalows, mostly white, lay nestled behind a row of golden-leafed maples, which were interspersed here and there with tall Lombardy poplars whose leaves flickered in the Indian summer breeze.

Elaine wandered aimlessly along the road in the direction of the nearby woods. She shuffled her feet through the summer's accumulation of leaves in an effort to block out the sound of the footsteps around her. But even when she succeeded in not hearing them, she could sense their owners' presence. They were always with her. She had managed, miraculously enough, to escape from the scrutiny of the press these last few days, mainly due to a sudden change in flight plans from Washington. They might as well have followed her; the Secret Service agents gave her the same shut-in feeling. She conceded that they were often necessary, particularly in big crowds, but here in Sitka on her holidays? But she could never convince her aide to leave them behind. Miller was rigid in his insistence that the Secret Service contingent must be on hand at all times, no matter where they were, vacation or no vacation.

"But Richard," she protested, as they continued to stroll, "this is Baranof Island—off the Alaskan Panhandle. No one even *recognizes* me here." He was about to answer, but was interrupted by a small group of schoolchildren who had suddenly materialized and who were gaily rushing Elaine for her autograph.

Miller stood by smugly while the Secret Servicemen carefully watched the cluster of well-wishers. After the group had departed, Elaine turned to Miller. "And if anyone does recognize me, it's precisely because this platoon of yours immediately draws attention to us."

Miller, choosing not to dispute the point with his boss, looked around him at the near-deserted street. "Ma'am, I feel safer in New York than I do here."

Elaine snorted. "You can't possibly mean that."

"Yeah. I mean it's so—so open up here. No protection."

"Open, my God! That's exactly why I came here. I can't fish in Manhattan. I'm tired of skyscrapers and pushy crowds. I like the openness."

"That's why we need all these men," said Miller, shaking his head.

"Well, I warn you, Richard. First gap I see, I'm off."

Miller smiled indulgently yet with dutiful respect. "You're welcome to try, ma'am."

Despite the lighthearted exchange, Elaine really did mean to have some privacy. The pressure was getting to her. She wanted to push Washington out of her mind, to forget about the daily invasion of her desk by hundreds of reports, all crying catastrophe. Long gone were the days when the Vice-President of the United States was considered little more than a parrot of the President. There had been six assassinations of key political figures since Kennedy, so now the Veep was expected to know as much as her boss, in preparation for the chilling possibility of waking up one morning and being addressed as President.

Elaine Horton, at thirty-seven the youngest-ever Vice-President, had once been described by an elderly Republican congressman as a "captivatingly plump" brunette. When she heard about it, Elaine had rolled her hazel eyes in pleased surprise and smiled—captivatingly. Soon the sheer force of her ebullient personality and her easy, efficient style had won over her potentially hostile male colleagues, not only in Congress but in the White House as well. And because she was attractive but not what the society journalists called one of the "beautiful people," she was not perceived as a social threat by those women in Congress who relied upon makeup as much as brains in vying for the prestigious administrative jobs close to the President. She had been raised on the homespun and oft-caricatured virtues of self-discipline and restraint and had carried them with her through a brilliant college career and into the cynical political arena.

The Vice-President became aware of someone coughing nearby. It was Miller's usual way of drawing her attention. She had been so preoccupied that she had not realized she had reached a cul-de-sac and had been standing still for several minutes. The Secret Service was trying to look inconspicuous, peering apprehensively through the trees that stretched far beyond the street. The Secret Service did not like trees. Too much cover. The chief agent had been frowning at Miller to do something, to keep the Vice-President moving. Already the long limousines had slid up behind her, engines purring faintly, sending out long breaths of grey-blue exhaust into the still, clear air. "Perhaps you'd like to ride for a bit," Miller suggested diplomatically.

She glanced at the vice-presidential limousine, heavy and somber with its armor plate and black paint. My God, she thought, it looks like a hearse. It reminded her of the almost successful attempt on the President's life last month in New Orleans. That had shaken her badly at the time. Even now the thought of it sent a slight shiver through her. For the country, it would have been the loss of a leader; but to her it would have meant much more. Their affair which had begun some years before when they were both just members of Congress was over—at least they had both done their best to convince themselves that it was. Theirs was now a strictly professional relationship. She shivered again. Was it?

Miller coughed again, a little louder this time, and Elaine shot him an angry glance. Miller, the agents, everything reminded her of her job. Most of all they reminded her of the President, and it was the President she was trying to forget. Suddenly she felt almost claustrophobic. She would have to break free of the official world—of the constant surveillance—if only for twelve hours or so. She needed somewhere quiet to rest and to think. It would be tough on Miller, but there was no other way. She would put everything right when she returned.

The agents were still looking anxiously about. One of the women spun sharply on her heel when a colleague crunched gravel at her back. Elaine looked around at her protectors, at Miller, and at the chauffeur dressed in black, all patiently waiting. Two of the women agents even accompanied her when she went to the ladies' room. "What's the weather forecast for tomorrow?" she asked, her irritation showing in her voice.

Miller, hardly ever surprised in his job, was momentarily stymied. "I don't know," he admitted reluctantly.

"Then find out, please," she snapped, getting into the car, her hands deep in the pockets of her jacket.

As the long black limousine pulled away from the wooded area, Miller lifted the phone and within a minute had the weather report. "They say it will be fine tomorrow—high of sixty-seven. Indian summer," he added, trying to cheer her out of the sudden depression. She managed a smile. "I'm sorry for barking at you, Richard. I'm tired."

"That's what I'm paid for."

"No, you're not," she replied quietly. "I'm just being bitchy, that's all." She drew a piece of paper from her purse. "Here's Harry Reindorp's address. He's the fishing captain I told you about—the old friend of my father's. I'd like to have him around this evening. Would you invite him to join me for dinner? We'll go back to the hotel now."

That evening was the most enjoyable Harry Reindorp had had—since the week before. A tall man of sixty-seven with fearless pale blue eyes, he was still in remarkably good condition after a long, hard life as a deep-sea fisherman off Alaska. After a few drinks, his usually taut, wind-polished cheeks rumpled with delight when he saw the silver-laden food tray being wheeled quietly over the soft, deep red carpet in the vice-presidential suite.

"Ah, now, Lainey, would that be the hot dogs?" he exclaimed happily. He would not normally have addressed her so informally, for although he'd known Elaine most of his life through her father's fishing trips and had called her Lainey as a youngster, he had never quite recovered from her becoming Vice-President. But tonight the relaxed atmosphere was reminiscent of their fishing trips years ago. Elaine smiled. Usually she couldn't get him to call her anything but ma'am, which she disliked, not so much because it was formal as because it made her feel old.

When the waiter bent to offer her a sip of wine, she waved him gently aside. "Oh," she said, "let Mr. Reindorp try it."

Harry held up his hand. "Not me," he said, "I'm a beer man. I wouldn't know if that stuff was swamp water. Just pour it, son. If it's no good, I'll use it to preserve my starfish."

During the meal Elaine pushed Miller, the agents, and the cares of office to the back of her mind as the old fisherman explained the new additions to his boat, *Happy Girl*. Any other time she would have been bored by the conversation, for she had been on the boat often in the past, but now she listened intently. An idea had started to take shape. But it wasn't until he told her of his special pride in the new lanyard quick-release mooring lines that she became really excited. During the dessert—baked Alaska, much to

Harry's delight—the Vice-President explained to Harry what she wanted him to do. Listening to the details, Harry—helped along by his fourth glass of wine—began to chuckle. He was looking forward to doing Miller and those miserable agents one in the eye.

Elaine was up before her seven o'clock wake-up call. As she stood under the shower she felt almost ashamed of her excitement about the adventure which lay ahead. The plan was so simple that she was now convinced it would work. It had to work. Three more days and they would be returning to Washington. She lifted the bathroom window slightly and marveled at the weather. Though the sun was not yet up, there wasn't a cloud in sight. She watched a gull dip effortlessly and heard it screech against the clear sky. She took it as a good omen.

As she lathered her body she thought of Walter Sutherland and what he would be doing back in Washington. By now it would be mid-morning in the capital. In the same instant she thought of his wife. She turned off the shower and walked naked through the hall to the sitting room, luxuriating in the sun's rays. Miller had tried to persuade her to keep a female aide with her, but she was adamant. No one would share her living quarters. Ironically, her decision was not so much a bid for privacy as a precaution against talking in her sleep. She would never have been aware of the danger if her mother had not asked at the breakfast table during a weekend visit, "Who's Walt, dear?"

"Walt?"

"Yes. You were talking about a Walt in your sleep."

"Oh? What did I say?"

Her mother had poured the coffee unconcernedly. "Oh, nothing I could make out." There was a slight pause before she went on, a little too casually. "It wouldn't be the President, would it?" Elaine had felt the heat of a blush. She gave a weak laugh. "Good heavens no. Me call the President Walt? Really, Mother."

Since then Elaine had refused to be accompanied by stay-in female aides. Donning a long, soft robe from the closet, she sat down and began to dry and style her hair with a hand blower, not bothering to call in her hairdresser.

She had breakfast and got dressed slowly, putting on a clinging red turtleneck sweater, black pants, and a heavy brown suede jacket. It was one of the President's favorite combinations. To disarm the agents she stuffed her light blue Windbreaker into her large handbag and, walking out of the hotel, kept up a stream of questions about cables, news, and the like, trying to appear as official as she would have been on a quiet day in Washington.

THREE

September 22

As Elaine climbed into the limousine, First Officer Peter Salish, fifty miles to the north off Chichagof Island, was in the last hour of his 4:00 A.M. to 8:00 A.M. watch on the bridge of the U.S. merchantman MV *Kodiak.*

Heading south, thirty miles off the northernmost part of the Alexander Archipelago, the ship was en route from Valdez to Cherry Point in Washington State. Unable to sleep, the junior officer who would relieve Salish at 8:00 A.M. wandered onto the bridge, coffee mug in hand.

Salish made a caustic remark in the log about the unreliability of the recently installed anticollision radar, pulled out his pipe tobacco, and walked past the helmsman to the starboard side of the bridge to check the Fathometer. The giant tanker stretched before him, its bow no more than a distant blur in the gray morning light. From his position on the bridge, the outline of the seemingly endless, three-hundred-foot-wide deck looked like an airstrip relentlessly pushing its way through the subdued sea. *Kodiak* was not like most other ships. She was bigger. Enormously bigger. Five times the size of the *Queen Elizabeth;* length 450 feet more than the height of the Empire State Building; as wide as two football fields; depth 150 feet; deadweight tonnage 1,000,000 tons—equal to the capacity of a 200-mile-long train of 20,000 tank cars, each car holding 30,000 gallons—enough to supply a nation Canada's size with its entire oil needs for three days. And her generators could produce enough electricity to light up a city.

But despite the ship's impressive capabilities, Salish, in the long hours of the dogwatch, was apt to reflect that it wasn't true that the bigger the vessel the safer you felt. Not in his book, anyway. These man-built behemoths, beside which the great blue whales looked no larger than porpoises, simply took too long to turn. For all their sophisticated electronic gear, they reminded him of huge, lumbering, prehistoric animals grown too big too fast, bullying the sea with their power rather than using its natural forces. On a "crash astern" testing run at her usual seventeen knots, the *Kodiak,* even after deploying her stern parachutes, side fins, and bow rocket thrusters, had still gone on for four and a half miles before she had braked sufficiently to actually begin to go astern. And at the same speed without using her auxiliary braking systems, it took her twelve miles to come to a complete stop from the moment her engines were shut off.

Nevertheless, Salish had stayed with the *Kodiak* for the reasons most people stay with most jobs: they know little else and the money is good. After a dozen trips from Valdez to the Washington or Californian coasts, he would be able to afford a down payment on some land and move his family out of their chicken coop of a city apartment. Maybe he would build a house on one of the secluded Gulf Islands off the coast of British Columbia.

As the junior officer, for want of anything better to do, moved across the bridge and scanned the log, Salish stopped thinking about his wife and two young boys and where they might live, and stabbed his pipe in the direction of the anticollision radar computer. "That bag of bolts is acting up again."

The junior officer looked down at the rows of tiny flashing lights and the small recorder, which earlier had been disgorging its paper strip at an alarming rate. "What's the trouble?"

"Damned if I know, but if it blows we're blind."

The younger man thought of his coming watch. He cleared his throat. It felt tight and dry. "How about the relative radar? We can steer by that," he suggested hopefully.

Salish was tired. It had been a particularly dark night watch, and like every sailor, no matter how much electronic gear was stowed on board, he liked to see where he was going as well as read it on a printout. "All right then, we're half-blind. The point is, we're in a major sea lane, and if the terrific Marconi Mark II anticollision computerized radar screws up because of a speck of dust in its guts, someone up here will have to do some pretty quick thinking to plot a new course with only the relative radar as a backup. And with this tub nearly two thousand feet long, we need a turning circle of at least a mile to get out of the way of anything. Right?"

The junior simply nodded; he didn't like Salish's instructor's tone.

"Now what happens if some other bucket is turning too? It's no good if only one of us is on anticollision radar, 'cause then we're back in the old ball park—he turns, you turn, he turns. The board of inquiry calls it 'human error'—official language for 'screwup.' "

The junior officer nodded again, looking worriedly at the gray crackle-finish computer housing. "Is it working now?"

"Oh, it's all right now, but it was off for a while. Maybe it was just the paper roll. If you have any trouble, call Rostow. Let him earn his bread."

"Will do. But the weather's holding. In this light we can steer visually anyway."

Salish handed the junior officer the weather report: a slightly rising sea over the next twelve hours, then patches of fog off the west coasts of Chichagof and Baranof islands, reducing visibility to zero. The junior officer looked at his watch. It was 7:08 A.M. According to the forecast the *Kodiak* would encounter fog in the next half hour. At least Salish would have the first of it.

At 7:30 A.M., when the vice-presidential party arrived at the harbor, everyone except the Vice-President was annoyed to find that Harry Reindorp's thirty-footer, *Happy Girl,* was the only boat tied up at Wharf 17. The agents looked uncomfortable. The mooring was exposed to an impossibly wide field of fire. Noticing that *Happy Girl*'s motor was running, and at a loss for any other way to express his disapproval, the chief agent looked at Harry Reindorp sourly. "Going anywhere?"

"No," answered Harry. "I just warm her up every morning, whether I go out or not. It's an old engine—like me. Needs exercise, otherwise she'll just as likely seize up."

The chief grunted, still annoyed at not having been told of the Veep's wish to visit the old man's fishing boat until they had left the hotel a short while before. He was a thorough man and liked to check things out well in advance. But as he surveyed the surroundings with a professional eye, he began to feel more relaxed. *Happy Girl* was undoubtedly an easy target but at least there wasn't the usual crowd of small craft normally found in marinas, a maze of hiding places where all an assassin had to do was fire from among the congested boats, drop the rifle overboard, and go on drinking his martini.

The chief agent's eyes followed the wharf, a long, wooden spear that jutted out from a rocky, oyster-strewn outcrop. He could see a small clubhouse four hundred yards further along the beach, which stretched southwards from the oyster bed. The beach itself formed the edge of a stubbly grassed headland, but the grass, golden in the sunlight, was far too short to hide anyone. The agent, satisfied that he had all the land possibilities covered, turned and hurried ahead to check over the boat before the Vice-President boarded. Harry showed him around, telling him about the new quick-release line which moored the boat to the wharf fore and aft. The agent wasn't listening. He couldn't care less about Harry's new lines. What he wanted to see were all the possible hiding places for bombs. Up forward, beside the wheel, he noted a small cedar cabinet. "What's in that?" he asked. "Liquor," answered Harry with a twinkle in his eyes. "Only bomb in there is a bottle of cheap tequila."

The agent was not amused. He opened several bottles, sniffing with the intensity of a bloodhound.

"Would you like a belt?" offered Harry.

"No thanks," answered the other sternly, adding, "We really should have a diver check the bottom."

"What for?" asked Harry. "Wrong time of year for oysters."

"There's no season on mines," replied the agent tartly. "What's underneath that bench?" He pointed to a long, coffinlike white box.

"That's where all my girl friends sleep," Harry answered mischievously, adding, "Matter of fact, might be one in there now." He knelt down, lifted the lid, and shouted into the box, "Are you there, Sheila?"

The agent swung round, his forehead furrowed with disapproval. He was about to say something, then checked himself and dutifully bent over, quickly glancing into the box.

Harry chuckled to himself. The chief, red-faced, had had enough. He turned on the old man angrily. "Listen, Mr. Reindorp, I'm not trying to invade your privacy, but I've a job to do. I know the Vice-President is only here to visit for a few minutes, but some of those nuts'll try anything, believe me. Poison in the drinks, bombs under chairs, in the toilet, anything—you name it."

Harry patted the younger man on the shoulder. "'S all right, son. Just kidding. I care about her as much as you do." The agent walked off, tight-lipped, and gave Miller the all clear.

Elaine Horton moved towards the boat. Miller followed and she turned back to face him. "James, it's already been checked out. I'd just like to indulge in a few childhood memories with Harry. All right?"

Miller didn't like it, but he nodded understandingly. "Sure. I'll be right here if you need anything."

Harry took her hand as she came aboard. She gave him a wink and he smiled back. He showed her proudly around the old boat, pointing out some of the new additions. Meanwhile the six agents and Miller ranged themselves along the jetty, looking strangely wooden and conspicuous in their dark suits, silhouetted against the hazy blue of the Pacific, which stretched far beyond.

Suddenly the boat's engine burst into full power. Harry pulled the lanyards on the quick-release lines and *Happy Girl* roared away from the dock. Beneath him, all Miller saw was a wake of white, foaming water as the old engine's screw churned full ahead. "Jesus Christ!" he bellowed. "Jesus Christ—do something!" he yelled at the Secret Servicemen, who ran towards the edge of the jetty only to stand there looking and feeling utterly helpless as they watched the fishing boat growing smaller and smaller and the Vice-President throwing them a cheeky kiss from the stern. Miller turned savagely to curse the chief agent, but he was nowhere to be seen. Having instinctively stepped forward to stop *Harry Girl* from drawing away, he had suddenly disappeared from view. It was against his principles to swear; instead, he was making strange muttering sounds and beating the side of a pylon with his fist, his sleek gray suit clinging to him like black sandwich wrap.

When two of the agents, gasping for breath, finally reached the clubhouse to commandeer a pursuit boat, they found it locked. By then, *Happy Girl* was almost out of sight.

Back in the limousine, the chauffeur passed Miller an envelope addressed to him. "The Vice-President asked me to give you this after she visited the boat."

Miller tore open the note. It read simply, "No Coast Guard, Richard. I need a day alone. Tell the news people whatever you like if they catch up—but keep them away. I'll take the heat for you, if there is any, when I return. I've gone fishing. My eternal gratitude, Elaine." There followed, in what was obviously Harry Reindorp's handwriting, detailed instructions on how Miller could reach *Happy Girl* in an emergency. Elaine Horton prayed there would be none. So did Miller.

Elaine lay back in the stern, gazed up at the clear blue sky, and began soaking up the sun, the cool sea breeze streaming over her, bringing with it the purifying smell of salt air and seaweed. The wind reminded her of the childish pleasure she used to take in swinging her hair about in front of Walter whenever they had been alone. She tried to put him out of her mind, but their affair kept returning like a happy dream, breaking down the guilty barriers created by the "homespun" virtues for which she had become respected in the official world of Washington.

Think what she might, she could not shut out the memory of his distinguished graying hair, his firm walk, and the quick, winning smile in the evenly tanned face. Above all, she could not forget the tenderness he had shown whenever they had been alone, before their rise in the political world had ended the relative privacy of their congressional life.

Before success had thrown them permanently into the public spotlight, they had had a chance now and then to disappear together. In the fall it had been Vermont, in the spring Virginia, and once, as part of a congressional fact-finding mission on the feasibility of dumping nuclear waste two hundred miles off Hawaii, they had managed to spend a magical three days on the islands. The books had all been left behind in Washington, and she had concentrated instead on packing the most tasteful yet alluring outfits she could find. Since then she had often been troubled by how easy it had been to ignore the fact that he was married. She tried not to think of the President's wife. Clara Sutherland was a remarkable woman, and the thought of hurting her was one of the main reasons Elaine had agreed to try to end the relationship.

Happy Girl's aging motor, tired by the sudden takeoff, coughed several times. Now that they had passed the headland and were out of sight of the agents, Harry throttled back.

Elaine began thinking about her return to Washington. She wondered just how strong her will would be. From here, three thousand miles away, her decision of some months before to stop seeing Walter in other than public matters seemed firm; but what would happen when she saw him, when he first spoke to her, when he smiled?

It was 7:32 A.M.

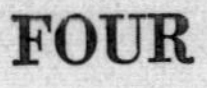

FOUR

By 7:44 A.M. the fog was thick about the MV *Kodiak,* and Salish had become aware of another ship's presence in the area. Normally this would not have worried him, but the anticollision radar was acting up again, spewing out reams of unintelligible printout. As a result, for the past thirty minutes or so Salish had been trying to pinpoint the other ship's position using only the relative radar, which was close to impossible.

Then suddenly the anticollision screen had gone completely blank. The junior officer, who preferred not to think about the increasing unpredictability of both the weather and the computer until he had to, had retreated to the galley to make himself a sandwich. Radar always reminded him of outboard motors; they always seemed perversely human in the way they would pack up just when you needed them most. Like now, with the fog bank rolling in relentlessly as a cold Arctic air mass came into contact with the land-warmed air of the Alaskan Panhandle.

What was worrying Salish was all this reliance on machines. Not only did it make men lazier in their surveillance duties and blunt their general alertness, but whenever one thing went wrong in the myriad electronic systems that guided the ship, it made him wonder what else was wrong below decks, deep in the "mine shafts," as the men called the labyrinth of tanks, pipes, and tunnels. Were the explosimeters or gas registers registering, or were there invisible and highly flammable pockets of vapor building up—pockets which only needed one spark to blow out the Butterworth tank covers like rockets and rip open the sides of the supraship as easily as one might explode a balloon? One spark. And the tanker wasn't afloat that didn't leak gas somewhere, somehow.

Salish had nightmares about leading inspection crews down into the tunnels to check the empty tanks after they had been automatically cleaned. The continual fear of such descents was encountering an unseen layer of highly concentrated gas lying quietly in one of the many bays that made up each tank, waiting to envelop a man the instant the movement of his body punctured the gas bubble. When that happened you blacked out in less than ten seconds. Five minutes more with the hydrocarbons rushing into your brain and you were a vegetable for life. Another minute and you were dead. And even in the emergency drills, it had taken twelve minutes to rush the Drager breathing pack gear down into the bowels of the tank from the nearest "pithead." On top of that Salish hated having to wear the big antistatic overalls and spark-free slippers which were mandatory. Not only did they make for awkward movement inside the tanks, but they were unbelievably hot. He didn't mind the inspection tours quite so much on a bright day, when at least reassuring pencil beams of light could be seen penetrating the somber tanks; but when it was overcast, there was no natural light. Even the soft shuffle of the slippers echoed in the vast zeppelin-sized interiors; the leaden tangle of pipes, ladders, and tanks within tanks seemed like cold, damp caverns in which primeval beasts dwelt and died, imprisoned in a world of unending darkness.

On the MV *Sakhalin,* a tanker of the same tonnage as the *Kodiak,* the helmsman was humming because he was bored. As they headed south off the Alexander Archipelago, the sea was calm, and Bykov had discovered that he could maintain the ship's course with fingertip control. Now and then long wisps of fog raced past like fleeing ghosts. Everything else around the Russian vessel was stone gray.

Third Officer Yashin turned away from the radar again to prowl nervously about the bridge. "Bykov, stop making that noise."

"Sorry, sir."

"See anything?"

"No, sir."

"I've still got a blip on the scanner. Keep your eyes open."

"Yes, sir." Bykov wondered what it was he was supposed to see in this pea-souper of a fog bank.

As Yashin sounded the foghorn, Salish started. After fourteen years in the merchant marine, he still wasn't used to the unnerving sensation the horn blasts gave him. He pulled the cord and answered the other ship, not knowing who she was or where she came from. Then, leaning over the dead anticollision radar screen, he thumped the side of the set with his fist.

"Goddamn it, that's the second time in the last half hour." He swung round, walked quickly to the bridge phone, picked up the receiver, and punched a number. He could hear only a long hum. He hung up and pushed the touch key again. After a few seconds a tired voice answered, "Yeah, Pete?"

"Sure hope I'm not disturbing you guys," Salish growled sarcastically.

"No. Just making a sandwich."

"Huh. Well, wake Rostow, will you? Tell him the anticollision's on the blink again."

"Completely out?"

"Completely. Not a sign of life. Dead. Kaput."

"Roger, I'll tell him."

"Don't just tell him. I'm running damn near blind on relative radar and there's another ship in the area. I want his ass up here—now!"

"Will do."

Salish put down the phone, satisfied that he had acted quickly and properly. He started to fill his pipe, glanced at his watch, and made an entry in the log: "September 22nd, 0749 hours—anticollision radar scanner and computer ceased to function—(third malfunction in 24 hrs.)."

The Russian was sweating. He stared at the blip three minutes longer, then made the decision. He went to the intercom, flicked down the officers' mess switch, and called the captain, something he had never done before on his watch. To his surprise a voice replied almost immediately. "Yes? What is it, Yashin?"

"Captain, I'm sorry to interrupt your breakfast, but . . ."

"Yes? Yes, what is it?"

"Sir, there's a ship chasing us."

There was a short silence that made Yashin wish he'd never called.

"Chasing? What the hell do you mean, chasing us? We're not at war, man."

"But I have him on the scanner, sir, and the horn hasn't managed to shake him. He seems to be running blind."

The captain answered irritably, "All right, all right, I'll be up in a minute."

Yashin had been on edge ever since the beginning of the watch, when the Old Man had ordered him to flush out the oil-and-water mixture from the bilge tanks off Sitka. They both knew it was contrary to IMCO's (Inter-Governmental Maritime Consultative Organization's) ban on dumping waste oil and water in coastal waters. But Yashin knew there wasn't much danger of their being found out, because the Old Man had craftily waited not only for darkness but until they were in what IMCO had designated a registered spill area, or RSA. These were spills caused by leakage of oil either from fissures in the earth's crust on the ocean bottom or from some tanker that had gone down and was still releasing its cargo as its tanks progressively corroded. The spills ranged in size anywhere from five miles by two miles to ten by one hundred in some cases, as in the

Gulf of Alaska. Yashin knew that by flushing bilge oil into an RSA, the Soviet master wouldn't be caught out, but he didn't like it. He was looking forward to the day when IMCO would be seeding each tanker's cargo, fingerprinting it as it were, with identifiable isotopes, so that in the event of any spill, offending parties could be quickly and positively identified.

Yashin was thinking a lot this morning, as the blip on the screen kept edging relentlessly towards him through the fog. That Japanese tanker that had collided with a Liberian freighter in Tokyo Bay in November 1974. She had burned like a torch for seventeen days. If she had not sunk, the experts said she would have burned for six months. Thirty-one tanker explosions at sea every year for the past ten years—that was one statistic which Yashin could remember, and its implications brought beads of sweat out on his forehead as he watched the oncoming blip. All that was needed to ignite a pocket of gas was a single, tiny spark from a man brushing his hair. A single spark, let alone the charges that would be generated in a collision. Yashin walked quickly to the starboard side of the bridge and gave a long blast on the horn.

Peter Salish jumped again. The helmsman smiled. Salish noticed and glared at the back of the man's head, then stood absolutely still, listening, trying to figure out the heading of the unknown ship. He wondered what kind it was, what his counterpart was like, and above all, how the sound of the horn had come so much closer since the last blast. There had been no reports of any other vessels in the area, and although this wasn't unusual, he turned to the helmsman. "Keep a sharp lookout, Henry."

"Yes, sir. I think he's on our starboard side."

"No, no—he's to port," answered Salish unconvincingly. "You're hearing the echo."

"Don't think so, sir. He sounds—"

Salish turned on the helmsman sharply. "Shut up and listen . . ."

Two minutes later the Russian horn sounded again. Salish's mouth went suddenly dry. This time he could feel the deep, booming vibration in his stomach. Both men strained their ears. Salish rang the watchman who had been stationed at the bow since the fog had started rolling in. "Bow, you see anything?"

"Only fog, sir."

Salish replaced the phone with a crash, ran over to the port side, and drew open the sliding door. The anxious watchman whom he could not see had anticipated his question. "Nothing this side, sir—least I can't see anything."

"Damn!" Ramming the door closed, he crossed back to the starboard side, flung open the door, and yelled into the wind, "Anything, Wray?"

"Nothing, sir—just fog. I think he's dead ahead."

"First light you see, holler."

"Roger."

Salish closed the door and looked at the scanner. It was still out. He turned to the relative position radar. He could see the series of black dots that had marked the other ship's previous positions—sometimes close, sometimes several kilometers from the *Kodiak*. But without the anticollision radar the relative radar was all but useless, given the time he needed to turn. It was pure guesswork now. Should he stay on this heading, hoping that the other ship would move, or should he change course again? Maybe her radar was out too. As he pressed the horn button for another blast, his stomach knotted and bile rose in his throat. Angrily he grabbed the phone and rang again for Rostow.

Both foghorns were blasting at each other now. Normal procedure had collapsed because of the Americans' malfunctioning anticollision unit. In the radio shack, the operator shook his head in exasperation. He couldn't understand a word of what was coming through the headset. The only message either ship would understand from the other was an SOS.

The foghorns' slow, mournful cries sounded like a dirge to Salish. Despite countless hours of training, his anxiety was approaching panic. With the sophisticated scanner out, he knew that he was helpless to anticipate the other's move.

Rostow arrived, sleepy-eyed, and began unscrewing the anticollision set's side panel.

Seconds after hearing that the bow and crow's nest watchmen could see nothing, Yashin heard the whine of the elevator bringing the captain up from the officers' mess five stories below. With the sweat now streaming down his face and feeling ashamed that he had had to call for help, the third officer decided to regain some lost pride by taking a sudden initiative. He ordered Bykov to steer zero eight three degrees, estimating that a course change eastwards would turn the *Sakhalin* away at right angles from the course of the approaching blip. But as he gave the order, the American, traveling faster, had also begun what he thought was an evasive turn to the southeast, steering one two seven. Yashin looked down at the blip and went pale as he saw that it, too, was turning. He pulled the horn cord and gave five short blasts, warning of impending collision.

Out of the fog the two giant ships suddenly became visible to one another, like two great leviathans that had unintentionally stalked each other through the fog-bound sea. The Russian, starboard aft on the American's starboard quarter and heading at a sharp angle towards the *Kodiak*'s stern half, was the first to see the unavoidable. Frantically, both helmsmen wrenched their steering levers back as far as they could go, but even at twenty knots, the ships were too close for any turn to save them.

As Salish saw the massive, two-thousand-foot-long Russian vessel loom up out of the night, bearing down on him, his brain raced. He thought of the enormous explosion that would follow if fuel from the Russian's forepeak tank cascaded into the engine room upon contact and met with a spark. Seeing there was no longer any hope of avoiding impact, he threw the

Kodiak's telegraph to "Stop Engines" and pushed the fire alarm button for "Abandon Ship." Then he bit clean through the stem of his pipe.

Had the Russian ship struck the American ship anywhere from bridge to bow, most of the crew, who were quartered above the boiler room, might have survived. Although some of the longitudinal steel stiffeners which reinforced both the inside and outside plates would no doubt have been sliced through like spaghetti, like those aft, the American ship with its lighter-than-water oil cargo could actually have been cut in half and yet remained afloat, buoyed up by unpunctured center and wing tanks. Instead, with a bone-splitting crash, the *Sakhalin*'s bow, smashed through the *Kodiak*'s port-aft side, punching a hole the size of a bomb crater in the American tanker's flank.

As the *Sakhalin*'s forepeak tank burst like a balloon, spraying thousands of gallons of high octane over the red-hot remnants of the *Kodiak*'s cavernous engine room, the sea, eager not to be left out, flooded in, cooling the engine room and reducing the possibility of a sparked explosion that could have torn the ships apart. But the implosion of thousands of gallons of seawater pushed the entire after end of the *Kodiak* downwards, drowning most of the American crew who had not been killed outright by the impact.

Within minutes the bow of the *Kodiak* angled steeply into the fog above, and the tanker began a slow backward slide into the debris-laden sea. All the while, the stricken ship's horn, now below water, maintained the subdued moan of some great and dignified beast being slowly tortured to death.

Amid the deafening confusion of sounds caused by burst high-pressure pipes, suddenly arrested propellers, and the crashing of everything from falling pots and pans in the galley to the splitting of solid steel plating, the Russians heard the loud "whoomp," like the crunch of a distant bomb, as a small explosion blew out the starboard side of the *Kodiak*'s fast-disappearing bridge. Momentarily the two huge black ships were silhouetted by the orange white flash—two dark monoliths doing battle in the shroud of fog, locked together in a grip of twisted, bending steel, the Russian lying with its bow being slowly dragged under by the after end of the *Kodiak,* whose own bow, acting counter to the sinking stern, was almost completely out of the water.

Yashin caught a glimpse of a lone man struggling in the oily sea eighty feet below. Within a second of the Soviet captain's ordering, "Engines full astern," in an effort to tear loose from the American's death grip before it dragged his ship under, Yashin dispatched a life-raft cannister overboard toward the American sailor.

But even as the *Sakhalin*'s diesels screamed in a wild fury, her three screws churning the sea about them into a spinning vortex of foam a hundred yards wide, the Russian captain knew he could not break free. After forty-five seconds, the *Sakhalin*'s forward deep tanks one and two, half-full of Avgas and situated immediately behind the forepeak tank, ruptured, and highly combustible aviation fuel gushed into the sea.

Meanwhile the strain on the bulkheads was beginning to tell, and leaks shot open in seven of the sixteen wing tanks along the port side. Yashin reported that the indicators showed that fuel was also being lost through foot-long fissures in the inch-and-a-half steel walls of numbers one and two center tanks. Even so, the Soviet captain decided to keep the engines straining full astern for another two minutes. It was only when the control panel showed obvious buckling of the plates in six, seven, and eight center tanks that he stopped engines. He was losing oil fast. The next moment he was flung to the deck as another explosion in the *Kodiak*'s engine room rocked the *Sakhalin,* blowing forward with such force that it burst four of the *Kodiak*'s after tanks, namely sixteen, fifteen, fourteen, and thirteen. Fortunately all the tanks were full. Had any of them been only partially so, allowing a buildup of gas inside them, the engine room explosions would almost certainly have ripped the *Kodiak* apart and turned her into an inferno. As it was, thousands of tons of crude were pouring into the sea.

When the lone American was brought aboard the Russian ship, he was vomiting violently, throwing up oil and saltwater. Cleaning him off and giving him coffee, Yashin tried to comfort him in halting English. The American had difficulty understanding how the two ships were stuck together. In the fogbound sea he had had no idea what had happened, only that one moment he had been reading in his bunk and the next he had heard the alarm; then he was suffocating in a sea of oil.

But the sailor had no difficulty understanding Yashin's concern when he asked the Russian officer for a cigarette. Yashin shook his head vigorously. "Sparking," he said, "sparking!" and then made a wide upwards gesture with his hands which very obviously described the arcs of an enormous explosion. At first the American was not as concerned as Yashin, because the *Kodiak* was carrying crude, and though it would burn, it was almost impossible to ignite by itself. But when he smelled the air, he finally understood the other's fear. The Russian, he guessed, was carrying a combination bunker oil and high-octane cargo bound for Cuba. The heavy vapor from the highly refined fuel was already spreading like a poisonous cloud through the fog about the ships and low over the sea's surface.

It was a cloud which would spread with extraordinary rapidity over wide areas of the ocean about them, a cloud which, despite the red identification dye of its liquid form, was all but invisible to the naked eye when spread so widely in the fog bank. Therein lay its danger. The American sailor, staring blankly at the mountainous hulk that was now a coffin for so many of his friends, began to shake uncontrollably from delayed shock. He tried to get up from the bunk, but fell back and vomited again. The smell of the gas was making him feel increasingly ill. As he gasped for air, all he could think of was the conservation movies he had seen during the gasoline rationing of a few years back. One of them had shown the ignition of a four-gallon can of gas. It had gone off like a bomb. And four gallons, he knew, was literally a drop in comparison with what the cavernous tankers were spilling. He didn't believe in God, but he began to pray anyway.

While the deadly vapor continued to spread silently over the sea, transported more rapidly now by rising winds, row upon row of tiny red, green, and white lights continued to play a silent and fantastic dance on the indicator boards of the *Kodiak*'s sinking bridge. Urgent messengers of doom, they continued to flicker their warning of impending disaster even as the ship's bow continued to rise and the saltwater sizzled briefly around the main computer's core, signaling the *Kodiak*'s end. Then, their frantic brain finally recognizing the hopelessness of the situation, all the lights died simultaneously, leaving the bridge in total darkness as Salish's crumpled body, supported by a life jacket, drifted aimlessly about, softly bumping into protruding islands of equipment.

The Russian captain had all his crew ready to fight any outbreak of fire, though they all knew that if fire did start in this ocean of oil, no number of extinguishers could stop it; it would simply ride on the sea's skin, glued like napalm on a helpless body. The boats and inflatable raft containers were readied too, though again, fire would render them useless. The captain had decided not to abandon his ship until she actually began to sink. Putting out life rafts in this fog, with the wind rising, would be a sure way to lose his crew. Yashin saw that all they could do was wait and hope that help arrived before any explosions reached the high octane or before the *Kodiak* dragged them further under. He noted the time in the *Sakhalin*'s log. It was 0802 hours.

FIVE

At 8:30 A.M., the knife-edged bow of the nuclear-armed destroyer U.S.S. *Tyler Maine,* speeding south from the direction of Cross Sound at a point twenty-five miles off the southern end of Chichagof Island, cut ghostlike through the fog that now and then mysteriously gave way to clear patches of sea.

Being the only ship anywhere near the collision site, the destroyer had been asked by the U.S. Coast Guard to answer the Russian Mayday. The sinking *Kodiak* had not even had time to send a distress signal, her radio room having been demolished upon impact with the Soviet supratanker. The destroyer's captain rang the engine room. "Chief, you got us on maximum revs?"

"That's what the dials say, Captain, but I could maybe squeeze another knot or two out of her. It'd be pushing her mighty hard."

"Well, push her. I want to get those poor bastards out before anything else happens. I don't want to be a hundred yards from 'em and have to give 'em up."

"Aye, aye, sir."

In the destroyer's chart room, the executive officer worked fast with dividers and parallel rule. The line he drew between the destroyer's position and that of the stricken tankers—estimated to be forty-odd miles west of Sitka—ran northeast to southwest. In the zero visibility, they would not be able to see the Russian ship until they were practically upon it. Till then it was up to them to reckon how close they were to the escaping oil. After a few more minutes, the navigator poked his head out of the chart room and called urgently to the captain, "I think we're approaching the pollution danger zone now, sir. At least we must be getting close, according to their position and the increase in wind velocity."

The captain received the information without surprise. "Shit. Don't need your charts to figure that out, Ex. My nose is the best goddamn indicator on this ship. You can smell it—stinks to high heaven." The first officer agreed. The captain coughed and spat into his handkerchief. "And I can taste it," he added irritably. "How far from the Russian?"

"Couple of miles sou' southwest."

The captain grunted. He took a cup of coffee from an orderly and instructed a junior officer, "Sound 'Approaching PD Zone' warning. We'll likely encounter the slick within the quarter hour."

In fact the *Tyler Maine* was already deep within the fuel oil slick, though no one aboard could have known, for the ship had entered a long, tonguelike extension of the high-octane vapor that had been blown into a clear area beyond the fogged-in Mayday position and the bulk of the spill. Having vaporized, the octane now lay in a highly volatile, invisible layer over the surface of the sea. The captain, confident that they were merely smelling advance fumes from the main spill, believed that he was giving ample warning to his crew. He added crisply, "I want a double check that there's no smoking and that the engine room and galley are in the sealed-off condition and operating on filtered air only. Got it?"

"Yes, sir."

Leading Seaman Jones, a newcomer to the *Tyler Maine*, wasn't what you'd call a big drinker, but standing alone outside on the bridge's starboard side lookout position, unable as usual to make out anything that came out of a PA system whether in an airport, train station, or aboard a destroyer, all he was thinking about was ending his watch and having a shot of the Jack Daniel's he'd smuggled aboard. It was a birthday gift from his wife. Every year she gave him the same thing, and every year he said it was just what he wanted. He lifted the binoculars and scanned the horizon, but all he could see was the ashy gray mist of the scattered fog banks. Letting the binoculars hang about his neck for a moment, he pulled out his tobacco pouch. At forty-two he figured that if lung cancer was going to get him, it was going to get him—same as old age. He'd tried to cut down his habit, and on shore he could do it, but here at sea, he asked himself, what the hell else could you do but eat and sleep and maybe drool a bit over *Playboy?* Besides, how could you cut it out when you'd already been at one and a half packs a day at sixteen? Using the bridge's flanged wing as a wind barrier, he held the cigarette paper low and deftly rolled the tobacco into it.

Inside the bridge, confident that the ship was completely electrically grounded in the event of lightning or electronic malfunction, the captain was receiving "sealed off" confirmation from various sections of the ship. Halfway through listening to the engine room report, he motioned to the executive officer.

"Yes, sir?"

"Better remind the new man on the starboard watch about PD drill. He might not hear it on the PA system in this wind."

"Aye, aye, sir." The executive officer pulled up his parka hood and made his way out to the starboard wing. As he opened and closed the bridge door, the wind howled past, causing his eyes to smart. Bending his head low, he held onto a rail with one hand and fumbled for a handkerchief with the other. The officer knew that two tankers the size of the *Sakhalin* and the *Kodiak* had never before collided. Compared to this, the old *Torrey Canyon* back in the sixties had been strictly minor league.

One figure kept coming back to him—the data from a spill on the Gulf of St. Lawrence in the late sixties. In just one day a spill of ten thousand gallons—only a fraction of the *Torrey Canyon*'s cargo—had covered an area a hundred miles in diameter. And the whole cargo of the *Torrey Canyon* had been only a sixteenth of the spill they were heading into.

For a moment he could see nothing in the hurtling

mist, but then he caught a glimpse of the vague outline of the watchman drawing on a cigarette. The officer roared against the noise of wind and sea, "What the hell are you doing, sailor?"

Leading Seaman Jones, startled, quickly took the cigarette out of his mouth, and before the other man could stop him, flicked it overboard. "Sorry, sir."

For a fleeting moment the executive officer watched with horrified fascination as the ship's slipstream plucked the lighted cigarette, carried it aft, and then whipped it down towards the sea. There was an enormous orange flash followed by a deafening CRUMP, then another and another, until soon the horizon itself seemed to be exploding in a distant, silent flashing of massed artillery.

The Russians and the lone American, like their would-be rescuers now a short distance away to the northeast, could do nothing; but their end was more agonizing, for they had time to see what would soon kill them. Standing and sitting, they were silhouetted like toy soldiers, clinging to their dying ship, staring in horror as they watched the long, orange roll of flame building up on itself, advancing towards them through the illuminated shroud of fog, like breakers from a closing and fiery surf. As succeeding pockets of gas exploded, each flash closer than the last, Yashin looked in numb dispair at the radar screen. The pulsating dot that seconds before had been the advancing American destroyer was now scattered in a thousand tiny points of lights which quickly faded, like so many meteorites suddenly extinguished by an inhospitable planet.

Yashin kept staring at the blank radar screen, momentarily hypnotized by the sweeping arm. He had seen a fire on a tanker once. It had happened in the Black Sea. Now he could see it in the screen. As the fire wave had struck, everyone at the deck level had died instantly, their bodies lit up like pieces of burning paper, first white, then saffron darkening to black as they curled up, shriveling in the flames. Any screams had been lost in the noise of the exploding tanks. A steel whale in a final agonizing attempt at escape, the tanker had first leapt hopelessly into the air, her back broken as she was thrown up by a series of explosions. No sooner had she collapsed back into the water than her bow disintegrated in a shower of shrapnel, a half-empty forward tank blowing out sideways, spewing tons of coal black bunker oil through the orange flame like volcanic bile.

Illuminated by the fire, the sea around the crippled tanker had taken on the semblance of a moving abstract painting as the translucent greens, mauves, and reds of the various dyed octanes curved and slid about each other in liquid rainbows, their ever-changing patterns invaded here and there by the dark brown molasses of crude that continued to ooze from the stricken ship. What amazed Yashin was that despite the force of the initial explosion, many of the house-sized wing tanks, though hurled hundreds of yards at a time and badly ruptured, were still afloat. What had once been the second-largest tanker in the Soviet Eastern Fleet was soon no more than two dozen hulks, each bleeding its cargo into the sea.

The explosions were very loud now. Sweat dripped onto the screen from his nose. His heart punching his chest, frantic to escape, he tried not to think what would happen when the fire wave hit the *Sakhalin*. He heard the captain yell his name, and as he turned away from the radar, he saw through the bridge windows that the fire, now blood red, was less than 400 yards away, rolling inexorably towards him.

Admiral Klein, commanding officer of the U.S. Pacific Fleet, refused to believe the first reports. He said flatly that it couldn't happen. But the satellite pictures showed that it had.

SIX

No one had ever seen so many gulls. By noon, fourteen miles over the horizon and beyond the fog bank, they came in tens of thousands. Some headed north and others south, over the wide mouth of Dixon Entrance and the green-dotted blue of British Columbia's island-strewn coast towards the snow-dusted peaks of the Coast Mountains which formed the common backbone of the American and Canadian lands. Old-time fishermen were puzzled, for there was no storm in sight.

Forty-three miles northwest of Sitka, *Happy Girl* lolled lazily on the long, glossy swells. Even had the Vice-President seen storm clouds following the distant claps of thunder she thought she had heard earlier that morning, she would not have cared. This was the first real break since her hectic election two years before, and her only concern this day lay with the big rockfish that inhabit the nutrient-rich upwelling of water about the summits of the undersea mountains that rise almost sheer from the ocean floor to within a few hundred feet of the surface. She cast her line again and smiled mischievously. This was the first time in her term of office that she had managed to elude her watchdogs.

There was no sign of land, only the hazy, pale blue-washed horizon of the endless Pacific giving her the illusion of a limitless world. She let the quietude seep into her as a lizard would the sun. She felt a tug on the line, reeled in the five-pound red snapper, took the hook out, threw the fish back, and wiped her hands on a clean rag. Harry looked over and made a wry face, friendly but slightly deferential. "Time used to be when you could eat 'em, ma'am."

"Time'll come again, I hope, Harry."

"Not in my life. Only fish I'll ever eat will have all the flavor steamed out. It's all that sterilizing stuff. The fish are all like that now. Like a goddamned sewer here."

The Vice-President said nothing. The last thing she wanted to talk about today was pollution. She looked eastwards, watching a long line of dots trailing the thin sliver of the horizon. "Harry?"

"Ma'am?"

"Have you ever seen so many birds?"

Harry's old eyes squinted at the clouding sky. "Nope, can't say I have. Must be a storm building out yonder. Don't look bad here, though."

Harry's mention of a storm made Elaine feel uneasy. Then, quite suddenly, she was assailed by an overwhelming sense of guilt. Despite her need for privacy, and no matter that other vice-presidents had made a habit of deliberately breaking out of their protective cocoon, she rebuked herself. No American vice-president had any business being miles out at sea, virtually alone, radio or not. She should know better. Any senator, any aide knew better. She began reeling in.

"Harry, I think we'd better head back."

Harry nodded and moved towards the cabin to start the engine. Still reeling in, Elaine saw a dark lump bobbing up and down by the boat. She pointed it out to Harry, who shook his head in disgust and fished it out of the water. It was a dead gull. Feeling its sticky body, he threw it back into the sea and showed Elaine his hands, which were now covered with oil. "Pollution," he grunted, and went into the cabin.

To starboard a tremor passed through the water as a phantom breeze broke the silken surface of the sea. The Vice-President looked up again at the multitudes of gulls passing over the horizon. "I wonder why they're all coming from the same direction."

Harry pushed the starter button. The motor did not respond. "Don't know," he answered. He pushed the starter button a second time. Again it did not respond.

SEVEN

At 5:35 P.M. eastern daylight time a military aide sat in the gallery of the North Virginia Country Club carrying the nuclear code box that always accompanied the President. Below the President and his close friend, Air Force General Arnold B. Oster, moved into match point in the sixth game.

An athletic six-footer who always looked as if he had just stepped off a reviewing stand, Oster served the ball into the President's corner. It dropped slowly. The President, his red face in marked contrast to the hospital whiteness of the squash court, moved quickly but not hurriedly behind the ball and drove it into the front right corner. Oster, anticipating him, had already moved across the court. He intercepted the ball on the rebound, flicked it across to the President's backhand, and stood in center court, waiting for the inevitable hard backhand drive, but it didn't come. Instead he could hear the plop of a dead ball dribbling forward from the back wall. Oster turned around. "You don't usually miss those, Walt."

The President, who at fifty was three years younger than the general, wiped the sweat from his eyes with his armband. "No," he answered quietly, almost dispiritedly, "no, I don't." His voice was almost apologetic. "You mind if we break off now?"

Oster picked up the ball with a deft flick of his racket. "Not at all. Walt?"

"Yes."

"You okay?"

The President smiled without conviction. "Yes. Hard day."

Oster glanced up at the aide sitting alone in the gallery. He decided to wait until they were in the privacy of the locker room before asking more questions. The President was his closest friend. They had been in school together long before the future President had gone to Harvard, and he knew that when Walter Sutherland couldn't kill an easy backhand, it meant he was either out of shape or he was worried. And the President was in shape. They had been playing an hour's squash three times a week for the past ten years. Sutherland had then been an up-and-coming congressman serving on the powerful Armed Services Appropriations Committee to which Oster had been an advisor.

Oster knew he had made himself unpopular in some circles for his frankness, but his blunt honesty had made him the President's closest confidant and friend. Walter Sutherland could tell him anything with the assurance that his thoughts would go no further. The President had to have at least one such friend in the White House, an ever-ready sounding board for some of the tougher decisions.

Clara Sutherland, the President's wife, was another thing. Though she had always been willing to support her husband during the tougher moments of his office, she was essentially nonpolitical. She was a deeply religious woman, whose beliefs did not dispose her to insert herself into the world of power and manipulation. When she first heard gossip about her husband and Elaine Horton, for example, she had discounted it, convinced that it was just crude gossip.

Until recently, staff, friends, and even the press corps had refrained from confronting her with her husband's infidelity, but a month ago a loud-mouthed young reporter, violating the self-imposed restrictions of the press corps, had blurted out, "Mrs. Sutherland, could you tell us whether you and the President have come to terms with your husband's liaison in Congress?"

There had been a hush in the pressroom before Clara Sutherland, with a smile on her face, had replied, "My husband's relations with Congress have always been extremely close. I believe that it's most proper for a President to maintain ties with Congress, don't you?" The First Lady got a solid round of applause for that one, but the story broke in some of the tabloids, and try as they might, the local networks couldn't avoid mentioning it. Finally, CBS and NBC had made passing, cautious references to it.

It was the networks' mention of the story only a week before which Oster had in mind as he entered the locker room with the President. After making sure that the Secret Service agents and the aide were outside in the corridor, Oster asked bluntly, "Walt, how's things with Clara?"

The President peeled off the sweat-soaked T-shirt and dropped it wearily to the floor. "She's very understanding."

The general nodded and began adjusting the shower tap. As the water began drumming loudly, he raised his voice. "Hell, I know that. She's a champion. But how are *things*?"

Walter Sutherland looked up at his friend. No one else would have dared press the question. He sighed heavily. "Things are—well, not so good. Truth is, Arnold, Clara's hurt, but she's so goddamn understanding I feel like a child-beater. That's how things are. It was that goddamn press conference that did it. In a way I was almost pleased that little bastard brought it up. At least, I thought, now we could talk about it. But Clara won't even do that. She never said a word. Any other woman and I'd think she was trying to get her revenge, but not Clara. She's forcing herself to keep cheerful about everything. Makes me feel even worse."

Oster soaped up and didn't say anything until he had sluiced the suds from his face. "Hell, Walt, she's not saying anything because she's too damn sensible. Knows it's all water under the bridge." The general paused. "Isn't it?"

Sutherland felt like a shower, but he was exhausted. He had made the decision to sit and talk, to unload his private burden, or as much of it as he could, on his friend. But now the bluntness of Oster's question inhibited him. He found himself answering vaguely, "Well it's finished as far as I'm concerned, but you know . . . I mean it's difficult when the two of us have to see so much of each other."

Oster as usual was quick to cut through the President's hesitancy. "You been fooling around with her again?"

"Goddamn it, you bastard, I should have you court-martialed."

"You don't want to talk about it, you mean?"

"No—yes. It's just that you're less subtle than a B-52."

Oster grinned. "The best airplane," he said proudly. "Straightforward."

The President managed a laugh. "No, I haven't been fooling around. But—" He found it hard to say her name. "Elaine, you see, she's still—well, she's . . ."

"Hot?" offered Oster.

"Yes. Never says so, but I know. Sounds conceited, I suppose."

"Horse balls," said Oster, toweling himself vigorously. "Elaine's a great woman—knows a great man when she sees one. I introduced you. Don't ever forget it."

"I remember."

"I only introduce damn fine women, Walt. Still, what's your problem? She wants to; you don't. You can keep your distance."

There was a long silence. Oster knew he had hit a nerve, but for once he didn't press. Sutherland got up and began to shower. He finished quickly. Eyes still closed, he reached for a towel. There were none on the rack, and Oster handed him one. The President wiped his eyes slowly, as if playing for time. "I don't know, Arnold. I don't know if I can keep my distance."

Oster's voice was lower now. "You still love her?"

"Yes. But I have to stop . . . that."

"Why?"

"Guilt. My job. My wife." He smiled, his eyes empty. "The President of the United States can't fuck around."

"Horse balls. If Roosevelt could run the country for all that time and enjoy himself on the side, why can't you? Just keep it quiet." The general hesitated, but only for a moment. "It can be arranged. I'd help—you know that."

"And what about Clara, Arnold?"

"She's a grown woman. She could do the same. She's got a mind of her own."

The President tightened his tie absently. "No. She wouldn't want to do the same."

"All right, she wouldn't want to. But she could, and that's the point."

"It's not right, Arnold. It's as simple as that. I know it reeks of God, Mother, and Boy Scouts but I was raised on all three and I can't shake them. What's worse, I'm not sure I want to."

Oster lit up a cigar, a practice which Sutherland abhorred but tolerated out of friendship. "Look, man, I'm your friend, not your pastor, and I tell you, a happy President is a good President—or a lot fucking better than a lonely President. Right?"

Thinking hard, Sutherland took his navy blue suit off its hanger. He was about to answer when an aide entered the locker room. "Mr. President, you're wanted at the White House."

"What's up?" the President asked calmly.

"Don't know, sir. Just told me it was top priority."

As the aide began to explain, Sutherland finished dressing, nodding from time to time. On his way out, he called back to the general. "Arnold, stay in Washington, will you? I need you nearby."

"Yes. Mr. President. I'll be here."

Walter Sutherland left his friend wondering how it was that a man who daily dealt with the enormous pressures of public affairs had such difficulty making up his mind about a woman. Oster didn't know whether Walter Sutherland would take his advice, but he hoped like hell that the problem would be solved before the strain on the Chief Executive started to affect the way he handled his other responsibilities.

At 6:00 P.M. eastern daylight time, a grim-faced President walked briskly along a brightly lit corridor beneath the White House. At the end of the long, polished floor, two immaculately dressed marines stood guard outside a door marked Authorized Personnel—A-1 Clearance Only.

Since special aide Bob Henricks, a discreet distance behind, had joined him a few minutes earlier, the President had said nothing—had not even acknowledged his presence, and all Henricks could hear was the loud, hollow echo of their footsteps in unison.

The President felt irritably in his pockets. He had forgotten his handkerchief, and in a crisis his hands sweated profusely. He could live without crises. Some men, like Kissinger, he remembered, had soaked them up, used them as fuel for their careers. Solving big problems kept them happy. Crisis cranks. They loved it. He didn't. After months of preparatory work, just when he finally felt confident enough to launch a massive legislative assault on a whole range of domestic and foreign policy problems—and incidentally secure his place in history—this catastrophe had to come.

The high shine of the guards' helmets pleased him. Although they looked impassive, the marines had already checked to see whether each of the approaching men wore the required striped I.D. card on his lapel. For the President, the guards were daily reminders of his personal control. He would need a firm hand on the reins this evening. His first question to Henricks was more of a snap than an inquiry. "How big's the area?"

"At the moment, two thousand square miles, Mr. President."

The President allowed himself the luxury of incredulity. "Two *thousand!*"

"Yes, sir."

"Sweet Jesus! Why wasn't I told immediately—this morning?"

Henricks, for all his calculated casualness, replied somewhat sheepishly, "Ah, the cable was put into the 'Urgent' slot by mistake, sir—instead of 'A-1 Priority.' "

The President's head turned sharply. "By mistake? We've got a million-dollar computer in our basement and you're telling me the cable was put in the wrong box?"

Henricks had a way of accepting responsibility while seeming to sidestep the major portion of blame. "I'm afraid so, Mr. President," he replied.

But this evening the President was unrelenting. "Not good enough. You should have been on top of it."

"Yes, sir."

"How long's it been burning?"

"All day. At first the experts said there was a good chance that it wouldn't spread. That's before we knew about the tanks breaking up."

Reaching the end of the corridor, the two men stepped onto a small platform under the eye of a camera-computer which verified their I.D. through an instantaneous check of their photographs and thumbprints. The guards snapped to attention as the oak doors slid open. Inside the windowless Special Operations Room, busy aides barely glanced at the President as he entered and sat down at the long, oval mahogany table which ran almost the entire length of the cedar-paneled room. On the east wall, a huge relief map of the world slowly descended from the ceiling as the equally large movie screen retracted. Superimposed over each of the capital cities was an illuminated digital clock face—orange for those ahead of Washington time and blue for those behind. As the lights began to dim, most of the aides left the main room to work in the Communications Annex nearby, which was filled with chattering telex machines monitoring the news services and receiving official cable traffic.

President Sutherland shifted his chair for a better view of the huge map, whose oceans passed from ultramarine to navy blue as the lights behind the screen dimmed, casting lighter-shaded ocean currents and green mountain ranges into greater contrast. The President turned to look for his top aide from the Environmental Protection Agency. "Where's Jean?"

Henricks glanced up from his attaché case. "She's taping a newscast of it now, Mr. President. The networks are covering it as a special report."

The President's fingers began drumming on the table. "That figures. The United States government has to wait for Walter Cronkite. What in hell is our Intelligence Service for?"

Henricks was drawing a red circle off a group of islands that lay adjacent to the Alaskan Panhandle. The circle represented an area of about two thousand square miles on the world map's transparent overlay. He turned about carefully on the small stepladder. "Intelligence is covering it too, sir."

The President smiled derisively, wiping his hands with a trail of Kleenex he'd pulled hurriedly from his jacket. "That's nice."

Henricks was relieved to see Jean Roche walk in carrying two video tapes. The President waved the Kleenex impatiently towards the bank of TV sets and video recorders. "All right, Jean, let's hear it."

Henricks watched her bend over to insert the cassettes into a Zenith recorder and mentally undressed her. She was petite, quite ordinary-looking, even plain, but with a striking figure for a woman of thirty with three children. It always surprised him how at times like this he invariably thought of sex. He wondered whether the President had the same habit—whether he thought of Elaine Horton.

The overhead lights were dimmed further as the video tape began to show up on one of the forty-eight-inch screens. After a few flickers, Cronkite appeared, shuffled some papers, glanced down to his right, showing thinning white hair, coughed politely, and looked up. "Good evening. A news flash has reached CBS reporting an international disaster of unprecedented proportions. An ocean area of almost two thousand square miles caught fire early this morning and is now burning fiercely off the North American continent. What is already being described as the largest fire in history was primarily caused by the vast and ever-growing buildup of escaping oil."

Superimposed on the lower right of the screen, old film clips of massive worldwide and local pollution formed the background for Cronkite's description.

"Environmentalists have long warned that continuing undersea oil seepage, oil from the hundreds of tanker sinkings, and the dumping of waste oil by ships in transit might one day combine to form a huge and potentially inflammable blanket of oil in the North Pacific. Only last week CBS reported the blowout of two Alaskan north slope offshore wells, each spilling more than ten million gallons of crude oil into the sea . . ."

As Cronkite continued, the background changed; two model tankers, both broken in half, were shown. ". . . Now CBS has learned that shortly after dawn this morning, two million-ton supratankers traveling south from oil storage depots in Valdez, Alaska, collided in heavy fog approximately thirty miles off southern Alaska's Chichagof Island, one of the northernmost islands of the Alexander Archipelago. Both ships were fully loaded, the American, the *Kodiak,* with crude, the Russian, the *Sakhalin,* with a cargo of high octane and bunker fuel. It appears that at least one of the ships either was not equipped with the recently developed Marconi anticollision radar or did not have it in operation at the time, although this has not been confirmed. Agents for the ships report that both supratankers, measuring more than nineteen hundred feet long and three hundred feet wide, were carrying a near-capacity cargo of a million tons. This means that a total of more than *six hundred million* gallons of oil is spilling into the ocean. UPI reports that there is little possibility of survivors. More details on that spill in a moment."

The President turned away from the set as a soap commercial came on. He had placed a hand over his eyes as if shading them from an invisible glare. "My God," he said slowly. "How many gallons did he say?"

It was Jean Roche who answered. "Six hundred million, Mr. President." She added hesitantly, "Actually it's higher than that."

"Six hundred mill—! I can't even imagine that much."

There was a long pause. When the President spoke again, he was more composed. "Jean?"

"Mr. President?"

"Why are we watching that damned commercial?"

His aide flushed. "Ah—there was no time to edit it, sir." And she added quickly, "We didn't want to lose any footage."

The President groaned.

When Cronkite reappeared, he mentioned something about a report from Juneau, and now a field reporter was taking up the story. "Years ago experts predicted such a freak combination of circumstances somewhere in the world. They warned that should a large amount of gasoline or high octane be present, there would be an imminent danger of fire. Well, the experts have been proven right. Ironically, the fire, which is now igniting the thousands of smaller natural and man-made oil slicks in the area, is suspected to have been started accidentally by a U.S. destroyer. The destroyer was answering the Russian tanker's distress calls. It has not been heard from since it itself issued an SOS, saying only that it was afire. Experts here believe that the destroyer, the *Tyler Maine,* entered an area of high gasoline vapor density while en route to the collision site, and that a single spark from an electrical malfunction aboard the destroyer may have set advance sections of the slick ablaze. The Coast Guard has said it will release more details as they become available."

Cronkite again. "Our reporter in Juneau, Alaska, tells us that if the northerly winds increase—as the forecast for the area promises—then the firespill could threaten the entire Pacific coastline. While the slick would normally be swept northwards by the Alaskan Current, these winds could push much of it southwards, since wind rather than currents is the prime mover of spills. The possible extent of the fire can be approximated by comparing it with a recent spill of only ten thousand gallons in the Gulf of St. Lawrence. This covered an area one hundred miles in diameter in only twenty-four hours—a rate of spread of almost three feet per second. The Alaska spill is sixty thousand times as big—and burning. The flames, experts explain, will reduce both the viscosity of the oil and the surface tension of the sea. This makes it much easier for the oil to spread even faster. In addition, the firespill will soon join up with and so ignite a particularly heavily polluted area off Sitka. The sea here is filled with oil, natural seepage from the sea bottom as well as oil from ships which have used the area as a dumping ground for bilge waste, contrary to international law. If the firespill is not stopped, in seven days it could cover an area equal to that of Florida. Over 55,000 square miles."

The President got up from his chair. "Christ—" he began, then turned to Jean Roche. "That's enough."

She turned the set off. The President took a fresh cup of coffee from an aide and asked no one in particular, "Are they right about that destroyer—did it start the fire?"

Henricks already had the report in his hand. "Don't know, Mr. President. It seems the only logical answer, although someone at EPA says that it could just as easily have been a lightning strike. As Cronkite said, the weather is about to change. A ship out there is like a tree in a desert. If lightning hits the ship itself, no great problem, but the destroyer could have attracted lightning around her. Maybe that's what set it off."

The President sighed and looked down at his coffee cup. "How many men?"

Henricks glanced at the file again. "On the destroyer? Two hundred and fifty, sir. It was on CBS after the main report—a news flash."

The President looked up at Jean, then at Henricks. "Sweet Jesus. What about our tanker?"

An aide whispered to Henricks and handed him a telex message. Henricks looked grave. "Last report the navy had from the Russians says that they only picked up one survivor."

The President stirred his coffee and asked quietly, "And the Russians?"

"Last we heard they radioed the Coast Guard that they were listing badly but still afloat. Trouble is, we haven't been able to contact them for several hours.

We're still trying. They're probably sending whatever messages they can direct to the Soviet Union—in code, knowing the Ruskies. The navy suggests we contact Moscow if we want to know any more."

"All right. Have someone call Premier Krestinsky."

"Hot line?" asked Henricks.

"No, no. Don't want to scare anyone. Priority will do. I just want to convey our official condolences—and maybe there's just a chance that a few more of our boys have been picked up."

"Yes, sir."

Within five minutes the Kremlin was on the line.

"Mr. Premier."

"Mr. President."

The Russian Premier's deep, gravelly voice was followed by that of his interpreter.

"Mr. President, I am very grieved to hear of the loss of so many Americans aboard the tanker."

"Thank you, Mr. Premier. I would like to express my regrets also at the danger your people are in and—"

Krestinsky's voice came on the line. The Russian interpreter spoke. "Excuse us for a moment please, Mr. President."

Sutherland switched over to a direct, noninterference line to his standby interpreter. "What's the trouble?"

"Apparently there's some confusion over who you meant by their 'people,' Mr. President."

Sutherland looked puzzled. "I mean their sailors."

The green light showed that the Russian interpreter was back on the line. "Mr. President, Premier Krestinsky thanks you very much for your concern but wonders if you have been fully apprised of the situation?"

Sutherland looked around questioningly at his aides. "I don't understand."

The Russian was talking more slowly now. "Mr. President, some hours ago the *Sakhalin* sent a final message. A fire wave was advancing upon her." The Premier paused. "We presume she is gone."

There was a silence on the line. Then Sutherland spoke. "I'm sorry. I didn't know. Last report we had—well, we didn't know. We would have sent in aircraft

—helicopters—but as you probably know, the fog made that impossible."

"Of course. The Premier wishes to thank you nevertheless." There was a slight pause before the interpreter added quickly, "The Premier also suggests that at some later date we might investigate what has gone amiss. He is sure that we would all be interested in improving safety measures to prevent additional environmental accidents."

The President readily agreed, and there the conversation ended—clearly badly. Sutherland had detected a hint of accusation in the Russians' closing suggestion, as if somehow the Americans were being held accountable for the collision. Both leaders knew worldwide repercussions would come out of this. But the President decided that this was not the time to make these Soviet innuendos an issue. After all, the disaster had struck both sides. Blame would have to wait. Besides, he thought, he was probably overreacting to the Russians because the spill had started in North American waters, and more particularly because the U.S. destroyer might very well have set fire to the whole mess. In any event, he didn't expect the Russians to help with either fighting the fire or trying to clean up. Right now, that was strictly a North American problem—the U.S.'s job, with what little help the Canadians could offer. If they offered.

One thing was certain: no country in the world, including the U.S., was even halfway prepared for what had to be faced now. The only really world-shattering problems that had struck him as remotely possible during his term of office were related almost exclusively to threats to world peace. God, the possibility of something like this hadn't even entered his mind. He walked over to the map and stood dwarfed by the Pacific Ocean. He looked closely at the Alexander Archipelago, which stretched down beside the Alaskan Panhandle. "Well, Jean, what do the Joint Chiefs say we can do about this fuck up?"

Jean gathered a sheaf of notes by her briefcase. "Not very much, Mr. President. It seems that any kind of extinguishing operation is out of the question. We could send fireboats, but even if they could go close enough, there's not much they could do. The trouble is that there's a lot of high octane, aircraft fuel, naphtha—all kinds of volatile stuff in among the oil. At one time tankers carried only one type of oil on each run; now they carry different types in different tanks. That's the problem. Normally the crude would be hard to set alight—it would just sludge around—but most refined oils vaporize quickly, and once they're on fire they evaporate any inhibiting water content in the crude. There's so much gasoline and high octane in this spill that after burning awhile it could raise the crude to its flash point and start it burning. If that happens, we're in real trouble. It's all but impossible to extinguish. We'd need a second flood."

The President sipped his coffee and stared up at the map, recalling what Cronkite had said about the possibility of the whole length of the western seaboard being set ablaze. "This fire is just a primer, then?"

"Yes, sir. It could burn out in hours, but the crude could burn for days once it's started—months at the tanker site. Besides, oil from the tankers is just part of it; there's lots more floating around from other sources." Jean flicked over a leaf of her memo pad. "The Canadians have offered their water bombers, but they aren't any use in a fire this size. Anyway, the smoke has put large areas in a condition of near-zero visibility. The Coast Guard ships can't do anything. At the very most they could only reach the perimeter—if the heat let them."

"Won't that weather dampen it? I mean, contain it somehow, at least for a while?"

"No, sir, not a fire this size—probably make things worse. Can't see what we're doing. It may clear later on, but it's like soup out there right now."

"Is there any other shipping in the area?"

A phone rang and Henricks picked it up. "Hello, Henricks here. Yes, Admiral . . ."

As he spoke, Jean answered the President. "We're waiting on shipping reports now, Mr. President."

"Jean, if by some miracle we do manage to control this fire, is there any possibility of a half-decent clean-up?"

"TOVALOP says no, Mr. President."

"Tovalop—who's he?"

"It's the Tanker Owners' Voluntary Agreement on Liability for Oil Pollution."

The President grunted, "Sounds like a disease." There were a few grim laughs. "What do they suggest —anything?"

Jean flipped over several of her Environmental Protection Agency charts hanging from a nearby stand. "First thing we have to do is to corral and contain the oil, possibly with booms. Then the oil has to be either vacuumed up or soaked up with straw."

The President was incredulous. "You mean the EPA hasn't advanced beyond *straw?*"

Jean Roche felt duty-bound to protect her organization. "No, it's still about the best the EPA knows of, or anybody else for that matter. We can spray on an absorbent, but the problem is, before you can use it you have to extinguish the fire completely; otherwise it can act as a wick in the crude and help it to burn."

"How big a spill can we handle?"

"There's a sweeping, skimming, and separating procedure which also stores the oil, called Vacusponge. It can vacuum a hundred and fifty acres every hour, but its operation is limited by eight-foot waves."

"How long would Vac-whatever-it-is take to clear this spill?"

Jean Roche hesitated. "In a relatively calm sea, about a hundred years, Mr. President."

The President shook his head in exasperation. "Terrific. Well, can we use these chemical dispersant things?"

Jean consulted her notebook. "Not for a spill this big, sir. On the *Torrey Canyon* spill, which was nothing compared to this, they had to use seven hundred thousand gallons to disperse the oil enough for the bacteria to attack it and break it down. In any case," she went on, "the best dispersal detergents are the most aromatic. But they're also the most poisonous. If we used them, the toxicity would be awfully high."

"How high?" asked the President.

"High enough to kill everything else in the sea. We don't have exact figures, but we do know that ten parts of detergent per million for one hour is fatal for most plankton, which are the base of the food chain and oxygen production. If it got into the coastal inlets, it would wipe out local oceanic industries."

The President turned and flipped over another diagram. "Not to mention the people."

She blushed, chastened. "Of course, sir."

The President was tired. Apart from having just played squash with General Oster, he had been up since 6:00 A.M. He looked at the bank of digital clocks. It was 6:30 P.M. in Washington, 3:30 P.M. in the spill area. A messenger arrived and handed Jean a package. She tore it open, clipped the film cassette it contained into the automatic projector, and pressed the "On" button. The room lights dimmed and the map disappeared into the high ceiling, to be replaced by the white beaded screen. The NASA satellite pictures showed the vastness of the spill, which could be seen spreading like a black amoeba over the turquoise blue sea. Then suddenly the sea was blotted out by towering columns of tar-black smoke, curling and writhing within themselves as they climbed in vengeful spirals to challenge the white cumulonimbus which lay at the higher levels.

As the satellite sped towards North America, passing above intermittent cloud cover over the Aleutians, the closeup lens zoomed in towards the red black heart of the firespill, which now looked dangerously close not only to the islands of the Alexander Archipelago but to the British Columbia–Alaska mainland which lay immediately behind them. From Juneau in the north to Stewart a hundred and fifty miles to the south, the whole Panhandle was threatened. Leaping in a kind of mad unison, miles of orange red flame could be seen licking hundreds of feet into the dense smoke, reminding the President of childhood horror tales in which primordial creatures bent on destruction would rise out of a volcanic sea to devour the earth.

The ocean was covered in parts with white-dotted areas, as if confetti had been carelessly strewn about by some giant hand—conglomerations of tens of thousands of seabirds caught by the fumes, unable to travel fast enough or long enough to escape the fire, which had quickly robbed them of oxygen.

The film ended and the map reappeared. When the lights reached full intensity, the President sat still for a few seconds, his hands clasped together, staring at the blank screen. Then he rose from his chair, and peered closely at a chart of the Vacusponge process, which showed a mass of vacuum hoses running out from a boat, like some mechanical octopus, cleaning up a small, textbook spill. Henricks had just finished talking to the admiral as Sutherland asked, "Does anyone have the slightest idea what a cleanup might cost the taxpayers of this country?"

"We're looking at about three billion dollars, Mr. President," volunteered Jean. "The oil companies have cooperatives for spill liabilities, but TOVALOP sets a limit around fifty million. No one dreamed of anything this big."

The President nodded, exasperated. "That's all we need in an election year," he said. "Whatever happened to all those special double-bottomed and double-sided tankers EPA was talking about?"

"One of the tankers—the *Kodiak*—was a double-bottomed ULCC, sir, but hit with that force—well, it doesn't count for much."

"ULCC?"

"Ultra Large Crude Carrier, sir."

"Just call them ships."

"Yes, sir."

The President rubbed his forehead slowly as he tried to visualize how many of the huge tanks like those at the New Jersey refineries it would take to hold six hundred million gallons. But at the moment all he could comprehend with any clarity was what he had just seen. And soon that monstrous two thousand square miles of blazing spill would spread, leaping from spill to spill in the already heavily polluted sea, and become ten—twenty—times as big—and more if it wasn't stopped. But how could they stop it? No one had experienced a spill anything like this. Sutherland wished he'd vetoed the bill which had allowed crude storage facilities to be built on the coast. They should have just stuck to the overland pipeline through Canada from Kitimat to Edmonton and then down to the lower forty-eight, instead of allowing million-ton supratankers as well. And he should never have authorized U.S. tankers to save fuel by traveling close to the coast instead of following the outer route. He looked about at the assembled aides. "How in hell is this possible?"

There was a silence as the White House staff shared their chief's bewilderment at the firespill's magnitude. Finally it was Jean Roche who again proffered an explanation. "We've had the warning signals for years, Mr. President. And the ULCC—I mean the supratanker—breakup, for example, has been very heavy lately—five tankers a month, let alone offshore blowouts and submarine pipeline leaks."

The President gestured towards the map. "If part of the Pacific Ocean can catch fire, what about our smaller seas?"

Jean was unhesitating in her assessment. "They're sludge pools, Mr. President—ready for ignition."

"Goddamn it, we've got rules against that possibility, no? The Great Lakes legislation, the Water Quality Improvement Act. Aren't they operable? What's the EPA been doing—sleeping?"

The other aides retreated to files and memos. Henricks was talking to the admiral again as Jean continued to bear the brunt of the President's frustration. "Yes, sir, they're operable but barely. Trouble is, we started too late, with Nixon impounding the nine billion allocated for water improvement, then Congress haggling over which agency got what. The Great Lakes are the highest risk. We thought something would happen there first. We've already had a big spill on Lake Superior, but fortunately no fire."

"Then we'd better send out a top priority immediately. I want those rules enforced."

"Yes, sir," answered Jean. She lifted the phone and began dialing the head of the Environmental Protection Enforcement Agency to get special emergency action on all antipollution laws. "Should I release it for international coverage, Mr. President?"

"Hell, yes. And make sure you let the Russians know. This is one thing we can agree on . . . maybe."

"Yes, sir. I'll also—"

Henricks, looking grave, cut in. "Mr. President, I've got some bad news from the shipping report."

Sutherland waved his hand towards the Communications Annex. "Throw it on the pile."

"The Vice-President is trapped by the fire."

Everyone in the room was stunned. For a moment no one spoke, and the only noise was the steady hammering of the Teletype machines. The President's face was white. He stared at Henricks. "I thought Elaine —I thought she was on a fishing trip . . . ?"

"That's just where she's been fishing, sir—deep sea off the Alexander Archipelago." He glanced down at his notepad. "Out of Sitka."

Two other aides entered the room with charts and files. Sutherland felt a dull, heavy ache begin above his left eye. Jean Roche moved towards him, convinced he was going to collapse. Just as she reached him, he sat down at the table. "Trapped." His voice was barely audible.

Henricks glanced apprehensively at Jean Roche. "Yes, sir. Admiral Klein just told me. You could probably see from the satellite photos that the blaze isn't a blanket fire. That is, there are pockets as yet not ignited due to differing wind and sea currents. The boat is caught in one of those areas." Henricks paused and then went on in a quieter tone. "Apparently its motor cut out. Repairs took most of the day. By the time it was fixed—well, they were encircled by the firespill."

The President coughed and reached into his pocket. "What's the size of the boat?"

"It's a thirty-footer, sir."

For the third time that day the President was utterly incredulous. It was as if the impossible were becoming the norm. "Good Christ!" he exploded. "What's she doing fishing in a tub that size?" No one answered. "Can it outrun the fire?"

The answer came from one of the new arrivals, Norman Blane, an EPA man attached to the White House staff. He was pinning up a satellite weather map which showed that beneath the cloud and smoke layer there were small pockets of clear sea standing out like blue islands amid the blackness. Despite his airy manner, Blane, who, like most of those present, did not know the extent of Elaine Horton's relationship with the President, only added to the growing mood of helplessness. "No, sir, not a chance. It's been caught in a pincer movement—completely surrounded by a large fire zone which could come in fast."

On the map Blane's finger moved westward from Sitka out to sea. "This is where the Vice-President is—about fourteen or fifteen miles from the collision site. You can see the spill was already in front of her, to the east, between her and Baranof Island, before it caught fire. Pretty soon after, two arms of it circled back around her, then joined up again and spread back of her, making a kind of bone-shaped spill. The clear area, with the boat in it, is in the center of the eastern part of the bone, as it were. Now, as I say, how fast the fire comes in towards the boat is—well, anybody's guess. It all depends on the hydrostatic head at what was the Russian tanker site."

Blane's cool professionalism irritated the President. "Come on, Norman, put that in English I can understand."

The aide's arms moved flamboyantly as he explained. "Hydrostatic head? Oh, well, it's the pileup of oil as it leaks up from the sunken tanks, sir. Like pouring whipped cream on coffee, only from underneath the surface." Blane smiled, congratulating himself on the analogy. "Its dispersal rate depends on wind and currents. And temperature. Oil will normally move at around four percent of wind velocity, but with strong currents and winds it can do a lot better than that. Those gases can race across the sea like a regular prairie fire."

Sutherland grunted. "Has anybody found out yet if any of our ships are in the area?"

Henricks quickly read the shipping report. "No, sir, no U.S. surface craft now that the *Tyler Maine* has gone. There is a Canadian sub. That's all."

The President thought for a moment, then asked, "What about our subs?"

Henricks checked the report again but shook his head. "No, sir. We have four nuclear subs on northwestern patrol—two in the Bering Strait, two in the Beaufort Sea—and one conventional a hundred miles south of the Aleutian chain. They're all too far away to get there in time, even at maximum speed."

Sutherland barely heard Henricks's last remark. For a moment his mind had fled from the present crisis to the memory of a much happier time—to Elaine's face, flushed with excitement, the first time he had shown her how to snorkel on Kauai, the northernmost island of the Hawaiian chain. He could still hear her voice, her words almost tripping over one another, eager to tell of the wonders she had seen for the first time: the kaleidoscope of colors; the polished black, yellow, and blue of the Moorish Idol gently nibbling the seaweed just a few feet below her; and the long white eels with their eyes like marbles, immobile and piercing, as they hung suspended like stiff pieces of kelp below the surface of the gently rolling surf. Her mood had been so infectious that the thrill of his own youthful discoveries had come flooding back to him.

It was the sheer vigor of her childlike curiosity which had first drawn him to her, had revived in him emotions far removed from the daily machinations of power, and had filled him with a desire to shrug off the inhibitions imposed by the often secret nature of his work as a congressman in the Armed Services Appropriations Committee. The long hours, the constant pressure from generals and admirals to increase the size of defense contracts, and the almost flagrantly ill disguised bribes offered by hopeful contractors had made him suspicious of nearly everyone in Washington.

But with Elaine, he found, he could relax. She possessed a candor so well balanced by a sense of humor that no one could take offense. He had once seen her fix a large and importunate electronics tycoon with a winning smile and announce, "I hope you're not trying to bribe me into voting yes on that new import quota bill, Jack, because if you are, I'll vote the other way, just to prove how crazy women are."

That had ended that episode, and it had been done with such disarming geniality that the tycoon had no alternative but to buy another round and leave, putting as good a face as he could manage on it. It was this mixture of childlike honesty and worldly sophistication that had constantly surprised and delighted Sutherland.

Henricks coughed politely, waiting for the President's orders, but Sutherland was back on Kauai, on the day he and Elaine had walked hand in hand along the deserted, straw-colored beach and swum in the cool green sea just as the red disk of the sun disappeared behind the macadamia trees. That day their lovemaking had been the best. Afterwards they had strolled along the more inhabited beach at Poipu, in the soft twilight, watching the torches of the hotels flicker and wave in the gentle trade wind, listening to the surf pounding over the reef and surging onto the curving, palm-backed beaches, awash with moonlight.

And now she might die.

Henricks coughed again, louder.

Sutherland tried to marshal his thoughts, to put the memories out of his mind, but the more he tried, the more they rushed back at him. "Are there any other surface craft out there?" he asked curtly. "Any nationality at all?"

"A Japanese LNG off Chichagof Island out of Juneau. She's under contract to El Paso Company—

heading towards Point Conception just north of L.A. But she's too far off at the moment, too."

The President slapped the table angrily. The telexes kept chattering like recalcitrant children as everyone fell silent. "Would you all stop trying to impress me with your technical expertise and talk to me in plain, simple English." There was a long silence. The President reached into his pocket and threw several small balls of Kleenex into the wastebasket. After a few seconds he asked quietly, "Now, Bob, what in Christ is an LNG? Just so a simple old Harvard boy like me can understand."

"It's a liquefied natural gas carrier, Mr. President," Henricks explained. "It's like a regular tanker, only it has three—maybe five—cylindrical tanks sunk into the deck."

Sutherland nodded his thanks. "Then it won't be any use at all. Matter of fact, it'd be downright dangerous having it anywhere near the fire. Right? Wouldn't the gas expand in those tanks?"

It seemed no one in the room had thought of this possibility. "Well, wouldn't it?" asked the President. "As I remember it, natural gas has to be refrigerated for transporting; otherwise it becomes extremely unstable."

Henricks answered, "Yes, sir, it probably would. Be dangerous, I mean."

The President wasn't listening. He pushed his chair back and jumped to his feet, slamming his fist on the table. "The Canadian sub! It can go under and get them out!"

It was a rough day for Henricks. Again duty obligated him to be the harbinger of bad news. "Sorry, sir, it's trapped like the boat—only beneath the fire. Admiral Klein has been in contact with Canadian Maritime Command at Esquimalt in British Columbia. They say it's a nonnuclear, conventional trainer type—post–World War Two, but not much. It's modernized, but apparently it will have to surface soon to recharge its batteries and replenish its air supply. Klein says it could perhaps make it under the fire to the boat, but in order to return it would have to recharge and reoxygenate." Henricks hesitated. "That is, of course, if the Canadians agreed to try it."

"Why wouldn't they?" enquired the President.

Jean Roche answered quickly. "Along with Washington and Oregon, they fought hard against supratanker routes down their coast, Mr. President. They've always been afraid of spills. They feel very strongly about it, I'm afraid."

"Of course," grumbled Sutherland, obviously piqued. "They don't have to import as much." He turned back to Henricks. "You said its batteries 'apparently' need recharging. Does that mean they'll need it or not?"

"Yes, sir, they will."

The President waved impatiently at the weather map. "Couldn't they do that in the clear area where the fishing boat is holding out?"

Henricks admired the President's inventiveness, but he shook his head. "It would take time, sir. Besides, the fire could have eaten up most of the area by then. As Norman said, we don't know how fast it's closing in on the Vice-President or any of the other patches which haven't caught fire yet. All we do know is that it's closing. Where it is now, the sub's only safely got enough power and air to retreat away from under the fire. If it goes further in, it could reach a point of no return."

Seeing how risky such an operation would be, Sutherland studied the weather map for some hidden answer. "Is there any possibility that the fire can be doused? By the weather, I mean?"

Blane's arms were windmilling. He looked like an enthusiastic professor unexpectedly given an opportunity to get in on the decision making. "There is an Arctic front coming down, but it's a close bet. It might not rain. Actually, that would be worse; you'd have winds pushing the firespill further in, right down the coast."

"Well, we can't depend on acts of God," said the President, turning to Jean for a glimmer of hope. "Jean, call General Oster. Ask him if there's any chance of a helicopter or parachute drop. And ask him to come over."

"Yes, Mr. President."

The general's voice on the phone was clipped and tense. "No way. Even if we could get them there in time, planes or helicopters couldn't work effectively in that smoke cover. They really couldn't work at all. Too dangerous lifting someone out of a fire you can't see properly. And they'd be burned themselves, as well as the Vice-President. I've checked with the Coast Guard; they've ruled out hydrofoils. They'd be useless in slick even if they could get near the fire, which they couldn't."

As Jean relayed the information, the President sat down. For an instant, he looked very anxious.

Clara Sutherland sat quietly in her White House study overlooking the tall, white, floodlit Washington Monument, waiting patiently for the phone to ring. He had not even told her about Elaine Horton's being trapped. Had it not been for an aide, she still wouldn't have known. She knew better than to call down to the Operations Room at a time like this, yet she had hoped that somehow he would need her. But the phone in her study remained silent. It did not occur to her to feel self-pity, but she did feel lonely. She gained no comfort from the warm feeling she usually experienced in the study which she had decorated in soft, autumnal shades of red and russet brown.

As the night darkened even further, she turned on the lamp in the mahogany stand near the balcony overlooking the still, light-bathed lawn. She opened a book, but try as she might she could not concentrate. Perhaps, she thought, he would ring later; perhaps they might have supper together. She pressed the remote TV control, changing channels only to see the same pictures of the fire reappear.

Back in the Operations Room the President, somewhat shamed that his attention had been almost entirely centered on Elaine's welfare, asked, "How about our agents down on the boat? How many are there besides the Vice-President?"

Jean Roche had been fearing this question, for although she was as upset as anyone else about the situation, she thoroughly disapproved of the Vice-President's behavior as reported by a distraught Miller from Sitka. She was afraid her disapproval might show. "None, Mr. President—only the captain, I believe. The Vice-President refused to have agents along on this trip."

The President made no comment though he instinctively felt angry that someone he loved had unnecessarily exposed herself to danger. And yet he realized, in her defense, that he, too, periodically tried to lose agents, as every president before him had done. "We'll have to ask the Canadians, then, even if it does mean risking a point of no return. We haven't time to wait for any other help."

Henricks was skeptical. He thought of the men aboard the sub. "It'll be touch and go, Mr. President."

Sutherland felt the stabbing pain above his eye. He instinctively raised his hand to protect it. "Well, Bob," he grimaced, "we haven't got anything else to go with."

"No, sir."

"Jean, get the Canadian Prime Minister. If he's out of the country, get him wherever he is. I want to speak to him personally. I'll take it in the Operations Lounge."

"Yes, sir."

"And Jean."

"Yes, Mr. President?"

"Get me the file on him before I talk to him." As Jean Roche pushed the buttons that would connect her to the records computer, Sutherland, looking up at the small red circle that marked the fire on the map, allowed himself an uncharacteristic moment of self-reproach. It was his fault that Elaine and that fisherman were trapped. If he had not met her, she would most likely never have gone to Alaska, would never have gone fishing. But then the ifs started to pile up.

If the tankers hadn't collided. If it hadn't been so foggy. If only none of us had been born. He smiled, without humor. Regrets and recriminations were useless. Steeling himself, he settled in his chair and reached for the file Jean placed in front of him.

EIGHT

Heading southeast at latitude 57°20′ north and longitude 137°29′ west, seventy-five miles west of the northern tip of Baranof Island and eighty-seven miles northwest of Sitka, H.M.C.S. *Swordfish* was homeward bound, gliding silently ninety feet beneath the spill at a steady eighteen knots.

Apart from some modifications to the casing which covered the two-hundred-foot-long, cigar-shaped cylinder, and the blackening of its formerly red forward and after messenger buoys, the sub looked like any of the conventional Ranger-class trainers built in the early seventies.

Ten weeks before, when they had put to sea from Esquimalt, Captain Kyle had been a reasonably contented man, and he had not allowed the incident with Lambrecker to darken his hope of an enjoyable patrol. Now he was worried, unhappy, and eager to be home. Alone in his cabin, he tried by way of distraction to understand one of the latest electronic equipment manuals, but he found it hard to concentrate. He was thinking that perhaps he'd made a mistake, and a bad one, in accepting this assignment.

Except for the old submariners aboard, few of whom had seen a shot fired in anger, most of the crew of eighty-four were newcomers. It wasn't their greenness that Kyle minded; he'd been steadily knocking that out of them during the last ten weeks, making himself unpopular by constantly drilling them until they were sick and tired of it. It was their attitude that disturbed him. No, it might still be a good navy, but it was different—so different that he had seriously begun to doubt his ability to command.

It had been as he'd suspected. There were those who wanted an explanation for every order—and worse, they could quote all the new regulations which required you to give them one. These were the men Kyle didn't need aboard the *Swordfish.* They merely increased the everyday tensions on a boat where in a sleeping compartment that measured six by ten by twenty feet, thirteen men were required to bunk for three months. It was this small core of troublemakers that had made this patrol one of the most exhausting of his career. Their questions were nothing more than a camouflaged hostility, a bitterness towards any authority. And it was their hesitation to carry out orders during an emergency that had continued to burden Kyle's command with unnecessary anxiety. Such hesitation, he knew, might cost not only their own lives but everybody else's on board.

He kept trying to teach the crew the lessons he had learned—to follow the same checklists day in and day out so that in times of stress the boat's safety would rest secure in habit and not hinge on memory alone or on individual variation. He'd told them how it had been in the Atlantic: you did what you were told when you were told, otherwise you might find yourself cut in half by a German destroyer. To his surprise, most of them had listened and learned well; but there were still a few who refused to conform.

A few times in the last few days Kyle had felt himself coming close to losing his temper with one or two of them who, though doing nothing overt in their refusal to execute orders promptly, had added to the host of petty insubordinations that constantly tried his patience.

He sighed heavily, knowing that he understood neither the "new breed" nor the latest electronic wizardry sketched out before him in the manual. He really did belong to another age. Even a few of the younger officers felt uneasy with a man of his years in charge. "To hell with them," he grunted, getting up from his bunk and shaking two aspirins from the bottle. His head ached. The air was getting foul.

He was a little concerned about the firespill, which was keeping them submerged much longer than he would have liked. Fifty-four hours, in fact. But it didn't worry him too much, for he'd instructed his first officer to plot the shortest course out from under the spill, and now they were on that heading. An hour or so to the south and they should be clear. Then they could surface, blow out the carbon dioxide, replenish their air, and run on the surface, using their diesel engines while recharging the batteries that powered them while they were submerged. He was comforted by the fact that they hadn't been caught submerged further inside the firespill. He would pity any poor devil in a situation like that. He decided that to allay any fears for *Swordfish*'s safety at home, he should report their position as soon as they reached periscope depth, where they could raise the transmitting antennae. Until then they could only receive from the trailing floating wire, and with the worsening weather they were having difficulty doing that. Wind and sea were whipping the aerial around, and long waves of static made reception very bad.

Soon he felt less fidgety as the aspirins started to work on his headache. Feeling drowsy, he let the manual slide easily from his hands. He looked forward to securing the sub in Esquimalt, already seeing in his mind the pleasant green hillsides which concealed the ammunition dumps of Pacific Command.

In the radio shack, the operator cursed. For the third time in the past hour, a roar of atmospherics had caused him to miss Pacific Command's bulletin on the extent of the spill.

NINE

In the short time it took Jean Roche to get through to Ottawa, Sutherland glanced through the file on the Canadian Prime Minister. The photograph made him look like a mild-mannered banker with balding head and a weak mouth. But in a few seconds Sutherland had found out that the picture belied Prime Minister Henri Gerrard's reputation as a strong, if quiet-spoken, leader of a large majority government. For the purposes of the request he was about to make, this was all Sutherland needed to know.

As he took the receiver, Jean thought it prudent to tell him that the call had taken the Prime Minister away from a cabinet meeting—presumably being held in response to the Canadian outcry over the spill. Sutherland nodded his thanks and indicated he would take the call alone. By the time she had closed the lounge door, he was already speaking to the Canadian leader.

"Mr. Prime Minister."

"Mr. President."

"I'm told I interrupted a cabinet meeting. I'm sorry."

"Not at all. I needed the break."

Sutherland leaned back in his chair, relieved at the other's friendly tone. "That's very kind of you in view of what's happened. I'm very sorry about the spill, damned sorry."

There was a slight, awkward pause before Gerrard spoke. "Of course. I understand. I gather that's what you've called about."

"Yes. We have a difficult situation down here," and he added hurriedly, "as I'm sure you do. I realize the

Canadian coast is in imminent danger as well as Alaska. I'd like to talk to you about that in a minute, if I might. But first I would like to ask a very great favor of you."

"Yes?"

"Well, as fate would have it, Mr. Prime Minister, our Vice-President has been trapped by the fire."

Again there was a brief silence.

"My God."

Sutherland didn't allow the other's shock to slow him down. The only thing that would help Elaine and the boat's captain was action. "It's particularly tricky, because while she's in a nonfire pocket at the moment, the firespill could close in very quickly. Well, the long and short of it, Mr. Prime Minister, is that we have no ships close enough to effect a rescue. We do, of course, have subs on western patrol, but fast as they are, it would take them too long to reach the boat."

Gerrard's response was instantaneous. "I'll give you all the help I can, Mr. President." Sutherland was deeply moved. He had met Gerrard only once, but suddenly he felt he was talking to an old friend.

"Thank you very much. Mr. Prime Minister, my . . . sources inform me that there is a Canadian submarine under the spill area. Of course, to have her go in would be—well, frankly, it would be very dangerous . . ."

"What precisely are the dangers?"

The President explained the risk of the sub's reaching a possible point of no return, given the depletion of her oxygen and battery power. "Under the circumstances, I couldn't blame you for rejecting the request out of—"

"Nonsense," interjected Gerrard. "These things happen. Naturally I will have to confer with my cabinet colleagues—for media consumption, if you get my meaning?"

"Of course. I understand."

Despite his headache, which now felt as if it would cleave his skull, Sutherland found himself smiling at the Canadian's innuendo. The President liked his style. The Prime Minister might wear banker's clothes, but underneath the blue suit he had a politician's eye for expediency as well as a human disposition for generosity.

The Prime Minister added, "Perhaps you could have your people send the Vice-President's position direct to Maritime Command Esquimalt."

"We'll send the coordinates immediately."

"Good. Can I ring you back, Mr. President?"

"Certainly—and thank you again. Ah—Mr. Prime Minister?"

"Yes?"

"I believe the name of the submarine is *Swordfish.*"

The Canadian leader laughed. "Yes, I know. We only have two of them."

Sutherland was hardly listening. Obviously, the Prime Minister was joking.

As Gerrard made his way back to the cabinet room from his third-floor office in Parliament's center block, he talked to his secretary in an unusually subdued voice. Despite the confident tone of his conversation with Sutherland, he was not at all sure that he could get cabinet approval to risk the Canadian sub. His biggest worry in the cabinet was Farley, the minister for health.

A one-time provincial socialist M.P., Farley had crossed party lines and joined the federal Liberals ten years ago, disgusted with the stagnation of his own party. Capable and cantankerous, he nurtured and championed the conviction common among many western M.P.'s that the United States, even more than the easterners, was determined at every opportunity to cheat western Canada out of its natural resources, from oil in Alberta to minerals in British Columbia. Gerrard had brought Farley into his cabinet not only because of his expertise as an administrator but also as a sop to a particularly vociferous group of backbenchers, most of them from the West.

The Prime Minister had at times regretted the appointment; not that Farley didn't do a good job with the health portfolio, but in cabinet he remained as divisive an element on Canadian-American affairs as he had been on the back bench. The little red-haired ex-Scot had a way of polarizing normally middle-of-the-road Liberals, and while he often guided his fellow M.P.'s to the best goals, he almost invariably brought out the worst manners.

Gerrard could only hope that Farley would not start asking awkward and irrelevant questions as to why U.S. nuclear subs were not available. He decided that he would just have to pass on what President Sutherland had told him. It should be acceptable, even to Farley, that the Americans would have looked after their own had they had a sub close at hand. Nevertheless, the P.M. knew that he would have to handle the affair cautiously; one never knew what tack Farley would take if given the slightest opportunity to steer the issue towards Canadian nationalism.

Sure enough, after Gerrard had explained the Americans' request as succinctly as possible, the air in the cabinet room was thick with tension.

The minister for external affairs, Eric Bern, was plainly all for sending the sub in immediately, but he had clashed with Farley even before the P.M. had finished his situation report. Now Bern was standing at a window with his hands in his pockets, looking out glumly at the mottled maples to the east of the parliamentary quadrangle. He rounded angrily on his colleague. "I might remind you, Farley, that that woman and that man out in that boat are first of all people, and then Americans—if that makes any difference to the members from British Columbia."

Farley's small, red face glowered up from the green baize-topped table that seemed to Gerrard like a moat between the warring east-west factions of his cabinet. The British Columbian's rasping voice spat out the words at his fellow M.P. "And what's that supposed to mean, eh? That I don't care? Let me remind—"

Bern, his face now as livid as Farley's, cut in. "I am merely making the observation that the Honorable Member for Vancouver East and some of his colleagues have repeatedly voiced what I consider, and I daresay what many others consider, an almost obsessive anti-Americanism and that this is neither the time nor the place to—"

Farley could hardly speak. "Good God! You've got gall calling *me* obsessive after your bloody performance in Washington! All that ass licking on import quotas. Why didn't you just sell them Alberta and be done with it?"

Prime Minister Gerrard was disgusted by the vehemence of the two members, especially Farley's willful vulgarity, but although he could have stopped it with a word or two, he sat quietly and let them air their mutual dislike. He had learned that in his cabinet compromise was invariably easier to achieve once these two had vented their spleen and were feeling a little ashamed of their loss of control.

While the other members sat quietly, waiting for the ritual name calling to pass, Gerrard's private secretary entered the room. Studiously ignoring the acrimonious exchange, he bent down and whispered to the Prime Minister, who simply nodded, then leaned forward again to watch the Honorable Members. He had the air of a man at a cockfight of which he totally disapproved but with which he still felt it prudent not to interfere. Several junior cabinet members glanced at each other; the minister for health looked pointedly at his watch. It was the external affairs minister's turn. "The trouble with you, Farley, is that with typical socialist fervor you love humanity but can't stand people—particularly those to the south of us."

Farley pushed his blotter to the middle of the table as if he were throwing down a gauntlet. He turned to Gerrard, dismissing Bern's remark as beneath contempt. His voice had lost its grating aggressiveness. He spoke slowly, without profanity, but with such pained restraint that the older cabinet members knew that if Gerrard did not step in he would soon burst into an uncontrollable rage. "Prime Minister, perhaps you can enlighten our dull-witted colleague and explain to him that the only point I wish to make is that whether we are talking about Americans or Chinese, there is a simple arithmetical equation involved."

He glared at Bern, who was staring out at the quadrangle again. "It is this. There are two people trapped by this inferno—which, I might add, would never have happened had we been more insistent upon policing tanker traffic on the west coast. As the chances of rescue hardly seem promising, the idea of risking the lives of eighty-four seamen—eighty-four *people* if the minister for external affairs would prefer—should be examined closely. In short, I'm saying that the minister and those colleagues who agree with him seem to be more impressed by the status of the unfortunate victims than by the number of rescuers who could well be lost. That is my point, and I fail to see how it can possibly be misconstrued as a petty display of nationalism."

Bern turned back from the window. "I'm fully aware of the . . . statistics Mr. Farley so assiduously quotes. The point I am trying to make, however, is that in such matters we do not, nor should we, make our decisions on the basis of slide rule projections. If we did, every missing child would be left to perish on the basis that we risk a hundred men in the search." The minister leaned forward, his weight supported by widely spread fingers drained white from the strain. "Clearly, *clearly* this is morally unacceptable—quite apart from being thickheaded."

Farley pushed the blotter further out and jumped up angrily, but Gerrard held up his hand. Enough steam had been let off for both sides' egos to have been satisfied. "All right, gentlemen, you've both had your say. All I can add is to say thank God cabinet meetings are not televised. This has not been a particularly edifying spectacle." There was an awkward silence as both Farley and Bern sat looking into the distance. "Be that as it may," continued the P.M., "I concede that both points of view have merit. I'm sure we all concur with Eric's argument, namely, that we cannot vote on matters of this nature simply on the

"Not a damn thing. I'm afraid," said Farley, passing a still on to Bern, "it's up to our American friends. All we can do is pray."

Bern was shocked by the proximity of the spill. Though they had been discussing its extent when the President had called about the Vice-President, Bern had not realized just how close the slick was. "My God. Just as well it's not too heavily populated out there. A flash fire anywhere along that shore would wipe out a town in a matter of hours."

Farley spoke with a tinge of sarcasm which even now he could not resist. "Well, of course there is Vancouver—that only has three million."

"I meant further north," Bern retorted.

"I'm talking about the whole bloody coast," said Farley. "These pictures were taken north, off Prince Rupert, but in a few days the situation'll be nasty in the south if those winds rise. It's been a dry, hot summer. Once those B.C. forests catch fire, there'll be a bloody inferno."

"And the same for Washington State," said someone, tired of Farley's petty vindictiveness.

"Quite," put in Bern. "In fact, it'll be very bad for the three contiguous western United States—especially California. Less chance of rain there, too."

Farley glanced over at the minister for external affairs. "Well, you see the point about the tankers; they're too bloody close in."

Bern nodded. "Yes, you're right," he said quietly. He paused, then looked straight at Farley. "I'd hate to be out there—wouldn't you?"

Farley nodded in return. Fair was fair. "Yes," he said, "I sure as hell would. Poor bastards."

Gerrard patted Farley on the back, then called out, "Gentlemen!" There was silence. "Gentlemen, I take it then we are agreed on the instructions to give the submarine. Important as the pollution problem is, we must give the rescue attempt our immediate attention. My secretary is waiting to transmit the message to Admiral Jolley at Maritime Command. And in any case, without wishing to be mercenary about it, in the light of what Mr. Farley has just shown us, the rescue mission may well elicit a much more favorable response from Washington apropos the cleanup. Those in favor?"

Every hand was raised. The Prime Minister smiled. "Thank you. I will notify Washington accordingly." He surveyed the room, his face suddenly alight with his famous conspiratorial grin. "I suggest we adjourn until we have more detailed information on the spill. I've been informed that Washington is sending satellite pictures. They should arrive shortly."

His secretary whispered and the P.M. held up his hand. "Oh, yes—before you go. The minister of defense has asked me if the press is to know of our decision. I would advise 'no comment' until I check with President Sutherland." He looked sternly at Farley. "He has enough trouble on his hands, and with the flack he's getting already, he may wish to keep it quiet, at least for a while. I'll let you know for sure when we reconvene. That's all."

As the room emptied and the last member filed out, Henri Gerrard, looking as fresh as if he had just shaved and breakfasted, turned to his secretary and asked quietly, "Has the message to the sub been sent?"

"Yes, Mr. Prime Minister. Maritime Command sent it thirty minutes ago."

"Good," said Gerrard, stuffing his pipe with his favorite cherry blend. "If Farley ever finds that out, he'll have a fit."

Sutherland put down the red receiver and announced, "The Canadians are going in." There was an audible sigh of relief in the Operations Room. He turned to Henricks. "Bob, have Admiral Klein radio the Vice-President. 'My lov—' " The President flushed. " 'My regards.' And tell them to hang tight. A sub's on the way."

TEN

O'Brien knocked sharply on the captain's door. Kyle, sleepy-eyed, swung off his bunk and instinctively reached for his cap. In his dream, he was still ashore. When he realized where he was, he replaced it, got up, and doused his face with cold water. Still waking up, groping for a towel, he asked his executive gruffly, "What is it?"

O'Brien handed him Admiral Jolley's message from Maritime Command. Kyle had a habit of moving his lips when scanning messages. Now his mouth was a thin, hard line, and a small muscle worked at the hinge of his jaw as he read:

RR RCWEWW
DE RCWEW 171
ZNR UUUUU
O
FM MARPACHQ ESQUIMALT
TO SWORDFISH
BT
SECRET OPS 143 FOR COMMANDING OFFICER
SUBJECT: VICE PRESIDENT OF UNITED STATES

1 PRIME MINISTER INFORMS US THAT US VICE PRESIDENT ENCIRCLED BY FIRESPILL LAT 57° 19′ NORTH LONG 136° 17′ WEST
2 SWORDFISH ORDERED TO PROCEED WITH ALL POSSIBLE HASTE TO ABOVE POSITION AND RESCUE VICE PRESIDENT AND COMPANION ABOARD FISHING BOAT
3 REALIZE RISK INVOLVED GIVEN YOUR SUBMERSAL TIME BUT NO OTHER MEANS AVAILABLE

4 SHOULD YOU CONSIDER RESCUE HOPELESS YOU HAVE PERMISSION TO ABORT
5 MARPACHQ WILL PREPARE ALL POSSIBLE ASSISTANCE
6 GOOD LUCK
BT

He stood silently for a moment. Then he coughed and looked up almost defiantly at O'Brien. "Well? You've got the coordinates?" He said it as if he were upbraiding a junior officer the first time out. O'Brien found his tone irritating, but he couldn't help admiring the Old Man. Admittedly the captain had been a little grumpy lately, but now here they were, instructed to rescue the Vice-President of the United States of America, the most important order either of them might receive in his career, and all old Kyle could say was, "Well?" as if his executive had wakened him unnecessarily from his afternoon nap.

O'Brien smiled. "Yes, sir, we've got the coordinates."

"Then we'd better get going—don't you think?"

"I guess so, sir. What speed?"

Kyle thought for a moment. Should he group up, full ahead together, linking up the sub's batteries and motors in series, which would give him maximum speed but at the cost of a high drain on the batteries? Or should he limit the rate of drain to full ahead together and keep some reserve power for later on? Keeping a reserve wouldn't help the Vice-President, but if they didn't reach her in time, they would need some reserve to get out from under the firespill. With or without the Vice-President. "We won't group up. Just keep it full ahead together."

"Yes, *sir.*" O'Brien saluted briskly.

He knew as well as the captain the condition of the batteries and oxygen. They had been under the spill for five hours, and while they didn't yet know its dispersal pattern, the sub's power and oxygen would very soon be so low that they would have to surface regardless. Before they had received orders to rescue the Vice-President, they had counted on being well beyond the spill. Now they would be going back into it. It all depended on the dispersal rate. If it was slow enough, they could safely come up. If not, they might find themselves covered by fire, in which case they wouldn't be saving anybody. Not even themselves.

Despite the risk, O'Brien felt a surge of exhilaration. It was the nearest he had ever come to active service, and it wasn't until he was halfway down the passageway that he realized how different the crew's reaction might be. He turned abruptly. "Captain?"

"Yes?"

O'Brien glanced around to check that they were alone. "Sir, I thought that—well, being as how the ship's company has been out so long and all, we might turn . . ."

There was a long pause. The captain frowned. "Secretly?"

"Well—yes, sir."

At any other time, Kyle would have rejected, and rejected rudely, the suggestion that prudence might best be served by turning his sub surreptitiously. The very fact that he was entertaining his executive officer's suggestion was a measure of *Swordfish*'s low morale on this cruise.

The administrators ashore often had difficulty understanding how the morale of any crew could drop almost in direct proportion to the time they were out, hitting rock bottom only days away from returning to base. But Kyle knew why. He had seen it happen many times before, and ironically it was at its worst in peacetime. In war the constant common danger from the enemy above and below brought men closer. In peace, when new men, already spoiled by the comforts of home, were away from home for long periods, perhaps for the first time, small problems and irritations festered and spread under the pressure of close confinement. Whenever Kyle had wanted to explain this to a desk sailor who had got his idea of roominess aboard a sub from Hollywood, he usually found some pretext for inviting him below decks. It didn't take long for the message to sink in when the visitor learned that the captain's cabin, the most spacious aboard, was no bigger than a double cubicle latrine, and often didn't smell much better after an extended patrol.

O'Brien spoke again. "It goes against the grain, sir, I know, but—"

"But you're probably right," said Kyle irritably. "This time round anyway. They're going to know sooner or later, but perhaps it's better later. No use asking for trouble."

"I didn't think so, sir."

"All right, do it as quietly as you can. Just inch it around and make the final turn as the watch changes. That should throw them off. No one knows where the hell he is when he first comes on watch."

"Yes, sir."

Although it was not yet nightfall, the control room, squatting below the conning tower, was "rigged for red" because of the heavy smoke layer which would make parts of the surface look as black as night through the periscopes. As he stepped into the blood red glow, O'Brien's earlier sense of excitement gave way to caution. Only yesterday the captain had confided to him once again that he was worried about the crew. Although he was a generation younger than Kyle, O'Brien well understood his concern. He too found it difficult to get used to the "democratization" of the navy.

As his eyes grew accustomed to the dim light, he gave orders to make a series of incremental turns and counter-turns, which he hoped would not alert the crew to the sub's unscheduled change in course.

Clara Sutherland was trying to work up some enthusiasm for the small filet mignon and wondering where her appetite had gone, when she heard a tap on the study door.

"Come in."

Sutherland entered, looking old in the soft yellow light of the lamp which stood behind Clara like a bonneted maid awaiting instructions.

"Have you eaten?" she asked gently.

"No."

"Should I ring for something?"

Sutherland gazed around the room without interest, his eyes finally settling on a Van Trier snow scene of an old cabin set amid a clump of bare beech trees. The detail of the cracked bark in the painting never failed to amaze him. He always felt he could walk right into the waist-deep snow, up to the old farmhouse, and seek solace from the cold. It would always remind him of Clara, no matter what happened.

"You can have my steak if you like," said Clara. "I'm not very hungry."

"Neither am I."

She held out a plate of toast. "You should have something—to keep up your strength."

Sutherland took a piece of toast and slumped down in the Colonial-style rocker. "Have you been watching it on TV?"

"Yes. It looks bad, doesn't it?"

"The satellite pictures are much worse."

"Aren't they the ones that have been on TV?"

Sutherland frowned irritably. "I mean the NASA clips," he said, his voice sharp.

"I'm sorry, I thought—" Clara began apologetically.

Sutherland lifted his hand above his left eye. The pain was getting worse. "Have you an aspirin?"

Clara began to forage through her purse.

"It doesn't matter. I'll ring for one."

"No, no. I have one here somewhere." Her voice was almost imploring. "Will a Midol do?"

"All right. Is there any coffee?"

"I don't think you should mix—"

"Mix what?" he snapped.

"Nothing," she said quietly.

Sutherland let out an exasperated sigh.

There was a soft tap on the door.

"Come in," Sutherland snapped.

The instant Henricks entered the study, he sensed his boss's annoyance at the intrusion.

"Yes? What is it?"

"Sorry to interrupt, Mr. President, but the people at Interior are pressing me about whether they should cancel the ball this evening, considering the circumstances."

"Hell no!"

"Ah—they're worried that—well, by the time we get a handle on this firespill, it might be pretty late."

"So it'll be late!"

"Yes, Mr. President."

"But you're tired," put in Clara. "Can't you postpone it?"

"No, I will not postpone it. How can I? It's the Sheik's last night here."

Henricks looked awkwardly at the Van Trier.

"I've told you before, Clara, and you, Bob," the President continued, "I've told my whole staff that that is precisely what the President shouldn't do in times of crisis. I must do everything as planned—to the letter. Any variation would be interpreted as meaning that —well, that events are overtaking us."

Which is exactly what is happening, thought Henricks; but he simply nodded loyally. Sutherland closed his eyes. "Anybody who opposes my administration would like to see me driven to bed. Well, they won't. I'll be at that ball. Besides, what does the Sheik say?"

"Well, being the guest of honor—"

"So he's attending?" cut in Sutherland.

"Yes, Mr. President."

"Then of course I'll have to go. Tell Interior I'll be there. It might be late, after midnight, but I'll be there to propose the official toast. We need that sheik's oil, and that's all there is to it."

"Yes, Mr. President."

After Henricks withdrew, there was a long silence, interrupted only by the ticking of the grandfather clock. Sutherland cut off a piece of steak as if it were part of some unpleasant reptile and chewed it, barely moving his lower jaw, loath to admit that he was suddenly hungry. Finally the silence was too much even for Clara, who was used to being and feeling alone. "I wish I could help," she said hopefully.

He cut off another piece of steak, more slowly this

time, furious that he could find no excuse for his ill temper in the face of his wife's desire to please.

"You can," he said.

Clara smiled. "How?" she asked.

Sutherland let the fork drop onto the china plate with a crash, his hand darting above his eye again, though this time it was less from pain than from humiliation. "You can stop being so damned—so damned nice. Just say what you mean. We have to talk about it." He pushed the plate away as if it were crowding him. "I just can't think properly. I just can't give my job all the attention it needs if you and I can't be honest."

Clara said nothing for a moment, looking out from the darkness of the study at the lawn, emerald green beneath the floodlights. "I've always understood that," she said, for the first that evening unable to stop her hurt from showing.

Sutherland rose angrily from his chair, reaching for a Kleenex and instead pulling out a whole train. He stuffed them back. "I know, I know—of course you understand, but—well, that's not enough. We have to bring it out into the open—especially now, before the papers start in on me. Before they start building public opinion against me. I can't veto public opinion, Clara —for you or for me."

"What do you want me to do, Walter?"

He turned abruptly away and walked towards the long French windows. He looked out at the great dome of the Jefferson Memorial, then swept his eyes over the expanse of lawn toward the tranquil pond stretching out before the Lincoln Memorial. His voice was firm, but so quiet that Clara had to strain to hear him above the steady, deep ticking of the pendulum clock. "I think we should talk about Elaine. I think—" He hesitated. "I think we should come to some arrangement."

The sound of the clock filled the room. Clara fingered the arm of her chair nervously, pulling at a loose thread. "Don't you think we can just forget it?"

"No. I don't think we can, Clara. It's become a wall between us. We're not talking anymore—or at least we're not *really* talking."

"You know I don't hold it against you."

Sutherland swung around. "Goddamn it, Clara, can't you see what I'm telling you? It's—I'm telling you I still love her."

He turned back to look out the window. "I'm trying to be honest with you, but you won't let me. You insist on slipping behind all your nice words every time I try to get you to face basic facts."

"You're angry because I'm not angry, Walter. Talking about it won't make me angry, if that's what you want. To make you feel better, I mean—to make you feel less guilty. You have to do what you want."

This time his tone was one of anguished triumph. "You think I should feel guilty—for not telling you before?"

"I don't know if you should," Clara said firmly. "That's not for me to say. I know that you do feel guilty. But I see no point in dredging it up to hurt either of us any more."

"At least," he said bitterly, "you admit you're hurt. At least you're being honest about that."

Tears were starting down Clara's cheeks. "I love you—that's why."

Without turning around, he knew she was crying. She did love him—he knew that—and he knew the game he was playing, trying to dissolve her civility so that he might rationalize not only his past affair with Elaine but any future liaison. Suddenly he felt very ashamed. "I'm sorry, Clara," he said in his gentlest tone, adding, "You know she's trapped in this thing."

"I know."

"God help me if the media dig up anything. They'll accuse me of trying too hard to save her. It'll be a real bitch for you."

"I'll ignore it."

He smiled fondly at her. "You probably will." He took her hand, the first time he had done that in months. "Tell me why you aren't bitter."

"You make me sound like Joan of Arc."

"You are."

"You're out of your mind," she said happily.

"Any other woman would have been—I'm sure of that. Why aren't you?"

"Because if I let myself have that, I'd lose you altogether."

After a few moments he asked, "Is that why you've avoided her so much?"

"No. I didn't avoid her to make it easier for you."

"Why then?"

"I don't like her. I never did."

Sutherland didn't answer.

Clara squeezed his hand. "Do you think they'll rescue her?"

"I don't know," he said. "I just don't know."

"I hope they do," she said.

Sutherland looked out into the night at the looming bulge of the Jefferson dome, then over at the Lincoln Memorial, and finally at the towering white obelisk in memory of Washington. Where, he thought, are the monuments to the wives?

O'Brien was knocking at the captain's door again.

"In."

"We've got some trouble, I'm afraid, sir. The whole crew knows that we're going further into the fire zone."

"How did they find out?"

"Damned if I know. I turned her about without a quiver. Not even Radar knew what I was doing. I did it as the watch changed, just as you suggested."

The captain ran his hands through his thinning hair as O'Brien continued, "I think the engine room boys must have guessed something was up. They formed a delegation as soon as they figured we'd definitely changed course."

The captain rinsed his mouth to rid himself, at least temporarily, of the dieseline taste of the sub. "Who's at the head of it?"

"Lambrecker, sir."

Kyle put the glass down and turned, massaging his

temples. "Delegation? Jesus Christ, what a navy. Delegations! All right, I'll see him in the control room. Let the others hear what I have to say." And he added with an unconvincing smile, "Might do some good."

"Yes, sir."

As O'Brien stepped over the sill, Kyle reached inside his locker for his cap. And because caps, like uniforms, were not usually worn at sea, O'Brien knew that Kyle was intent on denying Lambrecker the slightest informality.

"Bud?" There was a friendly intimacy in the question.

"Sir?"

"Any doubts in your mind—about going further in?"

"No, sir—but . . ." His hand moved in an evasive gesture.

"Go on. Say your piece."

"Well, sir, I wish some people would do their fishing closer to shore. This has been a long trip."

"I agree." Then, changing the subject, Kyle motioned ahead towards the sick bay. "Better check our medical supplies after you send Lambrecker up."

"Yes, sir."

O'Brien took the lead down the passage. The captain felt a twinge of envy at his subordinate's youthful ease and confident stride. "You think they'd try to rescue her even if she wasn't Vice-President?" he asked.

O'Brien's forehead bunched up as he pondered the question. "Don't think so."

The captain nodded to himself. "Neither do I—not anymore. No one gives a damn nowadays," he added bitterly, and headed for the control room, closing his eyes for a moment to accustom himself to the dim red light.

He stumped to the table wedged in the middle of the ten-by-twenty control room, between the attack periscope forward and the search periscope aft, bent down, and studied the chart. His eyes were drawn irresistibly to the green circle which represented the area of the spill. A seaman coming from the radio compartment just aft of the control room handed him a weather report. He glanced at it, then at the chart, wrote down wind direction and speed, and drew an arrow from the sub's position to the estimated location of the perimeter of the slick. He dropped the marking pencil, mumbling to himself, "Gale-force Arctic front anticipated within twenty-four hours. That's all we need."

He looked about him, checking that everyone was in position. Forward and to the right was the electrician, in charge of internal communications. In the forward left corner stood the petty officer, chief of the watch. Behind the chief, midway down the left side of the room, sat the bow planesman, controlling the sub's depth; then the stern planesman, who set the angles of descent and ascent. In the left-hand aft corner was the trim operator, responsible for the lateral movement of the sub, while the auxiliaryman stood in the right aft corner beyond a line of levers something like a railway change station, ready to open and shut the ballast tanks which would cause the boat either to surface or dive. Hogarth, officer of the watch, was walking about the control room, casting a watchful eye over the scores of gauges whose black needles constantly darted to and fro like swarms of frightened gnats.

The captain's head shot forward as he felt a man's breath on his neck. He swung around to face Lambrecker. The seaman was standing all but motionless, with a surly twist to his lips that seemed to register a petty delight in looking down on the smaller man. And although this evening he appeared somewhat anxious, the aggressiveness of his stare, even when he was standing rigidly at attention, showed everyone that he was absolutely unafraid of the officer before him.

After ten weeks on patrol, Kyle was convinced that the man was far more dangerous than anyone realized. He was the most senior seaman on the sub, but loyalty to old acquaintance, ship or man, meant nothing to him. If he bothered to believe in anything, it appeared to be only that familiarity did indeed breed contempt, for everyone but himself. Perhaps, thought Kyle, even for himself. He was what experienced officers colloquially, though without the slightest trace of humor or affection, referred to as a "hard case," and he would no doubt have been transferred long before had not the new regulations made such a move virtually impossible without overt evidence of persistent insubordination.

As he looked at Lambrecker's jeans, which to him epitomized the insolent sloppiness of the "new breed," Kyle's stomach went into a knot. "So, Lambrecker. What is it this time?"

Lambrecker made a point of not looking at the captain. It was a measure of his disregard for anyone in command. "The men are concerned. Sir."

Kyle pointed to the radar screen illuminating the area of the spill. "So is the world, Lambrecker. No one exactly enjoys having a floating inferno at large. The people of British Columbia, Washington, and Oregon, and I guess one or two other Americans are 'concerned,' as you put it." The captain gestured towards the chart. "And if this fire continues its free ride on the Alaska Current and gets blown into the California Current, then the whole western seaboard of North America could be barbecued. Are you, ah, concerned about that?"

Lambrecker looked past the captain as if talking to the rows of gauges on the bulkhead. Lately they had all started to look like Morgan's face, grinning stupidly at him. Keeping him trapped. "What's that got to do with us going further into the fire zone? Why can't the Americans do it? It's their problem."

The bow planesman looked hard at the deck, trying to avoid catching the electrician's eye, expecting the captain to explode. But Kyle disappointed them with his determination to stay calm. He picked up a pair of dividers and busied himself with the chart, not bothering to look up at Lambrecker. "We run on orders—or didn't you know that, Lambrecker?"

Lambrecker was still staring at the gauges. "All right, sir, so it's an order—but why are we going further into the fire? We're running out of air and our batteries need recharging. It just doesn't make sense."

Kyle quickly saw that if he allowed Lambrecker's insolence to go any further, his authority might be seriously undermined. He was now afraid that his calmness would be interpreted as outright weakness. He slammed down the dividers and faced Lambrecker with ill-disguised menace, his voice rising. "Listen, Lambrecker, you're here before me under sufferance. I haven't got to justify a thing to you. I've put up with you because of the new boys' policy of "feedback'—put up with you for three thousand miles of bitching, complaining, and inciting the men to damn near riot. But feedback doesn't mean insubordination, sailor. Now get back to your post or I'll have you thrown in the brig. Understand?"

Lambrecker's voice was calm. "I still don't see why we have to go into the fire. Sir."

Beads of perspiration had broken out on Kyle's forehead. "You're dismissed, sailor!"

Lambrecker smiled condescendingly down at the captain. "But sir—I don't understand—you haven't explained—"

O'Brien, standing a few feet away, was afraid Kyle might hit Lambrecker. Instead the captain, his face almost purple under the red light and his voice quavering, shouted, "Mister O'Brien!"

"Sir?"

"This man is under arrest. I want him in the brig—right now. This instant."

"Yes, sir. Come on, Lambrecker. Move!"

Kyle glared about the control room, then barked at the young third officer. "Hogarth, if there are any more complaints about us going further in, you inform me. Immediately!"

"Aye, aye, sir."

Kyle wheeled abruptly and left for his cabin as Lambrecker, smiling contemptuously, was escorted to the sub's tiny four-by-four-by-six office. The newcomer, Nairn, was assigned by O'Brien to stand guard so as to prevent any of Lambrecker's old associates from getting near him. Although Nairn had talked to him the first day, Lambrecker had hardly said a word since. After he'd sobered up, his generosity in giving Nairn the lower bunk had given way to a moroseness that always teetered on the verge of hostility towards the officers and to almost everyone else except for a handful of old-timers.

As O'Brien, sitting on a mess seat near the galley, made the entry on the charge sheet, Lambrecker's mood changed. He believed he had to handle the lieutenant differently. With the captain you played it cool, needling him and throwing him off balance by treating him as no more than your equal. With the lieutenant, however, the cool approach wouldn't work. He would just beat you down with his own quiet confidence. You couldn't get the lieutenant upset. You had to appeal to his common sense, and there wasn't any time to lose.

Lambrecker punched one of the small metal cabinets. "You hear what the captain said, Bud?"

The first officer, still filling out the charge sheet, was startled by the sudden familiarity, but he didn't look up. "My name's O'Brien, Lambrecker. Lieutenant O'Brien."

"You hear what he said, Lieutenant? He said to take me to the brig." O'Brien didn't answer. "Isn't any brig on this sub or any other. You and I know that, Lieutenant—everybody knows that. Even the green boys. Everyone except the captain." Lambrecker paused, watching O'Brien's reaction. "Doesn't that tell you something, Lieutenant?"

O'Brien, though not in the habit of talking about fellow officers with the men, saw that Nairn was listening intently, so he answered casually, "It was a slip," and then, before he could stop himself, he added, "He's been too long ashore, that's all."

Lambrecker's eyes glistened triumphantly. His arm shot out. "Right—exactly right!" He pointed a finger at O'Brien. " 'Too long ashore.' That's why we're in trouble, Lieutenant. That's exactly why we're in trouble —why we've got to get home fast."

O'Brien, his head bent, kept writing, taking care to complete a sentence before replying, *"You're* in trouble, Lambrecker."

Lambrecker slammed his fist into the cabinet again, yelling, "Why you so hell-bent on getting burnt up, Lieutenant? Medals won't do you no good then. You gotta take over. We'll back you up."

O'Brien finally looked up. For a few seconds he was silent, then he carefully clipped his pen into his pocket and said, "I think you're just scared, Lambrecker. I think you're wetting your pants."

Nairn gave a nervous laugh.

Lambrecker was staring wildly at O'Brien. "We'll back you up, Lieutenant."

O'Brien got up and walked away. He hated Lambrecker because he hated insubordination and he hated bullies, and Lambrecker, he believed, was a born bully. But at the same time, O'Brien hated chaos more than delegations, and at least Lambrecker had protested through channels so far. Delegations, whatever their problems, were better than mutiny, a possibility which had seemed remote to O'Brien until a few moments before. "We'll back you up," Lambrecker had said. Who was "we"? And how long would the radio operator keep silent? Sparks was duty bound to keep quiet, of course, but with the pressure and fear mounting, who could tell when the order would become known to the crew, particularly the part giving the captain permission to abort? Besides, he thought, they'll have to be told sooner or later. And worse, what would happen when Lambrecker and his gang, whoever they were, discovered that Kyle was taking them to a possible point of no return?

The sub took a slight roll, then righted itself as O'Brien made his way back to the control room. Soon they would be under the heart of the fire.

ELEVEN

What frightened Elaine Horton most was that she was powerless. Harry Reindorp was used to the vagaries of nature, and a life at sea had taught him that there were times when all you could do was pray, or rest, or both.

For Elaine, a situation entirely beyond her control was a new and frustrating experience. She felt like a farm person confronted for the first time by the terrors of a subway power outage. In the distance, over the oily, undulating swells, they could catch fleeting glimpses of the approaching inferno through brief gaps in the heavy smoke cover. An hour earlier it had been no more than a salmon pink line faintly lighting the sky behind the smoke-hazed horizon; but now it was a deep coral streak, shimmering like a living thing along the entire sea's edge.

"Wouldn't it be better to run?"

Harry turned about in a circle, his eyes following the line of the fire, his tanned cheek muscles bunching up as he squinted against the growing glare. "Nowhere to go, Lainey. We're better to wait for help to come here. We're not gonna find it out there. That's one hell of a fire. We've sent our SOS position; nothing else to do but hope the son of a bitch'll burn itself out 'fore it gets to us."

Elaine's habitual smile temporarily vanished, and in its place Harry Reindorp recognized the frightened little girl he'd once seen clinging to her father's leg as they cursed and hauled a feisty marlin aboard.

"Thing is, you see," he went on quietly, as she stared helplessly at the advancing spill, "to that sub they told us they're sending or to another ship, we're a dot out here. It'll be hard enough for them to see us anyway. We start moving away from our position, we'll only make it tougher. We've got to give 'em all the time we can. We move close in near that blaze and it might just reach out and grab us."

Reindorp didn't want to scare her any more than she was already, but he knew her well enough to gamble that the truth was not likely to make her hysterical.

A deep, icy gut feeling of helplessness swept over Elaine once more. She shivered, despite the fire-warmed air. Seeing her sitting there, completely out of her arena but still game, Harry Reindorp wanted desperately to encourage her, to give her solace, but all he could offer was what he realized was a rather lame reassurance. "Our best bet is probably the weather. Gales are forecast." But that didn't mean they'd arrive on cue. And even if they did, the odds were that they'd as easily blow the fire down onto the boat as put it out. Harry prayed for rain.

Elaine glanced overhead. The layers of smoke were getting thicker by the minute. She studied the line of fire, but could see no dent in it. Almost instinctively, she swung around, half expecting Richard Miller to be there awaiting instructions. Sensing that a wave of panic was gaining momentum, she forced herself to sit very still. She knew that trying not to think about the fire was the surest way for it to dominate all her thoughts. Instead she tried an old trick she'd learned as a congresswoman long before her party had chosen her to run as Vice-President. Staring at the advancing horizon, she deliberately thought of what the flames would be like, tried to think of every single flame, of the sky, the smoke, the strange, soft warmth of the acrid air—of everything around her. Soon her mind went blank, wiped clean like a slate. Overloaded by too many possibilities, it had temporarily refused to contain any. In their place, as always happened with her, only one thought returned. It was the memory of a Hawaiian night, recalled by the sensation of warm, moist air about her, that drifted into her consciousness.

Walter had taken her aboard the windjammer *Beau Regard* for a harbor cruise off Waikiki. The night breeze was playful about her hair and carried the sweet damp smell of mango and papaya. After leaving Fisherman's Wharf and passing beyond the big swells of the bar, the ship's engine stopped. Soon the canvas sails puffed out like the breasts of seabirds, and above the chatter of the other tourists they could hear the slapping of the rigging as they beat up into the wind.

In the distance, toward the deep purple of Diamond Head, they could see a lone light, barely visible, running close to the black surface of the sea. It seemed too low in the water to be a pilot light, unless it was a buoy circling at wide angles in the surf. Beyond the light, far up on Makiki Heights, they could see a rain cloud fast approaching. Those who had been watching the dancing, winking lights of Waikiki from the bow and stern made a rush for the midships tarpaulin, but she and Walter had stayed where they were, up near the bow. For a moment they lost sight of the light.

The rain quickly enveloped them in a mist so fine that they scarcely felt it. Elaine's hair, which she had spent an hour preparing, was ruined; it hung forlornly like long, oily strands of hemp. Walter proceeded to lift and drop the long strands like a forensic expert examining dead snakes.

"Maybe we can preserve them," he suggested. She laughed and dug him gently in the ribs. Feeling safe from recognition in the darkness, the congressman leaned over and kissed her, lingering over the fragrance of frangipani. Elaine lay back against the rail and pulled him towards her, pushing her breasts into him and fondling his hair. The shore swept quietly past.

Suddenly the lights came on as the tray dinners and Mai Tais were served. Walter Sutherland sat up immediately, but Elaine remained with her head resting softly on his shoulder, watching the stars moving against the dark, clean-washed sky.

"I'm sorry," he had said afterwards.

"It's all right," she had replied. "I know we have to be careful." She hadn't asked him then why he didn't leave his wife. The days when divorce hurt a politician's chances were long over, so he must still need Clara. What does she give him, she asked herself, that I cannot? She thought of being married and every night making love to him, uninhibited by the guilt they both now carried about with them wherever they went.

"I don't see the light," he said, bringing her out of the dream.

"What?"

"The light. That light that was running along the surface."

"Maybe it was a ship on the horizon."

"No," he said, "it was off Pearl Harbor. I think it was a submarine."

The thought of the submarine jerked her back to the present, and instead of the sweet smell of the trade wind, there was the acrid, throat-searing stench of burning crude.

In the crew's mess, the oilers were sitting down for the second shift of the meal. The mashed potatoes were lumpy as usual and the fresh milk was gone. The disgruntled seamen, wondering when they would be surfacing for fresh air and having their turn at a change of scene on the bridge, were becoming increasingly irritable with each other. Even the ruttish talk of sex had abated under the pressures of the unusually prolonged confinement. Long after their hunger had been satisfied, some men sat stuffing themselves, chain-smoking, or lethargically playing cards, simply because there was nothing else to do. Cards were sometimes dangerous under the circumstances, with tempers likely to burst at the slightest provocation. They had seen all the movies twice, some even three times, and the magazines, all the way from *Playboy* to *Reader's Digest,* were falling apart. Leading Seaman Ramsey stood glaring at the cook's helper, a young French Canadian. "I said no goddamn gravy!"

The cook frowned through the cloud of steam rising

from the greasy hotplate. "All right, Ramsey, keep your shirt on. Just scrape it off."

Ramsey looked murderous, and the helper's face paled. "Scrape it off yourself!"

The cook threw down a large, heavy spatula. "Jesus Christ! Here, give it over. I'll give you a new plate—all right?"

The cook took the plate, but Ramsey turned back to the helper. "No, it's not all right. Every night this stupid son of a bitch does the same thing! He's doin' it deliberately!"

The helper, still white-faced, was serving an oiler, looking down, terrified, at the deck. The cook handed Ramsey his new serving. "He's not doing it deliberately," he said evenly. "The lad just forgot. Just an accident."

Ramsey grabbed the plate with one hand while the other crashed around amidst the cutlery. "Huh. Suppose you're right. He's too goddamn stupid to do anything deliberately. He's just one big fucking accident."

The cook untied his apron. "Right, Ramsey, you've asked for it, you asshole, and I'm going to give it to you." His voice was thick with rage.

As he lifted the swing counter, a petty officer, coming to investigate the row, reached the door. "What's going on here?"

Ramsey, who had put down his tray, readying himself for the cook's onslaught, now quickly picked it up again and, scowling, moved quietly towards one of the mess tables. "Nothing."

The petty officer turned to the cook. "Cookie?"

The cook, who looked even bigger out from behind the counter, lifted the swing section up again and returned to the stove. "Nothing," he replied, looking at Ramsey and then at the petty officer and letting the counter slam down, causing Ramsey and several others to start from their seats. "Nothing," he repeated. "I was just about to do some mashing."

The petty officer raised his eyebrows. "With a cleaver?"

There were some stifled coughs. "Nothing to worry

about, Chief," said the cook, tying on his apron. The petty officer scanned the mess. Ramsey, still looking surly, was busy eating, stabbing viciously at his innocent pile of potatoes. "Good," said the petty officer. "I'm very happy to hear it. Let's keep it that way, eh?"

There was no answer. The petty officer left. Ramsey savagely tore off a crust of bread.

A few moments later the PA system crackled. "Now hear this . . . this is the Captain speaking. I know you're all tired . . ."

In the men's sleeping quarters, a sailor flipped over the well-worn centerfold of a girlie magazine. "He's kidding. We're not tired; we've only been out ten bloody weeks."

The captain continued, "It's been a long trip. I also know that you're as anxious as I am to get home." There was a pause as some static invaded the PA system. "However, I have received orders from Esquimalt, who, I should add, have received orders from Maritime Command in Halifax, that we are to proceed further beneath the firespill on a rescue mission. The Vice-President of the United States is trapped, surrounded by fire. We have been instructed to get her out."

"Who the hell—?" began Ramsey.

"Shut up, Ramsey," cut in someone else. "Let's hear it all."

As the captain paused for breath, Lambrecker gripped a lug on the bulkhead. His knuckles went white. In the sleeping quarters several men sat up, while in the overheated generator room, deep in the bowels of the boat, an engineer's assistant, having just made out the word *rescue,* tried desperately to hear what the captain was saying.

". . . Now I know that this asks us to stretch our resources to the limit . . ."

Ramsey was on his feet, yelling at the loudspeaker, "You mean stretching our fucking necks, don't you?"

". . . But," added Kyle, "it could be one of us up there. We are the only submarine close enough to help, and I don't have to tell you that if an American submarine was near enough to carry out the rescue in time, or if there was even a remote chance that helicopters could be used, we wouldn't have been asked. I should also tell you that the order apparently originates from a request by the Prime Minister."

In the crew's mess, a voice shouted, "That figures."

"In any event," continued Kyle, "it's our job to go in and get out as fast and as cleanly as possible. All off-duty officers will report to the wardroom in ten minutes. We know that at maximum speed we have four to five hours of battery power remaining and that the Vice-President is just under two hours away. We should be able to reach her. But if the Vice-President's boat has moved or we cannot make contact, for whatever reason, in two hours, we will abandon the attempt so as to allow us time to change our course and get out from under the spill."

The man straining his ears in the generator room, mishearing, inquired of no one in particular, "Danger? What the hell are we in now?"

The captain coughed, and momentarily the PA speakers gave off a high, piercing whistle. "Remember, all you have to do is to imagine that it's you trapped up there. I anticipate your full cooperation. Thank you. That is all."

For a few seconds, no one aboard the *Swordfish* spoke. Finally an off-duty oiler shouted, "That is all? Jesus, we're near bloody trapped down here."

Richards, the sick bay attendant, smiled uneasily. "Should never have voted for Gerrard."

His shipmate shrugged. "Wouldn't've made any difference. You'd've done the same."

In the wardroom O'Brien, stirring his coffee, was aware of young Hogarth watching him, as if waiting for some comment, some reassurance. After a few moments the junior officer asked nervously, "How much air have we got left, Mr. O'Brien?"

"Enough."

"I didn't think—"

O'Brien tapped the side of his white enamel cup

with a spoon. To Hogarth it was like a teacher calling a class to attention. O'Brien went into his "British Admiral" act, lifting his head with mock pomposity. "Now look here, Hogie old son—don't want to bother the chaps unnecessarily, do we?"

Hogarth smiled weakly. "I—I guess not."

"Good show. Stiff upper cock and all that, eh what?"

Hogarth reddened, grinning broadly. "Yes, sir."

Hunching over his coffee like a quarterback going into a huddle, O'Brien became serious. "You let the Old Man and me worry about air and the batteries and all the rest. We'll need a cool man like you to transmit orders. All right?"

"All right."

"Good. Pass the sugar."

The propeller spun in a steady blur, driving them deeper into the fire zone. In the engine room, eight sailors were arguing loudly. Petty Officer Jordan's forehead was shiny with sweat as he tried to reason with them. Sheen, an oiler, smashed a wrench into the bulkhead. His voice cut through all the others. "We don't care about no fire, Jordan, and no goddamned vice-president. We aren't gonna die in no fire 'cause some stupid son of a bitch wants to play hero."

The other men, momentarily silenced by Sheen's outburst, now angrily murmured their agreement. Sheen banged the bulkhead again. " 'Specially when the whole fucking thing's their fault. The Americans."

Jordan knew that he had to play for time, grasp at anything that would steer the talk away from their taking any immediate action against the captain's orders. He pretended ignorance. "I don't know what you mean, their fault. How the hell d'you know it's their fault?"

"Goddamned Yanks," shouted Sheen.

Jordan looked around at the circle of hostile faces, swallowed his pride, and spread his hands beseechingly. "Look, fellas, we don't know exactly who caused it. All we know is what the Old Man told us, right?"

For a moment, the only sound was the soft purring

of the propeller shaft. At least he had them thinking, and any time gained was to the good. If he could restrain the thought of rebellion here, he might prevent it from spreading through the ship. Next to Lambrecker, Sheen was usually the principal spokesman for the troublemakers aboard. At first the petty officer had doubted the captain's wisdom in putting Lambrecker under arrest, but now he was glad Kyle had acted so quickly. One at a time, you might be able to reason with them, but the chances of doing so when they were together were slim, if not impossible. With Lambrecker out of the way, at least they would listen.

Sheen answered, "Yeah, but what's the difference who started it? All we've been told is two great bloody tankers crashed and spilled their guts all over the bloody chuck, and we're s'posed to go and get some dumb broad out who was fishing from a bloody bathtub. I don't care who it is in there, I'm not going further in. You're just trying to play for time, Jordan."

Jordan detested having to argue. Like Kyle, he was of the old school, used to giving orders and having them promptly obeyed. But now he felt himself forced to plead. "What if it was, well, someone in your family?" he asked weakly.

"Jesus Christ, Jordan, if it was someone in my family, they'd tell me not to risk all my buddies."

The men began murmuring again. Sheen turned, stalked off, and called back defiantly, "Come on, we're gonna let Lambrecker out. We all shoulda backed him up earlier. He'll know what to do."

The petty officer grabbed him by the shoulder. "Listen, wait—"

The oiler shook free, menacingly lifting the wrench. "Let go! Petty officer or not, I'll bust your head if you touch me again."

Jordan took his hand off Sheen's shoulder, but he was boiling inside. The seaman would have been on a charge for this ten minutes ago. Before the captain had addressed the crew. Even then, many tempers had been near bursting point. Now Jordan felt as if they were all aboard a submerged pressure cooker without a safety valve in sight. He knew that if he tried to arrest Sheen, he would certainly have a mutiny on his hands right there in the engine room. He made one more attempt to pacify them. "All right. But listen to me, Sheen. All of you listen. You heard the Old Man. He said he'd set a limit of two hours—on the nose. If we don't contact 'em then, we quit. We go home. Okay?"

One of the young sailors shook his head like a frightened child, glancing at Sheen for support. "No, he won't. He'll keep goin' till we fry. He's lyin'."

"Yeah," added someone else. "What about that?"

Jordan shook his head at the sailor. "No, Smythe, he's not lying. Why should he? He doesn't want to kick off any more than you do."

The sailor was confused. Even Sheen hesitated, something which Jordan knew Lambrecker would never have done. The young sailor nervously sought a consensus from the rest. "I—I dunno. What d'you think, Sheeney?"

There was another pause, and it was then that Jordan thought he might have a real chance of stopping them. He spoke quickly, trying to keep the tightness out of his voice. "Okay, okay. Now look, you guys —you trust me? Well, do you?"

There were a few halfhearted mumbles. Jordan looked straight at Sheen. "Well?"

The oiler's grip on the wrench relaxed slightly. "So what if we do?"

Jordan lifted his hands in a gesture of compromise. "Look, I'll make a deal with you. If we don't pick up that fishing boat in two hours"—he glanced at his watch—"by twenty-thirty, and the Old Man wants to go on, I'll let Lambrecker out myself and we'll force the issue. We'll have to. Our batteries'll be halfway dead by then, so I'll be with you." He paused to let the proposition sink in. "Is it a deal?"

A few sailors nodded their heads slightly, but they still looked uncomfortable. The rest of them watched Sheen. He said nothing for a few seconds; then, pointing with the wrench at the petty officer, he answered for them all. "All right. Twenty-thirty—not a second longer, Jordan, or we'll waste you too. No shit!"

Jordan nodded his okay, and as the group broke up, he casually picked out several sailors for miscellaneous unimportant duties—checking stores which he had already checked himself, for example. Keep them separated as much as possible—a difficult job at any time aboard a sub, but even more difficult when they felt they had common cause for defiance.

As Jordan made his way out of the engine room, he was trying to imagine what it must be like to be trapped by a burning sea. Probably, he thought, it was like suffocating from lack of oxygen in a disabled sub. He resolved that if he were surrounded by fire, before the flames reached him, or came so close as to threaten him with the slow agony of suffocation, he would kill himself. But then, with an almost macabre practical bent, he wondered how you could do it on a small boat. There would be no quick way. Well, you could jump into the flames or try drowning yourself, but both seemed too horrible to submit to willingly. Of course, if there were anyone with you, they could do it. With a fish knife or something.

Jordan pursed his lips. When his time came, he hoped he would be permitted to die in bed with his wife. If he ever got to see her again.

TWELVE

In the White House the Presidential Press Conference had just ended. General Oster had watched his friend fielding questions from a battery of reporters. Though the Press Secretary had released news of the spill earlier, all the details of the Vice-President's situation had not been revealed, despite the fact that the press knew that she had made an early morning getaway from the Secret Service and that she and her companion were now trapped by the firespill. The conference was unusually restricted. Neither TV nor radio had been allowed in and the President had asked the news corps, on grounds of humanitarian concern, not to go into details of the rescue when filing their reports.

"What do you mean by 'humanitarian concern'?" one newsman had asked sarcastically.

"I mean," said the President, "that the next of kin of some of the naval personnel involved in the rescue operation have not yet been notified, and insofar as the rescue attempt does pose a certain degree of exposure to unforeseen circumstances, I feel that the next of kin should be notified before any further details are released."

Several reporters' hands shot up. Many of the faces looking at him wore openly suspicious expressions. The President continued in an even tone. "The same procedure, as you well know, is followed by local police all over the country in cases where media exposure may precede official notification."

"Are you telling us, Mr. President," called the L.A. *Times* reporter, "that members of our Coast Guard or whatever are in danger of their lives?"

"No. I never said that, Mr. Rawlins."

"But you said—" began Rawlins.

"What I *said,*" cut in Sutherland, "was that there is a certain degree of exposure to unforeseen circumstances."

Sutherland was sweating. He reached for a Kleenex and motioned towards another upraised hand. This time the young reporter who had asked Clara Sutherland about the Vice-President and her husband was on his feet. Sutherland instantly realized his mistake, but he couldn't withdraw his invitation of the question. Henricks glared icily at the young newsman as he asked, "Mr. President, you seem reluctant to talk about Vice-President Horton."

Sutherland was ready. "That's because we have very little information at the moment. You will be advised as we know more."

The reporter smiled superciliously. "Of course." Sutherland turned to face the other reporters. A young woman who had been waving her hand frantically for several minutes stood up. "Mr. President," she began rather shakily, then coughed and proceeded in a steadier tone. "Would it be fair to say, Mr. President, that the reason for this closed conference is to cover up the fact that in order to save the Vice-President you are exposing the rescuers to extreme danger—far more extreme than you would otherwise consider?"

The room fell quiet. Sutherland felt the perspiration stinging his eyes, but refrained from wiping his face. "It cert—it certainly would *not* be fair," he answered, trying to control his temper. "I would have ordered—requested—the aid of the men involved for any U.S. citizen—black, white—any U.S. citizen. I—for any U.S. citizen at all."

The woman smiled up from her scratch pad while some case-hardened reporters looked down at their shoes. "Oh, I wasn't suggesting that a president's, uh, special relationship with a vice-president would cause him to treat her, or him, any differently, but that in view of the worldwide outcry against the spill you might want her by your side." She hurried on as several heads turned to stare reproachfully at her. "Bearing in mind the historically high risk of assassination which you, as Chief Executive, face."

Sutherland spoke very slowly. "I'm sure you're overreacting to the world situation. I'm confident that despite these . . . local conditions, this administration—together with Congress—will continue to improve international relations with the United States." And with that he left the podium.

As the correspondents rose, the President and Henricks had already disappeared behind the red velvet drapes. "Who is that bitch?" snapped Sutherland.

"I don't know, sir," replied Henricks.

"Damn bitch."

"Yes, sir."

As Oster followed them into Special Operations, Sutherland asked Henricks, "How do you think the conference went?"

Henricks deliberated.

"The first part," Sutherland said pointedly, as if reading the other's mind.

"I really think it went all right, Mr. President, but I must confess I don't think they'll keep quiet on the rescue attempt too long. They'll give us a few hours at the most to notify next of kin, and then if we try to pull the 'humanitarian concern' bit again, they'll know we're stalling. And if that woman—if she or anyone else stumbles onto the fact we're using a vintage Canadian sub, they're sure to give us hell about not having one of our own in the area, as if we were expected to know exactly when and where this was going to happen."

Sutherland nodded thoughtfully. "That's all right," he said slowly. "By that time the rescue will be over. There'll be nothing left to speculate about."

"Yes," said Henricks, smiling with a confidence he didn't feel. As he walked away, leaving the President and the general alone, he muttered to himself that if the rescue failed, there wouldn't be any sub.

Encouraged by Henricks's smile, the President for a moment felt positively optimistic. He turned to Oster.

"Well, Arnold, how did the press conference go—the last part?"

"Lousy."

Sutherland's voice was surprised and indignant. "Oh, come on!"

The general deftly plucked a piece of rank tobacco from his teeth. "That skirt had you against the ropes, Walter."

Sutherland flushed. "You think she was right? That saving Elaine is screwing up my deeper responsibility?"

At the far side of the room, Henricks's head popped up protectively as he heard the President's voice rise. Oster lit another cigar. "I'm saying simply that she made you lose your cool. I'm just thinking that we're going to get more questions and that it's disastrous to let these people—"

"Excuse me, General," interrupted Henricks, "I wonder if you could help us over at the map."

Oster recognized Henricks's interruption for what it was—an attempt to let the President have some time to himself. For his part, Oster believed that time to himself was precisely what the President did not need, given the tug-of-war between his private and official loyalties. Nevertheless, the general followed Henricks across the room.

Sutherland massaged his eyes slowly, sat back, and toyed with a small, gold spoon stamped with the Venetian crest. It had been given to him and Clara on their tour of Italy two years earlier. He used it to stir the oily black coffee. That goddamn woman with her questions about the rescue and her snide innuendos about Elaine. Perhaps Arnold was right; maybe he had handled the press conference badly. Perhaps unconsciously he had called it simply in the hope that his willingness to meet with the press would be interpreted as a sign that he had nothing to hide and that he had exercised no special privilege in trying to have Elaine rescued. But he had asked the Canadians to help, to risk eighty-four lives—the happiness of eighty-four families—to rescue his Vice-President, his ex-lover. His not-so-ex-lover. The change in nationalities involved was hardly a change in risk. Would he have done the same for anyone else? Would he have done it just for the fisherman? He doubted it. More and more he doubted it. And would he even have done it for Clara? He was ashamed that the question should even occur to him. Where Elaine was concerned, it had never even suggested itself. He told himself that in this matter neither his political head nor his common sense had directed him—only his love of one woman, and that, he believed, might be unforgivable to his friends and his enemies. Most of all, it would be unforgivable to himself.

After several minutes he became aware of someone sitting next to him. It was Clara. Normally he didn't like her interrupting him in his work, especially in the Special Operations Room, but tonight he didn't mind. He always found her presence comforting when he was worried.

"Won't you come and rest?" she asked. "You'll be up late tonight."

"No," he said. "I can't sleep—not now."

"But you look so worn out."

"I can't sleep, Clara."

"All right," she said. "You will call? If you need something?"

"Yes," he answered, feeling angry with himself for snapping at her. "Yes, I will." Watching her leave, he marveled at her quiet dignity. How often it shamed his petulance! He must force himself to give his full attention to the spill, to submerge himself in the myriad details of the problem at hand, denying himself time to question his motivations, to agonize himself into a guilt-laden impotency.

He looked up as the clocks in unison clicked off another minute. In Washington it was 9:17 P.M.

THIRTEEN

For Elaine, three thousand miles away, it was just before sunset, and the firespill around the fishing boat was receding. A squall, while doing nothing to extinguish the main body of flames, had dispersed some of the advancing rivulets of burning oil.

Elated by the first spray of moisture sweeping over her, Elaine turned to Harry Reindorp, whose cough had been worsening by the minute. "You must have connections."

The old man managed a wan smile. He said something, but it was lost in the screaming gust of wind that announced the arrival of the squall proper. Then the black arch of cloud was gone as quickly as it had come, sucked dry by the spill, with nothing more to show for its run than a few disturbed swells that momentarily chopped the surface of the sea. The fire, like some giant momentarily disturbed by a fly, renewed its inexorable advance. Elaine felt drained of energy, her sudden optimism quickly dashed as the full hopelessness of their position came home to her again.

Feeling the depression closing in on her and shortening her already shallow breathing, Elaine tried once again to think of everything at once, to fuse her brain temporarily, to dull it against what seemed to her to be the inevitable end. But the trick did not work; instead, visions of fire filled her brain and overwhelmed any attempt at countermeasures.

She wanted desperately not to cry, not to blubber like a lost child. "You remember the time—" she began, but she didn't finish the sentence. A burning, sulphurous smell swept her breath away. "You remember," she continued gamely after the fumes had passed, "when we went fishing?"

Harry saw that she was on the verge of tears. "Yes," he said gently. "The last time in Prince William Sound?"

"Yes . . . yes. Father caught the big salmon."

Reindorp nodded. "I remember it. He never shut up about it for days."

The smoke, pushed aside by the squall, was now returning. There was a long silence as Elaine watched the fire creeping forward. She swung her head around to face her companion. "You used to fish in New Zealand, Harry?"

"Yes."

"Was it as good as our trips?"

"Company wasn't as good, but it was as beautiful," he said, trying not to cough. "Never saw more beautiful sunsets. You could smell the land, too. A sweet smell it was."

Elaine was staring at the fire. There was another long silence before she spoke. "They have thermal areas, don't they?" Before he could answer, she went on. "You ever seen anything like this over there? Not the fire," she added quickly, "I mean the smoke."

Reindorp's eyes were running constantly, and he could barely see through the stinging film of tears.

"Saw something like it in Rotorua," he said, "and White Island."

"Which was more interesting?"

Elaine's face was beet red. Harry reckoned that the temperature must be near a hundred and five Fahrenheit. "White Island was the most interesting," he answered dully.

"Why?" She swung back from the fire as she spoke and fixed her eyes on the growing darkness of the small fo'c'sle so that she could not see the whole circle of fire. Surprised that she had even heard him, Harry tried to remember why the place had stuck in his memory. "Well, it was an old volcanic island. It was kind of mysterious."

Elaine now sat facing him. Though she seemed to

have recovered some of her composure, there was a forced air, an intensity, about her quite unlike her usual unruffled poise. Reindorp wondered what he should do, and decided that under the circumstances the best contribution he could make was simply to keep talking. "The island was only five acres in all—the middle blown clean out of it. Nothing left but a few of those gas holes—fumaroles the geologists call 'em. All they did was hiss an' spit most of the time; blowing up sulphur fumes. Sometimes they'd just gurgle a bit and throw up a few puffs of smoke, but then before you could say howdy-do, they'd erupt with steam. Full of sulphur, that steam. Whenever you took a breath, it was like having a poker in your throat."

"What happened to the men?" asked Elaine, her vision drawn back to the crimson wall only half a mile away. Suddenly, Reindorp realized that Elaine must already know the story, and that she had deliberately steered him into relating it. What puzzled him was that he was almost sure he hadn't told it to her, though he couldn't swear to it.

"The men?" he continued. "Well, in 1916 there were about fourteen of them on the island, and the supply ship would drop off fresh food and whatnot every three weeks or so."

Elaine lay back on the gunwale, wiping the sweat from her face. She lifted her sweater a little and fanned her neck. "They were mining sulphur, weren't they?"

"What?"

"Sulphur, wasn't it?"

"Yes, that's right. For munitions. Well they—I mean the ship—they called around two weeks later and all the men had vanished."

"Without trace."

Harry nodded tiredly. He didn't want to go on with the story. It was the worst possible story in a situation like this, akin to talking of starvation amongst starving men. But Elaine looked over at him. "It was the fumes, wasn't it?" she asked, "a sudden buildup from the —what do you call them?"

"The fumaroles."

"Yes."

"Mind you," said Harry, trying his best to convey doubt, "it could have been anything."

Elaine's eyes closed. She shook her head, and when she spoke it was in a very matter-of-fact voice. "But there was no sign of anything. No volcanic debris, no bodies."

"They must have panicked," said Harry, pointedly. "Once you panic you're gone. They must have just run and pushed off in the few boats they had."

"But fourteen men? You'd think that there would have been some wreckage washed up on the island."

"There were no beaches," said Harry, feeling nauseated. Something seemed to be muddling his brain, making him think that it was of the utmost importance that Elaine and everyone else in the world should know that there were no sandy beaches on White Island, five thousand miles away in the Southwest Pacific.

"No sand," he mumbled. Each time he breathed, fumes seared his throat.

"But it was so rocky. You would think some—oh my God," she said, sitting up, eyes wide, staring unseeing into a cloud of smoke that reeked of kerosene.

Harry, snapped into full consciousness by her alarm, grabbed her by the arm and pulled her protectively towards him. "What's the matter?" he asked urgently. "What's wrong, Lainey?"

"It was the sharks," she said. "Now I remember. It was the sharks. They killed the men. That's why they were never found."

"Who told you that damned story?" he asked angrily. "Was it me?"

Elaine patted his hand softly.

"I should never have told you," he said, his voice full of self-reproach.

"You didn't, Harry. It was Father—you told him."

"Then I was a damned fool."

"No. It was my fault. I've been trying to remember him. All I could think of was that story. I can see him telling it now. Both of you—you were great story-tellers."

Harry looked down at her. "Were? Hey, girl, don't count me out yet. I've still got a few thousand miles left."

She forced a smile. There was a splash near the boat. They didn't bother to look for the dead bird as it popped to the surface; they'd already seen dozens fall, dead from the utter exhaustion of trying to outfly the fire.

"You remember your tenth birthday, Lainey?"

"The go-cart," she said.

"The red go-cart."

Elaine's eyes were closed again as she spoke, in an effort to lock out the smoke. "All the boys in the neighborhood said that girls didn't ride go-carts—couldn't ride go-carts."

Harry nodded. "*I* said girls didn't ride go-carts. That's what made your pa build it. It wasn't the boys that set his mind to it; it was old blabbermouth Reindorp."

"That was my dad," she said, "and then I had to go and gash my shin on the edge of the seat. I still have the scar."

"I don't remember that," cut in Harry. He was finding it increasingly difficult to believe that it was the Vice-President sitting across from him and not Lainey, a small country girl, speechless at her first glimpse of the sky blue Pacific.

"Oh, yes," she continued, "the boys laughed at that—little monsters—but Daddy just got a thick piece of rubber hosing, slit it almost right through from end to end, and glued it onto the edge of the seat." She paused. "I thought he was the smartest man in the world. I mean, he was always there to help, especially after Mother died. 'Course he had his faults, like anyone, but . . ." Elaine's lip began to tremble.

Harry leaned over, straining his back. "I know, Lainey," he said, patting her gently on the arm. "I know."

Elaine was winding and unwinding a grimy rope end around her finger. "I miss him," she said, but her words were lost in the explosion of a pool of high octane floating in amongst the heavier oil. More crude was burning, its water vapor driven off by the heat of the lighter fuel.

As the smoke all but blotted out the fast-fading daylight, they forced themselves to breathe as slowly as they could, to move as little as possible, in order to conserve what strength remained. The boat now lay near the middle of the lake-sized area not yet covered by the firespill. Afraid as they were, watching and hearing the roar of the fire wall encircling them in the near distance, they could not help but be struck by its awesome beauty.

The singed yellow flames of high octane did not leap up now, but rather churned towards the indigo sky in crimson fireballs belched up by the boiling sea. Now and then, surprised by the bellows of the rising wind, the flames would suddenly flare out, and the tar black fume clouds would roll further in towards the boat. Each time this happened, it seemed that the becalmed area was being reduced to nothing. For Elaine it was like watching a great black spider taunting its trapped prey. For minutes at a time they were blinded by the acrid vapor; then without warning the wind would fall, causing the smoke to retreat just far enough to reveal that the flames had not yet reached them. Harry, exhausted from coughing, was leaning on the gunwale, limply holding a hose, trying to cool the wooden boat. Beside him a pump chattered away, lifting and pushing the dirty seawater up onto the deck. He coughed again, his throat sore and burning. "You all right, Lainey?" he gasped as a new wave of smoke enveloped them.

"No—can hardly breathe."

Harry, convulsed by his coughing, lost his grip on the hose. It slithered along the deck like a tired snake, finally gushing up against the pump and flooding it. When his cough temporarily abated, Harry turned his attention to fixing the pump. "All we can do is to keep us hosed down. I've thrown everything overboard we don't need in case we have to make a dash." His eyes searched carefully about the boat for anything else that was expendable. Then, although the effort nearly made him black out, he managed to restart the pump. He slapped it affectionately, as one would a faithful pet. "She's a heavy old sod—weighs us down I know, but if that sub makes it I'll chuck her over all right. An extra burst of speed will come in mighty handy."

The Vice-President wasn't listening. All she could hear was a bellowing roar, and all she could see was the canyon-deep wall of fire which completely surrounded them. "Do you think we've got a fighting chance?"

Slumped against the life preserver, Harry was coughing uncontrollably. Finally he took a swig of fresh water, hot from the fire, cleared his throat, and spat blood over the side. After a while he answered slowly. "No, Lainey, I don't. A fighting chance is a fair chance."

More fumes swept over and around the boat.

"One in ten, maybe?"

"More like one in fifty."

They did not speak again for several minutes. Elaine didn't want to think of anything, least of all her slim chances of survival, but she knew that she must steady her mind against the panic she felt welling up again inside her. But the only thing her consciousness would allow was the thought of how much trouble she was causing. She heard the old man wheezing heavily. She looked at him sorrowfully. "I'm very . . ." she began weakly, coughing again. "I . . . shouldn't have gotten you into this . . . should've let those agents come with me . . . used a bigger boat."

The wind had changed direction again, and they immediately felt better as the suffocating fumes momentarily fell back. "Bigger boat wouldn't have helped, Lainey. Neither would a hundred agents. We'd still be stuck out here, and them with us. Besides, it's the motor's fault."

Before ceasing transmission to save their battery's

power, they had radioed Admiral Klein that if there were any risk at all to others, no one should try to rescue them. Klein, taking care not to tell them about the precarious position of the *Swordfish*, the dispersal rate of the oil, the deteriorating weather, or anything else which would make the rescue hazardous, had thanked them and then had told them that regardless of their desire, the President of the United States and the Prime Minister of Canada had decided that an attempt should be made. All Harry had said was "Damn fine of them Canadians." Elaine had readily agreed, buoyed up by even the faint prospect of rescue.

But afterwards she realized that there had been a certain inner calm in the acceptance of finality. Now that there was hope, however little, there was anxiety.

For her the most terrifying aspect of the fire was that there was no reference point, no steady marker against which to calculate the rate of its advance. It was even possible, she thought, that it might be slowly withdrawing, as it had earlier, in the squall. She tried to gauge the wind, but because much of it was being generated by the fire itself, it seemed to be coming from all different directions at once. Harry passed over some fresh water. Elaine felt that it was all she could do to reach out for the flask, and when she drank, it tasted of gasoline. She wiped her lips with a rag to rid them of their crust of smoke deposits. The next sip tasted worse. She capped the flask and handed it back. "How wide do you think this—this pond of ours is?"

"It was about five miles."

"Was?"

"The fire's coming in. Wind's rising."

A surge of panic passed over the Vice-President. "But—I mean—how can you tell? The wind's been eddying all around us."

Harry motioned towards the control console. "Drift indicator."

She looked at her watch. "How fast do you think it's advancing?"

" 'Round half a mile an hour. It's about four miles

across now, I reckon. Time we moved into the center again—need as much moat as we can get."

As Harry struggled to his feet to make his way towards the console, Elaine, her face contorted against the heat, asked, "You said four miles wide?"

Harry nodded and pressed the starter button.

"Then we've got four hours . . . before it reaches us?"

The boat started to move, slowly. "Less than that, Lainey. Four hours and it'll be right on top of us. Doubt if we can last less than a quarter of a mile from the flames. All the oxygen'd be gone. I'd say about two hours—maybe less."

Despite his fatherly tone of voice, his matter-of-fact delivery was alarming. Elaine suspected that the old man no longer believed that their chances were even one in fifty; he didn't believe they had any chance at all.

When they reached the center of the clear area and Harry turned off the motor, they could see rivulets of oil from the main slick curling about the bow in rainbows of colors, riding the wake and probing here and there in long tentacles. In the distance there was a loud crump as a new pool of high octane exploded, shooting a long, bluish yellow flash through the dull orange of the burning crude. Soon new columns of smoke could be seen arching towards them, riding on the advancing balls of flame which tumbled madly over and into each other, growing larger and spreading by the second as they cannibalized the primary fire in their path. As each wave reached the perimeter of the clear area, it collapsed, spreading out and hissing into the newly won space.

Soon the explosions of the high octane sounded like a creeping artillery barrage, raising the temperature of the whole spill, bringing more and more of the vast blanket of crude to its flash point. Unlike the variegated and dancing patterns of the high-octane fire, there was nothing especially dramatic about the ignition of the gellike crude—only a slow roll of tangerine flame. But once it was alight, the thicker oil would burn on and on, outlasting the high octane by days, even weeks.

Harry guessed what the explosions meant, but when Elaine asked him what was happening, he said he didn't know. More fire meant less oxygen and less time for the submarine to reach them. Suddenly a fierce gust of hot, skin-itching wind howled into the *Happy Girl,* sending Elaine's hair streaming behind her and flattening her against the gunwale. The fire was creating its own wind system, and this was its first assault. Harry knew that this too would get worse, for even though the high waves that would result from the winds at the fire's center might douse part of it, churning and breaking up some of the oil, he was sure that the winds had already pushed part of the fire onto the North American coast, and would push more. But he said nothing about this to Elaine. It would only make her feel worse about having asked him to bring her out here.

"What time do you have?" she asked.

He turned towards her and smiled kindly, answering her question as if it really mattered, as if they really did stand a chance. "Nearly six-forty-five."

By now the smoke and fumes from the crude were starting to envelop the boat, joining the night in forming a pitch black sheet about them.

By Elaine's reckoning the submarine had till eight-forty-five at the latest, to find them. And if the fire wind rose further, she knew it would be even less.

FOURTEEN

In Tokyo it was early afternoon. Through the unusually heavy smog that hung over the sprawling Asanami Shipyard, Police Chief Sunichi Yamada could see the towering, unfinished hull of a million-ton supratanker standing silently over the crowd of ten thousand demonstrators, like some great carcass besieged by swarming ants. Yamada's hand tightened on the pistol grip of the bullhorn as the crowd, mostly students, surged further into the shipyard, through the main gate, past the high, barbed wire storm fencing.

Raising the bullhorn, Yamada ordered, "Spearhead formation!"

In one quick movement, the aluminum-shielded, blue-black-uniformed Kidōtai—the mobile squads—changed from two lines of a hundred riot-equipped men into a double spearhead. If they began to move and one man fell in the forward formation, one from the second would immediately take his place.

Here and there Yamada could see that groups of workers had joined the demonstration against the builders of the now American-owned MV *Kodiak,* but in the main the police chief could tell from the signs that this was the work of the university students. For that reason he was surprised that the protest had been so ill planned. No doubt it was due to the fact that the firespill—unlike political events—had happened without warning. Normally the radical organizers would never have allowed the crowd to gather in a road that had no side alleys and only one exit—in this case, the gate through the shipyard beyond the half-built tanker, which could take them nowhere except into the cold waters of the harbor. The only other way out was past the Kidōtai, and for an angry mob that was no way at all. Yamada took a deep breath. This demonstration would become a riot. He glanced at his watch again, for the sixth time in the last hour, and lifted the bullhorn. "You are advised that you are on private property. This constitutes a violation of Civil Ordinance Number—"

His next few words were drowned in the roar of the crowd. He waited patiently for a minute, then added, "You now have five minutes in which to vacate these premises."

A barrage of rocks and bottles erupted from the crowd towards the Kidōtai. "Canopy!" barked Yamada, and the second row of shields clashed and rose in a single flash of sunlight, overlapping those that stood perpendicular, guarding the front line of men, forming an aluminum roof, covering the whole spearhead formation. The hail of projectiles bounced harmlessly to the already debris-strewn road.

The Kidōtai battalion stood steady, the rounded perspex helmet covers distorting their faces as they awaited the order to move. They had been through all of this a hundred times before. No one even looked round as they heard the caged buses roaring up the road and stopping behind them. They simply stood still, holding the five-foot shields in their left hands and the two-and-a-half-foot riot sticks in their right, like Roman legionaires. Immediately behind them, groups of regular police readied the tear gas guns, plopping the canisters into the stubby, black barrels. From this position the regulars could reload and advance in relative safety behind the cover of the Kidōtai.

Normally Yamada would have used the firehoses rather than tear gas, but someone had slashed most of the hose lines. At least they were that organized, he mused. He glanced at his watch for the last time. Now they had two minutes. It was hopeless. He knew they wouldn't listen, but he had to try. He sensed from long experience that the crowd didn't want violence, but it could not stop its own momentum. There were hundreds who were probably trying desperately to get out, but they were trapped by the crush of bodies which had taken on a collective will of its own, dictated by its sheer size and weight. But the drill was to give them a chance, until it was too dangerous to let them gather any more momentum. Some would inevitably be hurt, but better a few now than many later.

Suddenly the crowd surged towards the police. Yamada calmly lifted the bullhorn. "Fire cannisters!"

There was a series of "boomps" and the silver cannisters soared overhead and into the crowd. Pools of gas began to spread. As soon as he heard that the coughing was general, Yamada ordered, "Walk—advance!"

The spearhead moved in unison, the riot sticks shaking ominously up and down in expectation. A volley of rocks struck the black and silver line. One officer stumbled for a second, then a hand shot out to his side and he shuffled a little dazedly back into step.

Another volley of rocks struck the line, and two men fell. As two replacements came from behind, the long lines of clubs went up as one. "Charge!" yelled Yamada.

As the Kidōtai hit the first wave of demonstrators, scores of people went down amid a screaming panic. The crowd shrank to almost half its size, like a frightened slug. Now the regular police were mopping up, dragging and pushing the arrested over the littered road, back into the waiting buses. One student, a boy of about eighteen, dashed to the side of the street and frantically began to scale a shop awning. A regular policeman dropped his baton and grabbed an ankle. The boy kicked back, opening his captor's cheek. Feeling no pain in his fury, the policeman caught the boy's leg again, dragged him down, threw him against the brick wall, and kicked him in the groin. As the boy slumped, the policeman continued to kick at his face, squashing the nose so that soon the boy's arms, hopelessly trying to cover his head, were covered in blood.

By now two other policemen had arrived and were pulling their colleague off, one of them yelling, "That's enough. We'll take him. That's enough!"

As the boy was hauled away, his head fell limp over his chest like a squashed fruit. One of the policemen supporting the boy was nearly out of breath. Gasping for air, he murmured, "All this—because—because of some oil. Is it worth it, fella? Hey—hey—is it worth it? You bastard!"

Thirty-two miles east of the firespill, on the southwest coast of Kruzof Island, which lay like a protective arm guarding Sitka from the sea, the Tlingit village was deserted.

Backed by an apron of spruce and fir forest that stretched towards the three-thousand-foot Mount Edgecumbe, the small Indian settlement that just hours before had been inhabited by eighty men, women, and children could well have been mistaken for a ghost town. But quite apart from the fact that it was known to be a relatively new settlement, made up of families descended from the Angoon clans on Admiralty Island, the signs of recent habitation were everywhere. Inside the short-peaked plank houses, plates of food and unmade beds stood as evidence of the Indians' hasty retreat. Outside, washing fluttered on lines like the shredded flags of defeat, while racks of drying seaweed lay unattended and the tall, silent totem poles of Thunderbird, Beaver, and angry Bear glared across the village ground as if determined to do battle with the oncoming sea.

The Tlingit took their living largely from the ocean, but they feared it too. Some, though nominally Christians, still believed that if a man drowned and his body was not recovered, he would surely not be taken into the soft embrace of the afterlife. The men of the clan were modern fishermen, but this day the fear of the sea had swept ashore with the crashing of the waves and had moved them to abandon the motor-powered fishing boats that now lay rocking mutely like obedient animals awaiting an inescapable end.

Beyond the riot of devil club, cranberry bushes, and yellow pond lilies that grew at the edge of the thick woods, the village smokehouse, with its trapdoorlike chimney, kept streaming smoke as if it expected to go on forever. The smell of the cooking salmon wafted deep into the moss-laden spruce forest nearby and rose slowly through a clearing that had once been the site of an ancient gravehouse.

An old chief had been the first to see dark smoke scratched across the salmon pink horizon. He had hauled in his lines and buoys and headed in to alert the village. No one had taken any notice, saying that it was not possible that the sea was on fire. Not even the white men with all their madness could make such a thing.

In earlier times the old chief would not have informed them that it was wise to move lest the wind quicken and bring in the fire; he would have ordered them to move, and they would have obeyed. But now chiefs were elected, and the new leader, a younger man, had agreed with most of the other fishermen that the smoke was probably from a large ship on fire, nothing more.

By the time they heard the news of the spill, the wind had blown the northernmost part of the fire into the shape of a scythe whose tip, aided by the strong currents in the area, had reached the headland at Point Mary, several miles north of the village. Dry as tinder from a long, hot summer, the forested coast hills had caught fire within minutes of the first burning and oil-soaked log's striking the heavily wooded inlet. Soon thousands of cypress began to explode, splitting apart in grotesque shapes as the wind-driven flames raced across the treetops faster than the fires on the forest floor.

Unable to head out to sea through the horseshoe of blazing oil, the Indians had quickly packed what belongings they had and started north in a race with the fire to Shelikof Bay, their only hope being to cross the island on the five-mile logging road to Mud Bay and there to find a boat to take at least some of them down through Hayward Strait and across the sound to Sitka. As they began their forced march towards the road, the chief couldn't help but remember that his Tlingit ancestors had once burned Sitka to the ground, and now he and the clan were seeking its refuge.

The President was feeling shaky from drinking too much coffee, but he wanted to be alert for reports both of the rescue attempt and of the much larger danger facing millions of people should the firespill reach the coast. Perhaps the wind from the forecast Arctic front wouldn't rise and spread the fire after all; or if it did increase, perhaps it would reach gale force as the meteorologists had predicted and counteract the coast-bound movement of the spill, breaking it up into thousands of smaller, more manageable patches. But even then much of the shape and direction of the spill would still depend on the speed of the currents.

Sutherland began to pace before the map wall, glancing now and then at the bank of digital clocks which, in the neutrality of their constant clicking, took on the appearance of a row of automated referees disinterestedly counting off the seconds against him. He felt irrationally hostile towards them, so ordered and efficient in the face of human disarray. Here he was, president of a powerful nation, perhaps the most technologically advanced in the world, and yet he was helpless to stop the firespill's advance. All he could do, it seemed, was to react defensively, to continue to press plans for the mass evacuation of the entire civilian population of the Pacific Northwest.

The Canadian and American police in northwest British Columbia, the Alaskan Panhandle, the Queen Charlotte Islands, and the Alexander Archipelago were working as fast as they could to initiate what the authorities had hoped would be an orderly evacuation but what in fact was beginning to resemble a rout from a war zone.

East of Ketchikan at the Hyder-Stewart border crossing between Canada and Alaska, long lines of evacuees, panic-stricken by the news reports of the approaching fire, jammed the highway, their overloaded cars and trucks stretching back for miles. Children cried, grandparents tried to soothe, and impatient parents attempted, with varying success, to remain patient, their growing anxiety all the time threatening to push them into blind rage. The customs officials, who had as yet received no explicit instructions from above, continued to ask each immigrant, "Good evening. Where do you live? Where do you come from?" and "Are you importing anything into the country?" Finally the hereditary chief of a local Haida band had to be physically restrained from punching a police officer who, with clipboard dutifully by his side, had thrust his overworked face into the Indian's crowded car and asked quite ingenuously, "Are you landed immigrants?"

By now the President's staff had had time to assemble oil experts both at the White House and by phone linkups across the country, and observers had been sent to the coastal areas.

But as the minutes flew by, the President felt more and more like the coach of a losing team committed to a blocking action, and a futile blocking at that, as an apparently invincible opposition ate further and further into home territory. One of the telexes stuttered to life in the annex, and Henricks tore off the latest message. Sutherland turned anxiously away from the clocks. "Is it spreading?"

"Afraid so, Mr. President. Satellite pictures show that we've reached flash point. There's an immense pileup of smoke. They say that means a lot more of the crude is burning."

Sutherland thought of Elaine and at once regretted it. "Is it the wind?" he asked, as much to divert his thoughts away from her as to know the answer.

Henricks called over one of the oilmen. It was the expert's first time in the White House. He was a small, flabby man who walked comically but did everything else with the utmost seriousness as if to compensate.

His voice began at a nervous pitch. "Ah—partly, Mr. President." He cleared his throat. "Partly—I mean, part of the wind is made up of—well, the front coming down from the Arctic, and part is caused by the fire generating a wind system of its own. It's, ah, fanning itself, you see."

"Hmm," Sutherland murmured as he turned back to Henricks, leaving the oilman to back away. "The sub. How's it doing?"

"It's on maximum speed—eighteen knots submerged—but it's still about two hours from the Vice-President." Henricks grimaced and went on. "That is, providing the fishing boat's still afloat. The sub won't have it on its sonar for a while yet."

"If they are holding out in that calm area, can the boat wait that long for the sub with this increase in wind?"

Henricks exhaled wearily while he studied his note pad. "It's got about two hours—maybe—"

The President cut in. "About, about! All I've heard is 'partly' and 'about' and 'maybe'! Can't I have a definite time?"

The oilman nearby flushed with embarrassment, but Henricks was unflappable. "Well, Mr. President, just about all—I mean *all*—the satellite pictures can show us is black smoke and what little visible spill there is. We've no satellite sighting of the Vice-President's boat, and on board it they can't see anything to get a fix on. They haven't got Loran navigation equipment on a vessel that size."

"All right, Bob, I'm sorry. How long do you think they have?"

"No more than two hours. They probably figure they have longer, because they won't know yet about the wind from the north coming down on them. And it's impossible for us to tell with all this new smoke just what the fire wind is doing to the clear area they're in. Or were in. Not only that, the two wind systems could end up fighting one another, one pushing the fire towards them and the other pushing it away—or they could both drive the spill towards them."

"How about warning them that the wind's rising? I mean the ordinary wind—Christ, now I don't know what goddamn wind I'm talking about." The President's brow furrowed with anxiety. "Anyway, don't you think we should get some word to them? Alert them?"

Henricks admired the President's impulse to keep the Vice-President and her companion informed, but Search and Rescue Command had cautioned against it. He looked around for more coffee. "I don't think we should, Mr. President. There's nothing they can do anyway. It won't help them to be told that the situation could worsen."

The President agreed, but asked, "How about the sub? If the wind spreads the spill too far, they're in real trouble. What can we tell them?"

"Nothing at the moment. It's too dark for satellite pictures. But now the Coast Guard's sending out patrols to try to chart the edge of the fire. That way we might get some idea of how far the spill has come. We probably won't know until after the Vice-President's picked up, though. If she's picked up."

"All right, Bob, I'll leave it to you, but tell the Canadians as soon as you know. Those guys are pushing their luck as it is."

"Yes, Mr. President."

Feeling the strain of standing for so long before the map, Sutherland sat down. Facing him was a digital clock labeled Firespill Time. As the seconds flashed on and off, an old minute rolled over and disappeared from the electronic counting drum. Sutherland stared at the clock's imperturbable face, imagining in his fatigue that it was mocking him. In that moment, another second had passed.

As the estimated rescue time approached, inside the *Swordfish* Kyle had ordered the air-conditioning unit all but shut down to save power, and tempers were rising with the heat.

An oiler, Leading Seaman Evers, had collapsed over the spinning propeller shaft and had been taken to sick bay suffering from severe friction burns. In the redded-out control room it was already 103 degrees Fahrenheit and climbing, and the dials showed that they were using up oxygen faster than anticipated. The air was filled with the stench of rotting vegetables. Had Kyle known two days ago, during a deliberately prolonged and exhausting antiescort exercise, that they would be forced down for so long, he would have followed the normal procedure and opened the carbon dioxide scrubbers to maintain the carbon dioxide level at the time of diving. Now all the scrubbers could do was keep the present low level of breathable air.

Throughout the boat men began to shuffle rather than walk. The slightest aggravation could touch off a fury out of all proportion to its inconvenience. Those off duty lay or sat in a sweaty stupor. Conversation for its own sake had long since ceased.

Lambrecker sat slumped indolently against the bulkhead in the tiny ship's office, rolling a cigarette and sullenly observing his young and frightened guard. He had seen little of Nairn among the eighty-four-man crew since meeting him the first day out. O'Brien had moved Nairn to another sleeping quarter, and being on different shifts the two men had rarely encountered each other.

Lambrecker struck a match to light the cigarette, but the flame vanished almost immediately. Like an exhausted yet contemptuous hobo sitting in a gutter, he grunted up at the baby-faced seaman. "Hey, you." Nairn tried to look away, but there was no way his eyes could avoid Lambrecker's stare. "Hey, you—Nairn, isn't it?"

Nairn simply nodded, determined to say nothing. O'Brien had warned him not to talk to the prisoner. Lambrecker struck another match, sucking quickly and heavily on the cigarette, but even so only part of the tobacco caught light before the flame disappeared. He held up the blackened match to Nairn. "You see that?"

Nairn tried to look away.

"Hey, I said did you see that?" asked Lambrecker, still holding up the match.

Despite his earlier resolution, Nairn felt impelled to answer, if only to keep Lambrecker quiet. Besides, it seemed an innocent enough question. "Yes," he said, "I see it," adding with a surge of daring, "so what?"

"So *what?*" replied Lambrecker. "So why does a match hardly burn? Where the hell did you go to school, Nairn? That means we're pretty low on oxygen, dummy—that's what! That's why we're all sitting here sweating like pigs."

Nairn pointed the butt of his rifle towards Lambrecker in a futile attempt at a threat. "You'd better shut up."

Lambrecker sneered, "Oh, Jesus." After a few seconds he asked, "Ever screwed a woman, Nairn?"

Nairn blushed. "Look, you'd better shut—"

"You ever screwed anything?"

Nairn didn't answer.

"Well, don't worry," sneered Lambrecker. "Because you're never going to screw anything. Ever."

"What d'you mean?"

"I mean we're gonna suffocate, that's what, dummy." Lambrecker drew heavily again on his cigarette. "You feel drowsy?"

Nairn shrugged. "A little, I guess."

"A little! Don't bullshit me, sonny. Another hour and you won't be able to stay on your feet. That's the carbon dioxide in the air. That's what'll put you to sleep. Permanently. And you'll lie there like a dummy and let that incompetent old bastard do it to you, won't you? You'll go without a whimper. Like a fucking sheep to the slaughter."

O'Brien, on his way back to the control room after checking out the engine room, could smell a cigarette, but he decided not to say anything about it. While it used up oxygen, the amount was not enough to make any difference, and even if it were, most captains, he'd found, preferred to tolerate the habit rather than risk the tensions that would be aroused by banning it. As he neared the ship's office, he heard Lambrecker talking, against his orders. For a second neither Nairn nor his prisoner recognized him, because he was wearing the red goggles issued to all officers for night duty so that they could quickly adjust to the redded-out control room. O'Brien pointed his finger at Lambrecker. When he had mustered sufficient breath, he said, "Shut up, Lambrecker. Save your energy."

"What for?" Lambrecker contemptuously flicked his extinguished cigarette at Nairn's feet. "There isn't going to be any rescue, O'Brien, and you know it."

O'Brien glanced at Nairn and said, "If he opens his trap again, hit it." Then he moved on.

Lambrecker watched him go. "Anything happens to me, O'Brien, and I'll make sure they throw the book at you."

The first officer stopped, turned around, and winked at Nairn. "How you going to do that if we're all supposed to kick off, Lambrecker?" Lambrecker mumbled an obscenity and began rolling another cigarette, while Nairn stood grinning down at him.

Beads of perspiration were stinging O'Brien's forehead and penetrating the rim of his goggles like persistent insects. He wanted to walk faster down the passageway, but his position, he saw, was analogous to that of the sub. The faster he went, the more energy he used. He would need all the strength he could muster when, or if, they found the fishing boat. But while they must conserve energy, he knew that Lambrecker might be right. If they didn't get there in time, they wouldn't save anyone—including themselves. Passing from the white light of the sub into its red heart, he pulled the goggles off with visible relief. He looked up at the clock and checked his watch. It was 1930. In just over one hour, at 2031, they would have to turn back, with or without the Vice-President.

Deciding that there was nothing more he could do for Elaine or the old man until they heard from the sub, the President rang for Jean Roche, who arrived shortly with a special edition of the *New York Times,* together with a hurriedly gathered selection of papers from across the country and wire copy from the foreign press. He would have to prepare himself for the inevitable criticism and later press conferences. He waved Jean to a seat. She was obviously exhausted as she gratefully sat down and began quickly shuffling her notes into order. The President noticed that her face was drawn and that her hair, normally immaculate, was starting to show signs of strain. He smiled and patted her on the shoulder. "Take your time. Have you eaten?"

"No, but it's all right."

The President called out to a young press aide, "Get some food in here, will you?" He turned to Jean. "Coffee or tea?"

"Coffee, thank you. That'd be nice."

As the aide lifted the phone to order, the President asked, as jovially as he could under the circumstances, "Well, who's howling the loudest? About the spill, first."

"The Organization of American States, the Common Market, the States for African Unity—in short, the whole UN General Assembly."

The President sat back in his chair. "Good! That means everybody's feeling guilty for a change. Go on."

Jean gestured at the high pile of press clippings before her. "It's hard to know where to begin. Ralson of CBS got onto the story in Sitka. Unfortunately, he also recognized some of our agents."

The President started. "What agents? Jesus Christ, don't tell me they're trying to drag the CIA into this!"

Jean Roche was quick to cut in. If the President got onto his pet peeve about people seeing CIA spooks under their beds, they would never get through the press reports before the emergency pollution meeting scheduled for later that night.

"No, no, Mr. President, the Secret Service people who were supposed to be with the Vice-President."

The President was still angry. "Jesus! Now we really look dumb." He got up from his chair quickly, pushing it back so hard that Henricks, on the telephone nearby, had to reach out and stop it from tipping over. The

President pulled over a copy of the *New York Times*. "I don't understand why Elaine went a hundred miles out to sea in a goddamn bathtub."

Jean thought it prudent not to mention that it was forty-odd miles out to sea, not a hundred. The President's shoulders slumped a little. He paused, and then went on. "Well, I do know, I suppose. Poor girl—she's hounded every other second of her life." He glanced sympathetically at Jean. "Like you are," he added. For some reason she did not understand, Jean blushed. Sutherland went on. "A person has to get right away from it sometimes—don't they?"

"Yes."

The President sat down again. "What's the Secret Service say?"

"Chief Holborn is hopping mad, by all accounts. He's blasting agents from here to Anchorage."

Sutherland nodded. "Sure. He's right, of course." Then he looked at Jean and asked, "Still, what would you have done if the Vice-President of the United States had left you ashore so she could have some privacy?"

Without hesitation Jean replied, "I would have hired another boat and followed her, Mr. President."

Sutherland smiled. "Well said, Ms. Roche. They could use you over in the State Department."

Jean turned back to the press reports, commenting quietly, "I'd rather stay here."

Sutherland looked at her fondly. "Thank you, Jean."

"Mr. President," Henricks called out, cupping a hand over the receiver and rapidly jotting on his note pad with the other. Then he was on the phone again. "Yes, Admiral. Where? Hmm. How far?"

A middle-aged woman, a member of the kitchen staff, started to push in a squeaking trolley of fresh sandwiches and coffee. Henricks held up his hand at her. She stopped abruptly as the aide, his face taut, continued his conversation with the admiral. "I see—yes. What are they doing about it? . . . All right . . . Yes, I'll tell him right away. Thank you, Admiral."

Before Henricks had put down the phone, the President asked, "More on fire?"

"Admiral Klein has just received a report that the Japanese LNG—the liquid gas tanker out of Juneau—was caught by the fire near Chichagof Island. She turned about and tried to make a run for it, but the wind had blown a ring around her."

Henricks dropped his note pad dejectedly on the table. "She blew up eleven minutes ago. He said the gas tanks went off like missiles." Henricks didn't want to tell the President the rest, but he knew that he had no choice. "It's estimated she's added more than forty thousand tons of liquid methane gas to the fire, which means we've got a fire storm on top of everything else. Winds are reported to be a hundred and twenty miles per hour at the center. They'll probably sink some of the crude by creating huge wave action near the LNG area, but they'll still cause more than enough trouble by sucking up oil particles that will have to come down somewhere else."

Sutherland's voice was strained. "How does it affect the Vice-President's position?"

Henricks walked over to the map and pointed at the intersection of the coordinates the admiral had given him—a spot about sixty miles northwest of Baranof Island and twenty miles from the southern tip of Chichagof Island. "It doesn't affect them. It's too far north."

The President's eyes followed the long, curving arrows which indicated the counterclockwise sweep of the Alaska Current as it broke away northward from the Japan Current and the clockwise curve of the California Current turning away to the south. Then he turned to the diagram showing the joint effect of the clockwise movement of the Coriolis Force in the Northern Hemisphere and the strong alliance formed whenever the wind direction coincides with the direction of current. "But it will raise the crude in that area to its flash point and head it in for the Alaskan coast. Right?"

"I'm not sure."

"Get Mr. Partly over here."

Henricks looked puzzled. "Sir?"

The President motioned toward the telexes at the far end of the room. "The oilman—the fat one."

"Oh," said Henricks. "Mr. Parks."

As Jean turned, she noticed the maid, still standing frozen at her trolley. "Oh dear, let me have that," she said, smiling. The woman, looking terror-stricken, bobbed her head and quickly excused herself.

Parks heaved himself over, and in his nervous voice began giving his opinion on the possibility of the northeasternmost part of the spill reaching Sitka. "Ah, Mr. President, I think the slick might reach the coast—due partly to the Alaska Current and partly to the wind, which is coming from nor'nor'west. I mean the current carrying the oil northwards could be diverted by the wind. Part of it at least might be pushed sideways, more or less."

The President found it difficult to conceal his annoyance with all the ifs and buts of the so-called experts. "Mr. Part—Mr. Parks—what do you think *will* happen?"

"Oh, I think it will burn. Sitka. Go up like a matchbox. After that, the mainland will catch fire."

"Jesus Christ!" The President looked around at Henricks and Jean. "How will it do that? Surely it can't just leap ashore—"

Parks cut in eagerly. "Oh, I'm certain it will, unless the crude forms tar balls—very large tar balls."

Whether or not it was his unconscious reaction to the pressure of the crisis Sutherland didn't know, but he had to struggle to suppress the laughter he felt was about to explode inside him. Mr. Parks and tar balls seemed perfect for each other. "Oh?" said the President. "And what do they do?"

Mr. Parks was smiling broadly. "They're heavy concentrations of crude, formed if the sea gets rough enough to break up the spill. Then they sink and fall to the bottom of the ocean. But before they had a chance to form, I'm sure the fire would wipe out, well, certainly Sitka, and then the whole coast, right down through British Columbia and probably further south. Partly, you see, because the flames will simply leap ashore and head inland. What surf there is isn't strong enough to chop up the spill or douse the flames. And in the inlets, where it's so calm and there are often log booms, the fire'll find it even easier." Parks seemed to derive great satisfaction from his ominous forecast. As he walked back to the telex he rubbed his hands, as if anticipating fresh disasters.

Sutherland watched the oil expert for a moment and shook his head despairingly. "Where the hell did we get him?" Without waiting for a reply, he turned to Henricks. "Get Admiral Klein and find out the shortest estimated time before the fire is expected to reach the Washington coast on that California Current."

In Sitka, sixteen miles eastwards across the sound that separates the southern portion of Kruzof Island from Baranof Island, the old-timers didn't want to go.

The most vocal was an old man who insisted on calling the town by its original Russian name of New Archangel, in memory of the great trading days of the Russian-American Fur Company. Brandishing his stick, he stoutly resisted the attempts of the nurses in the Pioneers' Home to get him into the bus for the airport. They didn't have to tell him about the fire. Even if he couldn't see too well nowadays, he could smell the petroleum fumes mixed with the rotten odor of the pulp mill. But oil or no oil, he wasn't moving.

Most of the population, however, was packing as the seemingly endless flocks of birds came in from the burning sea that kept appearing and disappearing like a premature sunset, curtained by the pall of black smoke smeared against the horizon and the silhouette of Kruzof's Mount Edgecumbe.

The firespill swiftly spread through the water-veined archipelago, polluting its blue channels and sounds and darkening its quiet, rippled bays, creeping ever closer to the panhandle and the vast green hinterland beyond. It was clear that there were not nearly enough planes for an immediate total evacuation of the four thousand inhabitants, so first priority was given to the hospital and then to the women and children. What caused tempers to run high was that while the sick and disabled obviously had to be cared for first, the government had commandeered all civil aircraft for the task. Moving the assembled patients from the TB sanatorium, the orthopedic hospital, and the Pioneers' Home would have been difficult at the best of times, but with most of the town actively readying themselves to leave, it was next to impossible. Valuable time was being lost as the planes stood waiting—time which could have been used evacuating those already at the airport.

Of the hundreds of small boats that now lay sandwiched together, riding the swells in Crescent Bay, few were taken out by owners chancing an escape by sea. In the gathering twilight, one look at the blackening horizon and the imprecise reports of the shape of the firespill were enough to dissuade all but the foolhardy or very brave from making a dash through the sound to the open sea. By now the main body of fire, which had earlier sent offshoots to Point Mary and beyond to Kruzof Island, had completely sealed the northern exit to Juneau by blocking the Kakul Narrows, which separate Baranof and Chichagof islands. Some had been clinging to the belief that the western entrance to Sitka Sound, below the southern tip of Kruzof Island, might yet provide an escape route. But shortly after seven o'clock, a series of muffled thumps and tiny flashes in the distance told them what the others in the isolated town already suspected. Sitka was trapped.

Soon the few boats that had ventured out returned.

The President once again confronted the pile of press clippings editorializing the public outcry.

"All right, Jean. Where were we?"

"The *New York Times* objects to what it calls 'gross governmental irresponsibility in permitting massive tanker traffic. . . . Decisive action by the President and

Congress could have prevented the almost unbelievable condition which has allowed the *Tyler Maine*'s action to be so catastrophic.' "

"Tyler Maine?"

"The destroyer that started the fire."

The President, putting on a pair of half-moon glasses which made him look distinctly professorial, peered over at the clipping. "Bullshit. Why don't my friends at *The Times* stick it to the fucking oil lobby? How much real power do they think we have? Who wrote this?"

"Liley."

"Who else?" grumbled the President. "Still, he's right I suppose. What about the L.A. *Times?"*

Jean shuffled the papers. "I had it here somewhere."

The President spotted it, reached over, and pulled the piece from the pile. "Must be bad if you have to hide it from me."

Jean started to protest. "I didn't want to . . ."

"Forget it."

The headline of the editorial screamed, "Harvest of Incompetency," while the text strongly attacked the "obvious inadequacies of tanker legislation . . . undue oil influence . . . behind-the-door deals" and "what seems to be the President's total inability to inspire confidence, either in his Cabinet or in the nation, during the continuing energy crisis."

A junior aide approached Jean hesitantly and whispered. She excused herself, but the President was so engrossed in the article that he did not notice her leaving.

Outside the Operations Room, a red-lighted sign above the two marines was flashing In Conference. Beside the guards stood a military courier holding another video tape container. Before she returned to the Operations Room with the cassette, Jean noticed a sea of pickets and police in the darkness outside the White House. The wailing of sirens came to her, muffled by the bulletproof glass.

When she returned, the President was still reading. He jabbed his finger irritably at the L.A. *Times* editorial. "I went to college with this donkey." He sat back in his chair, rubbing his eyes. "At least Liley's constructive—not like this son of a bitch."

Jean busied herself leafing through some of the foreign press reports, hoping to shift the President's attention away from domestic criticism. Sutherland replaced his glasses, however, and leaned forward as if to demonstrate that he was ready for anything they threw at him. "What about *Le Monde?*"

"They went to press before they got the news. But we do have a telex translation of Dupré's editorial on French television."

"What's he say?"

"He blames both the Russians and us."

The President folded his hands with some gratification. "Not bad for a change—the Russians getting it."

Jean deliberately shielded an unflattering U.S. news cartoon of the President and the Soviet leader wallowing in an oily pigsty, captioned "Home Sweet Home." She went on quickly with a summary of Dupré's remarks. "He warns against 'the immediate danger to the vital planktonic guarantors of what little marine food remains, not only for North America but for all the Pacific nations and indeed the world . . . a lesson every schoolboy knows.' And 'the danger to our smaller seas—' "

The President cut in. "Meanwhile he uses gasoline to take his copy to the studio. Besides which, he's full of shit—they always try to make it out to be the end of the world. Don't they know oil's a natural compound? It'll break up eventually. Jesus, some of the bugs thrive on it. I don't mind these guys throwing the fire at us. That's okay, because that's the real threat. But all this killing plankton business—they just don't do their homework—think oil's like goddamn DDT." Sutherland pushed away the press file. "It'll soon be time for the pollution meeting. I see you've got more video. Should we see it?"

"I think we should, Mr. President."

Sutherland was unconvinced. "What's the description say?"

"Demonstrations."

Sutherland straightened up. "Demonstrations? So why should I want to see demonstrations?" He waved his hand in the direction of the crowd outside. "I've got one going on right outside, right this moment."

Obviously the press reports were beginning to get to the President. Jean hoped that at the meeting, just when he needed to be at his coolest, he wouldn't be too aggressive. What he needed, she thought, was hard evidence on his side to do the talking for him. She pointed at the video container. "This is a film of major outbreaks, Mr. President. We're not the only ones with demonstrations in our front yard. I think these clips would be very useful in pushing for those emergency oil control powers you want. It will only take a few minutes."

Sutherland sighed with resignation. "I could do with some ammunition all right. Particularly with the Texas bloc. Get them to move their asses for a change."

"Exactly, Mr. President."

"All right, you've convinced me. Run it through."

While Jean loaded the tape in the video deck Sutherland inquired, "How many Japanese killed in that LNG, Bob?"

"Thirty-three, Mr. President. The whole crew. Those things go up like bombs."

"Sure do," came Parks's nervous voice, obscenely cheerful amid the chattering of the telexes.

The President studiously ignored the intrusion and turned towards the huge TV screen.

The scarlet flames darted fitfully out into the thick darkness around Harry and Elaine like the tongues of monstrous, unseen lizards in search of prey.

Half-choking for want of air, the Vice-President and the old man were now up to their waists in the oil-streaked sea, clinging to the rope loops which Harry had earlier strung from the gunwales in anticipation of the scorching heat that would accompany the fire's final advance. The pump was only just managing to suck up the water from several feet below the surface and spray it onto the deck. While this lessened the chance of the wood catching fire, at least for the time being, the laminated decking buckled and rose, twisted in grotesque shapes by the heat. Harry's shoulders knotted in spasms as he coughed violently, bringing up more blood.

While a small, clear area remained around them, the lava red rivulets of burning oil were coming closer by the minute. Harry was using a bailer to douse the small patches of fire that broke away from the main streams and came too close. Nearing the end of his strength, he handed the bailer over to Elaine. She longed to take a deep breath and go underwater to cool her head, but Harry had stopped her, afraid that the oil in her hair would make her a human torch if a flame caught it.

Thinking constantly of Elaine, the President found it difficult to concentrate on the newscast of the riot at the Asanami Shipyard. When he managed to focus on what was happening on the screen, what immediately struck him about the disturbance was that such violence should break out in a country which, with little or no oil of her own, needed crude more than anyone else in the industrialized world. It was a grim omen. He glanced at his watch. He would soon have to leave for the pollution conference, but he was glad that Jean had talked him into viewing the film. This would jolt the State Department, if no one else, into putting pressure on Congress. Any fool could see that no matter who was really to blame for the spill, American foreign policy would suffer, and suffer severely, from such a level of outraged opinion.

The President rose. The lights came on as the TV picture disappeared into a silent dot, creating the illusion that with the flick of a switch the world had returned to normal. "Jean, bring that video with you to the Green Room."

"Yes, Mr. President."

"And the clippings. Some congressmen are mentioned by name too. They might as well share the flack."

"Yes, sir."

The guards came stiffly to attention as they passed. Through the windows of the long corridor that led to the west wing they could see the dense mob of protesters, broken up here and there by clusters of white-helmeted riot police. They looked reassuring yet frightening with their gas masks hanging passively on their packs like shrunken heads. As one squad moved to a new position, it seemed to Jean that the heads had suddenly come alive, jerking and swinging freely in the blood red glow of the flashing lights. Her eye was caught by a young woman who from a distance looked like the Vice-President. She wondered if she would ever see Elaine Horton again.

FIFTEEN

Hogarth was watching the trim and planing of the boat as they tried to maintain the maximum speed of eighteen knots as nearly as possible along the course O'Brien had mapped out earlier. The captain, who normally didn't stand watch, now stood by for periscope duty, his eyes constantly searching the control room for the slightest sign of trouble. He was particularly worried about leaks. The Ranger type XXII was a good sub, but every class had its weak spots, and as with every other submersible, the pressure doubled on her hull every hundred feet she dove. On top of this, *Swordfish* was now the oldest of her type in service. She wasn't running at anywhere near her maximum depth of seven hundred feet, but Kyle still had to keep her well below the surface because of the danger of hitting crude oil patches in the process of forming large tar balls, or of hitting tar balls themselves, slowly sinking on their long journey to the seabed. Run into one of those, and Kyle knew that the treaclelike crude might easily wrap and glue itself about the fiberglass casing which made up the outer layer of the sub's bridge and sail. If that happened and *Swordfish* were to surface too near a fire zone, she could quickly catch fire herself.

The men on trim and the two seamen who had been called in to operate the planes manually, to save power which would normally have been fed to the automatic control, were edgy and soaked with perspiration. Hogarth, very conscious of the captain's presence, tended to pounce on them for any power wasted by the slightest variation in either the horizontal or the vertical motion of the sub. The auxiliaryman was nervous too, anxiously waiting for the order to blow compressed air from the cylinders into the ballast tanks and take them to the surface.

O'Brien wiped his forehead and looked down at the chart table, watching the pin-sized light which darted and jerked under the chart as the automatic gyrocompass fed it coordinates. He traced the light for a few minutes to see how much the sub had deviated from the present course, then double-checked by switching on the depth sounder for a minute or two, comparing the soundings with those down on the chart. He worked swiftly with dividers and then called over to Hogarth, "Correction. Steer zero seven two for six minutes."

Though the sub heeled sharply on the course change, the sonar operator, dripping sweat from the effort of his concentration, never stopped watching his screen or listening for incoming noise. In order to extend its range, he had turned the set on to the passive mode, where it would not send out a pulse but would only pick up incoming noise, such as that of a boat's engine. But if he didn't hear anything soon, apart from the sound of the fire, the operator was ready to ask the captain for permission to switch on to the shorter, active range so the set, in addition to receiving sounds, would send out a pulse that would bounce off a solid object. If luck were with them, that object would be a fishing boat. So far they had been too far from the Vice-President's reported position even to hope for an echo; but now they should be coming within range.

The phone rang, and the indicator panel showed that the call was from the forward torpedo room. O'Brien lifted the receiver. "Control room."

At first it seemed that there was no one on the other end. Then he could hear the faint sound of a girl giggling. "Control room," he snapped. "What the hell's going on there?"

Hysterical laughter. Someone was saying between paroxysms, "He—he wants—to know—he wants to—"

O'Brien put down the receiver. "Somebody's gone stupid. Oxygen starvation, I guess. Must be bad up for'ard."

Kyle was perturbed, but all he could do was nod his head lethargically at the runner nearby. "Gofer, burn off one of the oxygen generators."

O'Brien, not sure that the gofer had lit one before, held up his hand reluctantly. "I'll do it," he said and slowly donned the hated red goggles. As O'Brien left the control room, the gofer asked the captain, "'Scuse, sir, but how long'll them oxygen generators give us?"

"Two hours. About an hour each," Kyle grunted, showing his fatigue. "Don't worry."

The seaman was more worried than ever. He knew enough to realize that while each generator would give them more oxygen, it would simultaneously build up the pressure within the sub, which would increase the effect of the carbon dioxide and the risk of carbon dioxide poisoning.

Walking towards the ship's office to get the generator, O'Brien stopped short. Nairn was lying unconscious on the deck, and Lambrecker was gone. O'Brien looked around as if half expecting Lambrecker to be hiding nearby. He quickly unclipped one of the white six-by-twelve-inch cylindrical generators from the rack, placed it in the stainless steel sheath welded to the deck, and struck the firing pin on top. There was a crack as the .22 blank cartridge exploded down into the chemical, and within seconds the chlorate candle started to burn, generating the vitally needed oxygen. Hissing quietly, it looked to O'Brien through his red goggles like a huge stick of dynamite.

The first officer decided not to tell the captain about Lambrecker's escape immediately, as it would only add to the tension in the control room just as they were entering the general rescue area and listening intently for the faintest echo. Instead he went to the petty officers' mess. P.O. Lane and Chief P.O. Saxton were sitting lifelessly, as if in the throes of sunstroke. "You guys up for a quick lap?"

The younger P.O., Lane, dragged himself off the bench. "What's up, Ex?"

"I want some help with Nairn. He's out cold. Lambrecker's gone." O'Brien looked at the other P.O. "Ted, I want you to round up some of the boys, find Lambrecker, and put him under guard. And this time tie the bastard up."

The P.O. raised his head sluggishly. "Will do."

All Nairn could remember when he came to was that Seaman Sheen had brought Lambrecker a meal tray from the crew's mess. The chief petty officer shook his head. "Sheen and Lambrecker! Jesus, son, didn't you ever watch *Gunsmoke?*"

Nairn's head was pounding. "I—I—beg pardon, sir?"

"Never mind. Here, come with me. I'll fix you up. Man, that's some bump you've got there. The bastard."

O'Brien made his way back past the hissing oxygen cartridge to the control room. It was now 1945, forty-five minutes before the rescue deadline. Where in the hell is Lambrecker, he thought, and more important, what's he doing?

Nearing the control room, he noticed that the boat had fallen unusually quiet. Probably because of the heat, he reflected; no one had either the energy or the inclination to move. But the first officer was not satisfied that the heat was entirely responsible for the sense of foreboding he had experienced when he found young Nairn stretched out on the deck. It wasn't just the picture of the unconscious youngster that troubled him. He felt that there had been something else he should have seen, something even more disturbing than Nairn knocked unconscious, but what it was he could not remember. And the more he tried to remember what it was, the more it eluded him.

The two petty officers, each with an M.P.'s riot stick, split up, the chief P.O. heading towards the forward section and Lane towards the after space and below to the generator room.

Passing the inert bodies strewn across bunks and slumped against the weeping bulkheads, Lane felt the heavy sullenness which permeated the crew's silence.

By the time he'd passed the crew's mess, the empty officers' mess, the ship's office, the perishable cabinet, and the two twelve-bed sleeping compartments and had reached the engine room, he felt the open hostility towards his presence. A small, bearded oiler, glistening with sweat from working in the after compartment's one-hundred-and-ten-degree heat, glared at him from behind the blur of the oil-slicked prop shaft. Lane met his eye and turned to face him. "What's wrong with you?"

The sailor squirted some oil on a bearing. "Nothin'."

"Then what are you staring for?"

"Wasn't staring."

The P.O. was too tired to pursue it. "You seen Lambrecker?" he shouted over the noise of the shaft.

"Who?"

Lane had to take several deep breaths before he could speak again. "Lambrecker."

"Don't know 'im," came the reply.

"What do you mean, don't know him? He's an oiler."

"Must be on a different shift."

"For Christ's sake! The guy who was under guard?"

"Oh yeah, I've seen *'im."* The oiler dropped his eyes and unscrewed the cap of the long-nosed lubricating can, as if signaling the end of the conversation. Lane drew his arm across his forehead. "Well, where'd you see him?"

The oiler was intent on refilling the can. Too intent. Lane realized something was wrong. "Where's the officer on duty here?" he asked quickly.

One instant the P.O. saw a pencil-thin shadow streak across the prop's spinning surface, and the next he lay crumpled on the deck. Three sailors including the oiler helped Lambrecker carry Lane out of the engine room down to stores, where Jock McMahon, the engineer, sat, his hands tied behind him to a cleat on the starboard bulkhead. The Scot's face was a heavy purple, and when he saw the unconscious P.O., he exploded, "You're mad, you bastards. You'll not get away with this lot, I can tell you."

Lambrecker had been thinking about Fran and Morgan constantly. All his waking hours were devoted to fantasies of forgiveness and bloody revenge, and the long hours of troubled sleep were empty with longing for her. But he could do nothing about it, absolutely nothing, until he got back. He heard McMahon's voice from far off. It was filled with Morgan's infuriatingly confident tone. He could even see a resemblance to Morgan in McMahon's soft, pudgy face.

Lambrecker's punch slammed into McMahon's solar plexus, and the engineer doubled up like a rag doll, the air driven from his lungs in a great sob. While Lambrecker bound Lane, Haines, the oiler, went back up the stairs and surveyed the passageway. In a few moments he returned. "What if they heard him?" he asked Lambrecker.

"If who heard him?" demanded Lambrecker contemptuously. "Control? They're too far forward."

"I mean the others—the rest of the crew."

Lambrecker pulled hard on a knot. "Most of them know what's going on. They won't stop us."

"How do you know?" Haines asked nervously. Lambrecker took the stub of a cigarette from between his thin lips, threw it to the deck, and scuffed it with his heavy boot. "I know because one, they're too tired to care; two, they know that if we don't turn now, we'll drown like fucking rats when our power's gone or get roasted alive if we surface to make a run for it; and three, they want to get home same as us. They'll let us do the dirty work. If it works, they'll back us. If it doesn't work, they'll say they didn't know anything about it. It's called playing it safe. They won't interfere. All right?"

Haines still looked worried. "Okay," he began unconvincingly, "but what if they send someone else to look for you?"

"If we're fast, we'll be on them before they know what's happened. They just think it's me loose—they won't know there's five of us till we hit 'em. It'll be too late for them to do anything then. Now get back to the keel and take a look at the off-duty officers. Make sure they're tied up tight, then bring Sheen and the others back here—fast."

"How about the fourth officer and the chief engineer? And Chief P.O. Jordan? We haven't got them yet."

"The fourth and Jordan are off watch up forward. The chief engineer is forward too, checking the fuel tanks. Don't worry—we'll get them on our way to Control."

Haines felt better now that he thought he understood. Good old Lambrecker. He grinned knowingly. "Right. I'll get the others."

When Haines left, Lambrecker gagged McMahon and Lane and checked that the two men were bound securely. P.O. Lane's muffled groans could be heard even under the gag as he started to regain consciousness. Lambrecker bent down, lifted the petty officer's head, and dragged him away from where he would be in full view of anyone entering the stores room. As he propped the P.O. up against a steel cabinet near McMahon, Lambrecker noticed that the hand which had held Lane's head was covered in warm blood. He looked at it for a moment, then quickly wiped it off on his trousers.

Suddenly Haines, his face ashen, appeared in the doorway. The oiler was trembling in panic. "He—he's coming this way!"

Lambrecker's hand shot out, grabbed Haines's overall collar, and pulled him down the last two steps. The oiler's boots skidded on the metal deck and his arms flailed at the air as he tried to right himself. Lambrecker dragged him hard up against the bulkhead. "Listen, you asshole, keep your head or you'll screw up everything. Now slowly, who's coming this way?"

"A—a—Petty Officer—Saxton—a chief. I turned round and came back, soon as I saw him."

"Where is he?" snapped Lambrecker.

"He's up at crew's mess, but he's coming this way. He's been searching for'ard."

Lambrecker shot a glance up the stairs to the open doorway leading to the passageway. He looked at his watch, then back at Haines. "All right, let him find me. We can't waste any more time."

"What—I don't—"

Lambrecker's grip tightened until Haines began to gag. "Go get Sheen and the others and come back here on the double. We've got to move now, before they realize I'm not alone. Understand?"

Haines nodded vigorously. Lambrecker loosened his grip, and the oiler gasped for air. "What if he—the chief—"

Lambrecker's brain was racing, and he had already anticipated the oiler's question. "If he finds me before you get back, I'll hold him, but I might need some help if he tries to play hero. So step on it."

Haines scrambled up the stairs. "Walk, you fucker," hissed Lambrecker. Haines stopped short, looked around, and fighting back panic, shuffled away down the corridor.

Before Chief Petty Officer Saxton reached the door leading down to the stores room, he passed a leading seaman checking the level of the starboard fuel tank. The sailor tapped the glass on the reluctant gauge. The chief's voice was heavy with fatigue. "Ramsey, have you seen Johnny Lane anywhere?"

Ramsey tapped the gauge a second time from habit. "Ah, sorry, what's that, Chief?"

"P.O. Lane—he should have been down here looking for Lambrecker. Have you seen him?"

The seaman seemed to be having trouble getting a reading through the humidity-fogged glass. "Yeah. Saw him in the engine room a while back—talking to Haines, I think."

"You sure? I've been looking for him everywhere."

"Yeah—I think . . ." Ramsey hesitated. "Come to think of it, I never saw him go through aft. He may have ducked down to stores."

The chief caught a stanchion as he temporarily lost his sense of balance, dizzy from the effort of walking and breathing in the oppressive atmosphere of the after compartment. Ramsey reached out and held him steady.

A moment later he felt better. "Thanks," he said. Relaxing his grip on his truncheon and letting it swing freely from its wrist strap, he began to descend the stores room steps, calling out, "You there, Johnny?"

He never even saw Sheen come from behind him with the wrench. Now only the fourth officer, the chief engineer, and Jordan stood in the way of complete surprise. They would be next.

All O'Brien could hear when he returned to the control room was the distinctive ping of the sonar. It told him that Sparks must recently have switched it from passive to active mode, and if he expected an echo it must mean that by now they were within ten miles of the fishing boat's approximate position.

But the captain, sensing what O'Brien was thinking, shook his head discouragingly. "We were getting too much background noise from the fire on passive. Goddamn thing's making a hell of a row." He stopped for another breath. "Almost impossible to pick up their engine in that. Have a listen."

The sonar operator switched from active back to passive as O'Brien lifted the earphone. All he could hear was a deafening, splitting crackle like the sound of a cypress forest fire. He handed back the earpiece and glanced at the chart. "We should be in the area, though."

The captain was leaning against the search periscope. The temperature in the control room had risen to 110 degrees Fahrenheit, and all the salt pills were gone. O'Brien felt uncomfortable about not having reported the Lambrecker incident, but the captain's shining, haggard face and labored breathing vindicated his decision. They all needed to hold together just a bit longer. Once the rescue began, if it began, everyone would be too busy to worry about his own troubles. Besides, Lambrecker would be found sooner or later.

As the remaining minutes slipped by, and the sonar sent its ping racing out through the deep layers of ocean, Captain Kyle watched the sweep of the sonar illuminating the screen in frosty, short-lived segments.

O'Brien was right; they should be just about within echo range of the fishing boat—if it still existed. But even if it did exist, he had no way of knowing how far the firespill had forced it away from its original position.

He worried too about the sub's fast-depleting battery. If electric power were to drop much further, *Swordfish* would be largely disabled, unable to drive quickly to the surface or to take evasive action. He thought of the old days in the Tench class subs. Running at maximum speed in these conditions then would have meant that your battery would be out in an hour. The Ranger class had extended that time, but even so, *Swordfish* would have no margin to spare in getting out after the rescue. He chewed at his lower lip. Maybe he should call it off now.

He ran his eye over the chart. They were approaching the blue X which O'Brien had marked on his preplotted course as the limit of their power capability at full speed—their point of no return. If only they could have half an hour's running on the surface, thought Kyle. It would be slower—the sub reached maximum speed only when submerged—but it would allow him to reoxygenate and at least partially recharge the batteries.

The clock's minute hand jerked forward. It was almost 2000. Kyle watched one more sweep of the sonar's arm and went back to the chart. The area of the firespill given earlier by Pacific Fleet H.Q.'s satellite pictures resembled a huge dumbbell, with two roughly circular areas joined by a narrower waist.

O'Brien was going over the course again, trying to find the delicate balance between the highest possible speed and the longest time available. If they kept up their eighteen knots, they would have to turn back soon. But if they slowed down, not only would it put the Vice-President in jeopardy, but any power they saved would be useless if the spill had widened so much as to make escape from under it impossible. And less speed meant that they would be down longer, increasing the danger of suffocation.

At 2003 O'Brien cursed lightly. His sweaty fingers

had slipped on the dividers, smearing some of his penciled calculations, and the perspiration from his forehead continued to blur his vision as he tried to concentrate. Kyle moved back to the sonar and asked, "Rescue team ready?"

O'Brien frowned. He had told the captain that all was ready an hour ago, when he had checked the team huddled beneath the forward hatch. "They're all set, sir."

Kyle bobbed his head by way of tired acknowledgment, his eyes fixed on the screen, as if his very presence might somehow induce a blip to appear. Without looking up he asked, "What's our power supply?"

O'Brien had told him that too, five minutes ago. They had half an hour left before they would have to turn back and about two hours to try to outrun the firespill. "Approximately two and a half hours, sir."

"I want it on the nose, Number One."

The starboard planesman shifted slightly in his seat. "Watch what you're doing," snapped Hogarth. O'Brien deliberately took time to mop his neck and face before answering the captain, hoping to convey to him that it was doing nothing to reduce the strain on everybody to ask the same questions every five minutes.

"Power supply is two and a half hours, Captain."

"That was ten minutes ago."

O'Brien murmured to himself in exasperation, then answered, "Two hours and twenty minutes power remaining, Captain."

"All sectors conserving?"

"Yes, sir. Air conditioning and lighting at minimum."

The captain had not taken his eyes off the sonar screen. "I want the air conditioning shut down completely—including food refrigeration unit."

"Sir?"

"Shut down *all* air conditioning—including food refrigeration unit."

This time both planesmen looked straight at Hogarth. The officer said nothing. "Yes, sir," answered O'Brien wearily. He was about to use the phone to convey the order but changed his mind; any more talking would only irritate Kyle further, glued as he was to the screen, tense for the faintest echo. Instead O'Brien spoke quietly to the gofer. "Go tell whoever's looking after the air-conditioning generator to shut it down."

"Yes, sir."

Slade, a short, red-haired assistant engineer of Irish extraction who had just dragged himself from his forward torpedo room bunk to stand relief duty in the small midships generator room, couldn't believe the order. "Are they crazy? It's over a hundred and ten fucking degrees in here. I'm relieving a guy who just passed out."

The gofer shrugged. "It's hotter'n hell in control too."

Slade threw a switch. "All right, all right—I'll shut the bloody thing down. They made contact yet?"

"Nope."

"We're gonna have to turn pretty goddamn soon, you know that?"

Again the gofer shrugged noncommittally, not wanting to be held at all responsible for anything that went on in the control room. As he stepped over the bulkhead on his way back to his post, Slade called after him, "Hey, gofer. You hear about Lambrecker?"

The gofer looked puzzled. "Being arrested? Yeah, I heard."

"Arrested, bullshit—he's out. Broke loose from the ship's office."

"Jesus! Where is he?"

"Don't know." Slade breathed heavily and used an old oil rag to wipe his face. "Want to know something else?"

"What?"

"Evers—the guy down with burns in sick bay."

"Yeah—what about 'im?"

"Sick bay attendant thinks he's gonna kick off. He's in shock. I just saw him. He's been throwin' up all over the place. Looks like a fucking ghost. That's all Lambrecker needs, I can tell you."

"Jesus."

Slade's hand stopped moving over his throat; the

dirty rag hung loosely down his chest. "You mean you never heard about that in Control either?"

"I—I never heard nothing."

Slade stuffed the rag in his back pocket. "Huh—they probably don't even know themselves, the assholes. Who's running this son of a bitch anyway?"

The gofer shrugged once more and walked off. Back in Control he reported to O'Brien. "I told Slade, sir. He's shut 'er down."

O'Brien merely nodded, and the gofer stood silently in a corner, wondering whether he should pass on what he'd just heard.

The captain was back at the chart table, one ear still on the sonar, annoying O'Brien again with more questions. "What's our air supply?"

"Four hours maximum."

As casually and quietly as he could, and so the others could not hear, Kyle, picking up the report that had just been passed to him from the radio room, asked, "From your calculations, will that get us out?"

O'Brien answered just as quietly, "No, sir. Not the way we came in. The fire's spread all around the back of us, if these coordinates from Esquimalt still hold."

"No reason to suppose they don't, is there?"

"Well, they can't tell us a thing from satellite pics anymore. There's too much smoke. And even if they could, our aerial is whiplashing so much that reception is unreliable as well. Most of the time Sparks is just getting static. We haven't received the U.S. Coast Guard's report yet, but my guess is that we might have, well, overstretched ourselves already. The firespill may have spread much more than we anticipated."

Kyle tapped the waist of the dumbbell-shaped area. "If we aim to run across here on our way out, will that give us more time in the search zone?"

O'Brien looked at the figures that crisscrossed his note pad. "No, sir." His finger rested on the middle of the eastern bulge of the dumbbell. "Last we heard, the Vice-President was here in the middle of the eastern sector. We passed from the western sector—where we first got the message—under the narrow waist, which incidentally isn't so narrow—it's estimated to be a hundred miles across. It will be easier to keep running and try to come out under the end of the eastern bulge. That's closest to the coast, where someone might be able to reach us. If we turn back to the waist hoping to break clear north or south, we might find the waistline has expanded, especially if it's met up with that Japanese LNG spill. Then we'd be right back under a fire zone with no one anywhere near the sub. And we'd be completely alone."

"What makes you so sure we'll get out under the eastern rim?"

"I'm not, but we might just as well try to outrun the front of the spill as go back into it." O'Brien swept his hand across the whole area. "I'll lay ten to one that given these currents, that so-called waist no longer exists."

The chief engineer, cursing the wear and tear that such long patrols invariably put on a submarine's hull, rang the control room and asked for the captain.

"Yes, Chief?"

"We're losing pressure in one of the for'ard fuel tanks. It's not much, but it looks like a leak." There was a pause as the captain wondered what this new information might do if conveyed to the crew. For an instant he almost wished himself back in an O class sub, where such a leak, though common enough, would have been impossible to detect. As nonchalantly as he could, he replied, "Right, Chief. Wouldn't bother anyone about it, though. What d'you think?"

"I understand," said the chief and hung up. But the gofer in his corner could tell that something was amiss. He decided that he should contain himself no longer. He certainly didn't want to be held responsible for withholding information from the officers; besides, he was afraid of what might happen if any of the crew took matters into their own hands. He turned to the auxiliaryman and blurted out, "Lambrecker's escaped."

Everyone in Control turned towards him. For a few seconds, the only sound was the lonely ping of the sonar. Kyle swung round at O'Brien. "Did you know about this, Number One?"

"Yes, sir. But I have a search party looking for him. I thought it best not to worry you about—"

The captain grabbed the phone and rang for Second Officer Grant. The gofer had also intended to tell them about Evers, but the expression on Kyle's face silenced him.

There was no reply from Grant. Perspiring heavily, his already reddened face showing purple in the control room light, Kyle lifted the phone again and rang O'Brien's cabin. O'Brien said nothing. Kyle smashed the receiver down and rang for the fourth officer, embarrassment fueling his anger.

"Yes?"

Kyle took a second to get his breath. "This is the Captain. Lambrecker's escaped. On a boat this size it—it—" Again he had to pause for breath. "Goddamn it!" he exploded. "It shouldn't have taken more than five minutes to find the son of a bitch. I want him under arrest—in a straitjacket if necessary. Understood?"

There was a click on the other end.

Kyle stood still, sweat pouring out of him, his eyes fixed on O'Brien. Maybe, he thought, maybe O'Brien had been won over, and that was why he hadn't said anything about Lambrecker's escape. He kept looking at O'Brien for several seconds. O'Brien had been in charge of all navigation. Maybe now they were heading out of the fire. He should have plotted and checked the course himself. He'd trusted O'Brien completely. Finally, as O'Brien steadfastly met his eye Kyle decided that suspicion had temporarily distorted his reason. If he couldn't trust Bud O'Brien, there was no hope of beating them anyway. He pointed to the phone. "That was Lambrecker."

"Jesus," muttered O'Brien. "That's why everything's been so quiet."

Suddenly the three officers and seamen felt isolated—cut off from the rest of the *Swordfish*. They all knew that now Lambrecker and his followers, whatever their number, must have taken the remaining officers and N.C.O.'s prisoner along with anyone else who had resisted them. With a few strategically placed men it would not be difficult to seize control of the sub.

Everyone in the control room now realized that Kyle had unwittingly forced Lambrecker to show his hand. He would have to move quickly before his initiative could be thwarted by countermeasures from the control room. O'Brien glanced at the clock. It was 2031. The two-hour maximum promised earlier by the captain was up.

Then it was 2032. A mutiny had begun.

Within seconds of closing the forward and after doors to the control room, the men on watch heard the sound of voices approaching. It was only then that O'Brien realized what had made him so uneasy when he had found young Nairn unconscious. The rifle issued to Nairn for guard duty hadn't been anywhere in sight. O'Brien looked over at Kyle, his voice taut with alarm. "Lambrecker's armed."

SIXTEEN

The fire was now within a quarter of a mile of the fishing boat, and the sulphur-pale moon had long been eclipsed by the jet black smoke that completely enveloped them.

A blast of furnace-hot wind tore over them, bringing with it a shower of flaming oil droplets, a few of which landed on Elaine's sweater. She screamed as the wool burst into flame, and letting go of the rope, she began to splash herself frantically, forgetting Harry's warning in her panic. Luckily, her splashing mixed enough water with the oil to extinguish the flame. It had lasted only two or three seconds, but by now most of the sweater was gone and her upper right arm was scorched. In her shock she had also let go of the bailer, which was instantly swept away by the wind, forcing them to use their hands as they tried, unsuccessfully, to douse the advancing threads of fire.

The pump, its filter finally overcome by the thick crude, gave a few coughs and died. The wind changed slightly, as it had a hundred times that day, and drove some of the burning rivulets back twenty or thirty yards, as if mercilessly prolonging their agony. Even with the wind's most recent reprieve, Harry was sure that it would all be over in another half hour. If the heat didn't kill them, lack of oxygen would.

Despite their fatigue, the men in the control room worked quickly in response to Kyle's sharp orders. A transformation had come over them. The final challenge to the captain's authority had suddenly pushed dissatisfactions into the background and quashed any doubts they'd had about his ability to command. Now there were no ifs or maybes. There were only two alternatives, to fight or to capitulate, and the latter never occurred to them. They knew Lambrecker would be in the control room any minute. Kyle looked ten years younger as he turned to O'Brien. "Number One. Unlatch the fire extinguishers. You take the for'ard door and I'll cover aft."

O'Brien threw back the spring clips, pulled the two red cylinders down, and quickly jerked out the safety pins.

Kyle called to the third officer. "Mr. Hogarth, when I give the word *roll,* I want hard astarboard, then hard aport."

"Yes, sir."

"And Sparks, whatever happens, you keep watching that sonar."

"Aye, aye, sir."

The captain grabbed an extinguisher from O'Brien and readied himself beside the aft door. "Gofer, you help the first officer and me, whoever seems to be in the most trouble. Got it?"

"Yes, sir."

"If any of them hit the deck, use your boots, and make bloody sure they don't get up." The gofer looked blank with fright. "Got it?" the captain snapped. The gofer nodded his head vigorously. "Yeah—yes, sir."

Kyle now spoke to all of them. "Remember, they can only come in one at a time—two, if they try both doors. That's our ticket. Get them just as they start through. And everybody brace yourself for the roll. That's our only chance to—"

Footsteps were approaching in the passageway outside. The captain's right hand went to the control panel and settled on the corridor light switch. He threw it down, plunging the passageway into complete darkness. The footsteps ceased for a minute; then they could hear raised voices and someone yelling for a flashlight. O'Brien gripped the handle of the forward door. He felt someone trying to open it and pulled back with all his strength, looking around for something to jam into the spokes of the door wheel. There was nothing. He heard Sheen shouting, "I'll open the fucking thing."

A cannonlike crash reverberated in the confined space. O'Brien's hand flew from the door wheel, and he was thrown back hard against the attack periscope as an axe smashed down a second time against the wheel on the outside of the door. One of the planesmen started from his seat. "Jesus Christ, what the—"

"Keep her steady," intoned Hogarth, gently pushing the man down in his seat. O'Brien grabbed for the extinguisher as the door wheel began to spin. He glanced across at Kyle. The captain inclined his head towards the door, saying quickly, "Get the man with the rifle."

"And the fucking axe," mumured the seaman on the trim control.

The sonar pinged again. It was answered by a hollow thong. Sparks called out to the captain. The ping sounded again, and once more there was the thong of an echo, this time accompanied by a small blip on the screen.

The captain shoved his extinguisher at the gofer, grabbed the mike from the public-address console, and turned it to full volume. "Now hear this. We've found the boat. We have found the—"

The forward door burst open. A flashlight darted forward. O'Brien squeezed the trigger on the extinguisher, and the man screamed as the chemical foam covered his face and began burning into his eyes. The flashlight clattered to the deck.

"Roll!" yelled Kyle.

Instantly the sub lurched violently to starboard. O'Brien kept spraying the doorway, and bodies tumbled and crashed over each other as they tried to crowd in from the passageway. The gofer realizing that the mutineers were coming in only from the forward section, fell to the floor, and pulled the trigger of his extinguisher so as to spray those who had fallen or somehow evaded O'Brien's field of fire.

A figure holding an axe cannoned into O'Brien as the sub swung hard aport. O'Brien rammed the cone-shaped muzzle of the extinguisher over the man's head and pulled the trigger. The nozzle hissed, and the swoosh of foam instantly blinded the sailor. As he clawed his eyes and turned to escape, he ran into a savage kick from the gofer and crashed to the deck. The falling axe, barely missing Hogarth, smashed to the deck like a thunderclap. The captain, still shouting into the mike, slipped in the foam, grunted angrily, and reached for a handhold. Someone tried to wrench the mike from him, but Kyle quickly released his grip, and as his assailant pitched forward with the roll of the sub, he drove a bone-crunching fist into the man's face. As the man's head smacked the periscope column, there was a clatter on the deck, and a shot roared through the sub, followed by the sound of splintering glass as the bullet tore through the banks of pressure gauges and embedded itself in the starboard bulkhead. In the deafening noise and confusion, it was only then that the captain realized the man was Lambrecker and that he had been holding the rifle. Kyle kicked the weapon aside with one boot and slammed the other into the mutineer's head, making sure he would stay down.

As suddenly as it had started, it was over. There were a few groans and obscenities from a foamy pile of bodies around the forward door, but no one had any fight left in them. The captain flicked up the passage light switch. He saw one of the mutineers, Ramsey, writhing on the deck just beyond the door and the gofer lying near him, badly winded. Sheen, shaking his head like a punchy boxer, was slumped against the forward bulkhead, and two other accomplices, one of them throwing up, were stumbling away through the foam that had spilled out into the passageway. O'Brien lay back on the search periscope, bleeding slightly from the lip.

The sonar pinged, and back came the echo. Sparks, his headphones still on and looking like a comic book Martian, glanced contemptuously around at the human debris before turning back to his beloved set. He had already plotted the fishing boat's position and now handed a piece of paper to the captain, who was steadying himself against the bulkhead, trying to catch his breath while proudly surveying the damage. "God!" said Kyle, counting heads with the air of a hunter tallying game. "There were only five of them!"

Hogarth, helping the gofer lift an insensible Lambrecker out of the chemical suds before they suffocated him, said, "I think there were more, Captain."

Kyle didn't know whether they'd given up because they'd heard the sub had made contact or because of the control room's defense. Probably both, he decided.

Soon the fourth and fifth officer, with a small band of P.O.'s and crew behind them, rushed in. The second officer began, "They took us by surprise and tied us—"

Kyle was listening to the sonar. He held up his hand, cutting the officer short. "Explanations later, gentlemen. We're going up." He pointed to the fourth officer. "Crowley, you're responsible for cleaning up this mess. I want it clear in ten minutes. All right?"

"The mutineers, sir," began Crowley, incredulous. "Don't you want them in custody?"

Kyle glanced about at the men who had somehow thought they could take over his ship. "Later," he said. "Hose them down and put 'em on standby."

Crowley, in sympathy with Petty Officer Jordan, who was rubbing his wrists where Sheen had had him tied after he'd refused to cooperate at the 2030 deadline, started to protest. "But, Captain, Lane's head was opened up and—"

Kyle bellowed at him, "Then get him to sick bay. Get the place cleaned up and put these bastards on standby! In our condition, we'll need all hands. Have them assemble with the rescue team. Now!"

"Yes, sir."

Kyle drew the black curtain which cut off the control room from the white light of the passage and positioned himself by the search periscope. "Bud, I want you here." Hogarth, who was grinning broadly while watching the bodies being carried off, heard Kyle give the first order to surface. "Take her up to sixty feet."

"Sixty feet, sir."

The sub started to rise towards the fire. Kyle glanced at his watch. It was 2034. He phoned the second officer. "Grant, I'll sound action stations in ten minutes and I want you in the forward torpedo room with two fish set to go."

"Yes, sir."

O'Brien was perplexed by the captain's last order but said nothing as he worked quickly at plotting the shortest escape course from their new position. Given the estimated area of fire from the new coordinates Sparks had just received from H.Q., it looked increasingly hopeless. If they didn't have enough time or room on the surface to recharge their batteries, their chances of getting out were nil. But there was nothing they could do about it now.

Hogarth, watching the trim, began to call out the depth every ten feet. "Two sixty . . . two fifty . . ."

At a hundred feet the captain pushed the battle stations horn. Throughout the ship, men who had been at each other's throats just minutes before hesitated, looked at each other confusedly for a second, then instinctively sprang to their attack posts. As bulkheads for the watertight compartments banged shut and locking wheels spun, Second Officer Grant readied the torpedoes. Hogarth began reading off the depth at every five feet. "Ninety-five . . . ninety . . . eighty-five . . ."

All this time the sonar pinged, its echo becoming louder and louder. As they neared periscope depth, Kyle asked, "Range?"

Sparks watched the arm sweep round the screen. When the blip appeared, he verified the distance in a deliberate but unhurried tone. "Four thousand yards."

"Bearing?"

"Zero five three."

Hogarth called out, "Seventy feet."

"Periscope depth," ordered Kyle.

"Periscope depth," came the confirmation.

At sixty feet the sub stopped rising. "Search periscope."

"Search periscope, sir."

The hydraulic motor wheezed softly, and the long,

shiny steel column slid up through the control room. Hogarth started the defrosters and water pressure wipers to clear the high magnification lenses of any oil that might obscure the captain's view. Even before the scope stopped, Kyle had flipped down its arms, and with the bill of his cap turned back he stood glued to the eyepiece, turning the column smartly yet unhurriedly through three hundred and sixty degrees.

He saw a stretch of calm, oily sea end abruptly against a precipice of black smoke and blood red fire. Now and then he could see glimpses of fire-free sea beyond small breaks in the flames, but nothing more. He swung the scope around again. Still he could not see the boat.

In the middle of the thick, pitch black night it looked as if the whole world were on fire. He stepped back quickly, snapping up the scope's arms. "Down periscope."

The hydraulic motor wheezed again, retracting the steel column. "Slow ahead." The telegraph rang. "Slow ahead, sir."

Kyle used his sleeve to wipe the sweat from his eyes. "We're in that calm area the fishing boat reported, but it looks like it's been cut in half. Can't see any sign of the boat, only fire and smoke. We'll have to get closer in."

Hogarth had responded quickly and was already beginning to edge *Swordfish* towards the blip shown on the screen. Sparks's voice was again slow and distinctive. "Four thousand yards and closing."

The captain moved to the chart table, speaking to O'Brien. "If there is a fire-free zone left somewhere inside that furnace, there's no way they can come to us. There's a wall of flame right round them. They'd go up like a piece of paper. We'll have to clear a way for them so they can come to us."

O'Brien looked doubtful. "Their motor might be out . . ."

Sparks interjected, "Excuse me, sir, but I checked that out on passive a moment ago. We do have a sound from the blip."

O'Brien was dubious. "You're sure it's the main motor, not just something else?"

"No way of being absolutely sure, sir. Could be a smaller engine, but it's certainly a motor."

The captain made his decision. "Their engine could be out, but we have to bet that it isn't. And there's no way we can send in the inflatable raft even if we do clear a way. Even if it didn't stick fast in the slick, its outboard would be gummed up in no time."

O'Brien watched the blip on the screen worriedly. "I suppose we can't risk going further in—under the fire wall—and coming up where they are? We need to recharge as well as get them out."

The captain shook his head. "No way. If there is a fire-free zone in there, it's bloody small. We'd either capsize them or drive them into the fire with our wash. Besides, if we hit them with our fuel leak or puncture one of our fuel tanks, that's it for everybody. No, we'll just have to clear a way for them and hope to hell they can run for it."

"Three thousand yards and closing."

Suddenly O'Brien saw the captain's plan. You had to hand it to the Old Man, he was good. Very good. And they had all thought he had spent too much time ashore!

Kyle was watching the range. "It's the only way," he murmured to himself as he lifted the phone and called the forward torpedo room. "Grant, those fish ready to go?"

"Yes, sir—short fuses."

"Right. Stand by."

"Aye, aye, sir."

Next Kyle rang the forward hatch room. "Jordan, when I surface I want that rescue team ready to go topside in a hurry. But don't move till you get the word—and have fire extinguishers ready."

"Aye, aye, sir."

The thong of the echo was getting louder.

"Two thousand five hundred yards."

"Search periscope."

"Search periscope, sir."

"Bearing?"

"Zero five five."

The captain flipped down the arms and began to rotate the scope. He stopped and turned it back slowly two degrees. "I've got it."

Everyone except Sparks turned around. "Can you see them, Captain?"

"Yes—just a glimpse. Damn, the fire's closed in all right. They're cut off."

O'Brien felt a surge of apprehension. "How big's the clear area?"

"About the size of a duck pond from here—radius maybe a quarter of a mile at most. Probably less." Kyle stepped back from the scope. "Hold position. Down search scope. Up attack scope."

Hogarth's response was terse and precise. "Position holding, sir. Down search scope. Up attack scope."

As the longer attack scope rose, Hogarth took the sub down another ten feet to compensate for the scope's extra height above the water. A few seconds later Kyle bent forward, draped his arms over the attack scope's handles, and called for the range.

"Steady at two thousand five hundred yards, sir."

Through the scope it looked to Kyle as if the fishing boat, blurred by the heat, were changing position every few seconds, but he soon realized that it was an illusion caused by the constant dancing of the flames. "Bearing?"

"Zero five seven, sir."

O'Brien cut in. "Sorry, sir—but why can't we surface and fire in the clear area above us?"

Kyle swung the attack scope to zero five seven. "Because if they're alive, they might see us and try to make a run for it—straight into our line of fire and the firespill wall. I want to blow out a hole for them, not blow them out of the water. Stand by. Bearing—mark!"

"Zero five five."

"Shoot!"

"Set."

"Fire one!"

"Fire one," repeated O'Brien.

"Fire two!"

"Fire two. Number one and two fired and running, sir."

A shudder passed through the sub as the torpedoes blasted out of their tubes, streaking towards the fire wall at fifty knots.

"Down scope."

"Down scope, sir." As the attack periscope withdrew into its protective sheath to prevent blast damage to the delicate optical system, O'Brien, his fingers above the console firing button, counted off the seconds to detonation. "Five—four—three—two—" He pushed the button and gripped an overhead pipe. The boat shook violently, heeling hard to starboard, then to port, flinging the crew about like toy soldiers, as the two almost simultaneous explosions ripped convulsively through the red black sea, hurling tons of burning slick into the poisoned sky.

As the sub came back on an even keel, Kyle ordered, "Prepare to surface."

Hogarth checked that all compartments were closed off. "Ready to surface, sir."

"Surface!"

Hogarth swung round to the auxiliaryman. "Blow one, two, four, six, and seven."

There was a hiss as the compressed air forced its way into the tanks. "Blowing one, two, four, six, and seven, sir."

The moment *Swordfish*'s nose broke through the black surface, Kyle instructed Hogarth, "Secure the blow-open upper conning tower hatch." He rang the forward hatch room. "Rescue party on deck." Remembering the chief engineer's report of the ruptured diesel tank, he added, "And two men to see where we're leaking fuel."

By the time O'Brien, taking over as officer of the watch, had given the all clear and stationed the lookouts, the captain was standing behind him on the bridge.

Kyle saw immediately that the gap made by the torpedoes was too small for the sub to risk passing through, particularly with fuel spilling from its tanks.

But he had to give them the best chance he could. He rang for slow ahead, wishing he could have had time to fire more torpedoes. The telegraph answered, and the sub started to edge towards the gap. The rescue party and the standby crew clambered through the forward hatch and breathed the air gratefully. It was hot and fume-laden, but it was air nevertheless and better than they'd had for the last twelve hours.

While the sailors readied their lines, Sparks, down below, was receiving another message from H.Q. in Esquimalt, informing the commander of *Swordfish* that the spill had expanded far beyond earlier estimates.

Three-quarters of a mile away, the Vice-President and Harry, gagging from smoke inhalation, did not see the explosions although they heard them and felt them as the underwater shock waves punched into their bodies, doubling them up and knocking them to the surface like stunned fish. After Elaine had partially recovered from the blow, her ears ringing and her vision still distorted by the impact of the blast, she strained to see through the clouds of sulphurous smoke.

Before the concussion hit Harry, he thought that the noise had come from above the fire, and now, his brain dull from lack of oxygen, he gazed dumbly skywards. Then they heard what sounded like the popping of small firecrackers, barely audible through the crackling and sputtering of the fire, which was now no more than four hundred yards away. Harry squinted again into the red black sky and saw the green starburst. It lasted only a few seconds. "It's a flare," he gasped hoarsely. "It's a flare! There's someone—the sub! The sub—it's here!"

When Elaine looked up, she could seen nothing, but gradually the gap which had been punched out of the fire wall by the torpedoes became visible. It was almost a minute, however, before Harry realized that the sub had stopped on the other side of the gap and was no longer coming towards them. He clambered aboard the boat frantically, pointing. "There—there, through the gap. It's not coming to us—no room. We'll have to run for it. Quick—get aboard! They've blown a path for us."

Elaine tried to pull herself up the short ladder but fell back, splashing into the water, now strewn with dead sea life amidst the oil. Harry put out his arm. She grabbed it and slipped from his oily grasp back into the sea, swallowing a foul-tasting mixture of high octane and crude. Harry reached down, grabbed her neck and dragged her aboard. She screamed as her injured arm brushed against the poker-hot gunwale. Harry stumbled forward to start the boat's motor, shouting, "Hang on! I'll have to give her full throttle to get through."

The motor roared into life, and the boat surged towards the gap.

On the sub's bridge, O'Brien wiped the oily slick from his face—he had opened the top hatch as they surfaced—and watched the rescue team standing by somewhat awkwardly under the eye of P.O. Jordan. They could do nothing to help until the fishing boat crossed the gap. The *Swordfish*'s diesel generator was now running at full speed, sucking in what air it could in the short time they had. O'Brien shook his head. The scene around him was like a medieval painting of hell. Everywhere he looked there was fire and smoke. The life-jacketed crew, twisted and distorted by the leaping flames, seemed like demonic invaders waiting anxiously for some charred and ruined prize from the fire storm around them.

Unable to take the sub in any closer, the captain had been watching the boat approaching the gap through his binoculars. A hundred yards or so on the other side of the open space, it stopped and began to rock helplessly in its own wash. He shouted through the bullhorn, "Their engine's cut! Get the raft overboard!"

Aboard the fishing boat, Harry worked frantically at the controls.

Kyle asked O'Brien, "Have they found that fuel leak yet?"

The first officer turned about, nearly losing his footing, and spoke to the men rigged with safety lines proceeding carefully along the deck, searching for the telltale trace of diesel. They shook their heads.

The gap in the fire was closing. At its widest, it had offered only a narrow channel. Kyle swallowed and raised his binoculars again. The boat was moving, but only at about quarter speed. "Too slow, too slow," he murmured. "Must be clogged to hell and gone with muck."

Harry had the throttle all the way down. He too saw the gap closing. "We'll never make it like this," he yelled to Elaine. "We'll have to jettison weight. You steer?"

Before she realized what was happening, Harry had pulled her under the canopy and put one of her hands down hard on the throttle and the other on the wheel. "Whatever you do, just steer straight ahead at the gap. When we get near the sub, push the throttle up. That'll cut the motor. Got it?"

Elaine nodded feebly while Harry made his way quickly but as carefully as he could towards the stern and the heavy water pump. The sea was choppier than before, and he fell heavily on the deck. Elaine looked around. He was on his feet again, yelling above the fierce roar of the fire, "I'm going to get rid of the pump. That'll give us more speed. How far are we?"

Elaine peered through a small hole in the smoke. "About two hundred yards."

As the boat sluggishly approached the closing gap, Harry grappled desperately with the pump. He fell several times, gasping for air before he mustered the energy to drag the heavy little engine over the distorted planking and up to the gunwale so that he could push it overboard.

The gap was now only about fifty yards wide, and the fire was closing even faster than before. There was a heavy, dragging noise, the sound of Harry cursing and coughing, then a loud splash. The boat's nose lifted slightly. Then *Happy Girl* pushed forward with a new vigor and leaped for the gap. The clear space was almost sealed now, and long tendrils of flame rolled greedily across the open water. Elaine pushed down on the throttle with all the strength she had, but still the fire enveloped her. For a moment, she thought the boat had stopped; flames were licking round her and the canopy was on fire. Then she realized that the fire wall was behind her. Tears streaming down her face, she shouted, "We did it! Harry, we're through!"

A black cloud lifted, and there was the sub—dead ahead. She cut the throttle and tried to swing the boat about. Too late. *Happy Girl* glanced off the *Swordfish*'s starboard quarter and slid along the side of the sub, the flames from her canopy spreading to the sub's oil-covered fiberglass casing.

One of the standby party in the inflatable raft, which had narrowly escaped being punctured in the collision, managed to leap aboard the boat, grab the Vice-President, and jump overboard with her while his shipmates tried desperately to fend off the burning wreckage. O'Brien had an extinguisher on the casing fire within seconds, but the flames continued to spread, racing about the bridge and sail. Kyle grabbed the bullhorn. "Get her aboard fast. Everyone else clear the decks. Let's get out of here!"

Petty Officer Jordan, wielding a long boat hook, had grabbed the sailor who held the Vice-President and dragged the two of them to the edge of the sub just as the fishing boat's gas tanks exploded aft of the bridge, showering *Swordfish* with burning gasoline. In the flash of the explosion, Kyle saw that the man in the water with the Vice-President was Lambrecker. Kyle had no time to ponder whether the mutineer's action had been motivated by bravery or expediency. He would have to give him the benefit of the doubt.

In a few more seconds the rescue team were lowering the Vice-President down the forward hatch. The moment he saw her head disappear from view, Kyle ordered, "Clear the bridge." The lookouts scrambled below and Hogarth in the control room heard the captain's order come over the intercom. "Dive the submarine!"

Kyle, drawing down the upper hatch, recited the

litany of the dive. "Upper hatch shut. One clip on—two clips on. One pin in, two pins in." He pushed the Klaxon alarm twice. On the second raucous blast, the ballast tanks' vents opened and giant bubbles broke the surface of the burning sea. The control room watchkeepers were still securing the lower conning tower hatch when the captain instructed O'Brien, "See if the Vice-President is okay."

"Yes, sir."

At an angle of ten degrees, the sub was diving to a leveling-off depth of sixty feet. The captain would have liked to go deeper to avoid the danger of tar balls, but from H.Q.'s last report, together with what he had just seen, it was now clear that the firespill had spread well beyond the maximum distance the sub could attain on her two remaining hours of battery power. Kyle cursed. If only *Swordfish* had had time to recharge on the surface!

Kyle now realized what O'Brien had feared just prior to the rescue, namely that without the admiral's "all possible assistance," *Swordfish* could not escape. He rang the engineer. They would have to stay at sixty feet, the minimum distance from which the sub could transmit a direction-finding signal. "Damage report, Chief?"

"Where would you like me to start?"

"Can we run at sixty feet?"

"We can—just. She's sprung a few wee leaks after that last bang. We'll have to watch her bloody closely."

The captain sent a message to Pacific Command that the Vice-President had been rescued and that *Swordfish* would need help. Though what could help her now God only knew.

Down in the sick bay the Vice-President, near complete exhaustion, was asking for Harry.

SEVENTEEN

Informed within minutes of the rescue that the Vice-President was aboard *Swordfish,* the President hastily adjourned his pollution meeting with congressional leaders in the Green Room and hurried down with General Oster to the Operations Room.

He still did not know about the extreme precariousness of the sub's position, and his face, though gray with the strain of the long vigil, broke into a wide grin as he strode past the marine guards, barely giving them time to glimpse his I.D. Entering the Operations Room, he saw Jean Roche, haggard-looking, dwarfed by a series of large-scale aquamarine-colored maps of the Northeast Pacific. "How is she?" he asked.

Jean had just received the post-rescue report from Canadian Pacific Command. "A little shaky, some first-degree burns apparently, but otherwise okay. The sub's making a run for it now."

"Well?" said the President happily, looking around at Henricks and the others, the tension draining from his shoulders as he took off his crumpled suit coat and let it fall on a chair. "That's great. There'll be a nice big thank-you when that sub docks, I can tell you. Does the press know?"

Jean's expression told the President that she couldn't care less about the press. "Mr. President, they're still in grave danger. They have a long way to go and the fire's still over them. It's spread much further east than we thought."

The President reached for his chair. "Didn't they recharge when they surfaced?"

"Not enough time, sir. The fire-free zone was cut in

two. They had to get out very quickly. Besides, they have a fuel leak." Jean handed him a cable from Canadian Defense Forces Pacific Command requesting help in extricating the sub.

The President poured a cup of ice-cold water, drank it in one gulp, crushed the paper container, and still gripping it, asked, "You mean they grabbed air only—no battery recharge at all?"

"That's right, sir."

"Where are they now?"

Henricks used the long pointer to indicate the position on the map.

"What have we got on the way?" asked the President in a gloomy voice.

Henricks wearily flicked over a file. "U.S.S. *Finguard*. A cruiser—nonnuclear."

"Can she help them?"

"No, sir. She can only stand by on the perimeter. As long as that fire burns, we can't do a thing."

There was a long pause as the President looked slowly about the Operations Room, sensing the air of exhaustion and defeat. Only Oster, pulling out another long cigar, looked fresh and relatively unconcerned. Sutherland stood up and went to the map with his hands on his hips and his head bowed in thought. The digital clocks continued their silent race.

The general tore the wrapper from the Tabacalera, squeezed the cellophane into a tight ball, aimed it carefully like a missile, tossed it across the room, and watched it drop into the center of a wastebasket overflowing with spaghetti-piled reams of telex tape. With the unabashed satisfaction of a connoisseur, he rolled the olive green cigar between his lips, lit it, and blew out a long stream of smoke. His aide, the air force colonel, knew that the Bomber was thinking hard. The general paced several times up and down the length of the long mahogany table, the tip of his cigar brightening and dimming regularly. Then he looked up in a haze of smoke that rose in a veil across the world map. "Jean, how long does the sub have?"

"At the time of rescue, Canadian Command at

Esquimalt reported it had two hours' battery power remaining. That's traveling at fifteen knots." Jean glanced at her watch. "But she's been under way for fourteen minutes now. One hour and forty-six minutes left."

Deftly flicking open a pair of dividers, the general measured off the distance that the sub would have to go to break out. He frowned. "At that rate she'd barely make thirty miles, and there's over a hundred miles to go before she'd clear the fire with even a minimal degree of safety." He put down the dividers; they could tell him no more than he already knew. "She's got no chance as it is."

Sutherland, desperate for the least sign of hope, said without conviction, "They have got air, though. They could stay down and breathe." His voice trailed off lamely. "Couldn't they?"

Jean Roche's reply was not encouraging. "You might call it air. It's full of fumes. But the main problem is that they haven't enough spare power to cool the ship, which means they can't keep the air temperature down to a safe level." Jean picked up the message that had come in from Canadian Pacific Command. "The real trouble comes when the batteries go out completely. And this last report from Esquimalt confirms that all batteries will be dead by 2249 their time—0149 our time. Without any power to cool the sub even a little, the temperature will soar."

"Soar!" grunted the general. "In that humidity, it'll kill them. Must be damn near boiling inside that sub right now."

Stunned by what he'd just heard, his hopes suddenly demolished, the President hardly heard Jean agree with Oster and inform the general that Esquimalt had reported that without proper cooling, the heat from the electrical systems alone would already be pushing the temperature in the sub to over 120 degrees Fahrenheit.

Oster looked morosely at the map. "If the calm area was cut in two by fire, how in hell did that sub get the boat out?" he asked.

Jean's voice was beginning to sound hoarse from

fatigue. "Apparently it blew a gap in the fire wall, General."

"Torpedoes?"

"Yes."

The general grunted and began to pace again, his cigar bobbing from one corner of his mouth to the other with an alarming rapidity. The colonel was intrigued; this was one of the general's "bombing" moods if ever he'd seen one. Suddenly the general stopped, the cigar abruptly stilled and sticking out defiantly like a small cannon. "Mr. President!"

Soon the two men were huddled over one of the smaller tables, where the three-dimensional satellite pictures of the fire had been assembled. Jean Roche heard Oster say, "It wouldn't have worked with the fishing boat, but it just might work out for the sub." She lost the rest of the conversation amid the rustle of photos being moved as the general hastened to explain his idea.

Sutherland listened intently, nodding, his face flushed, his excitement communicating itself to everyone in the Special Operations Room. Finally he stood up, beaming, and slapped the general on the back. *"Interesting?* By God, Arnold, it's brilliant, that's what it is! We'll go to war with the son of a bitch." The President signaled to Henricks. "Bob, get me Strategic Air Command—Bombers."

The aide hesitated as his hand rested on the red phone. "Nuclear Wing, Mr. President?"

"Christ, no—not the B-1's. We're not starting a nuclear war. I want the largest conventional bomb-loaded carriers we've got on standby. The B-52's. Right, General?"

Oster blew out a short puff of smoke. "Sure as hell is, Mr. President," he answered with obvious pride. "Still the most versatile bombers we've got—carry any damn thing—A-bombs to hand grenades."

"Good," said the President. "Where's the nearest conventional wing base?"

Henricks hurriedly leafed through the computerized list of bases. But Oster, flicking off a long ash and stabbing his cigar towards the map, already had the answer. "Closest is Freeth Air Base in Alaska, between Valdez and Cordova, four hundred miles northwest of the spill. But we'd better hurry. We're getting damn close to the wire—ninety minutes, to be exact."

The president motioned urgently to Henricks. "Right. Bob, get me Strategic Air Command Headquarters at Offutt, Nebraska. I want to speak to the commander, Conventional Weapons Wing."

After he had explained the general's plan, Sutherland was surprised to see that it had failed to excite much interest among his aides, but his exasperation with the lack of any alternative spurred him on. Henricks put their doubts into words. "We'd need an awful lot of conventional bombs."

Sutherland's eyes moved slowly from aide to aide, and with acidic understatement he observed, "If there's one commodity this office has available upon request, it is exactly that. We have some left over from Vietnam, you might remember. Besides," he added in a buoyant tone, "we might even be able to stop the whole fire before it hits the U.S. and Canadian coasts. If this mission works, we'll send in every B-52 we have."

Oster's eyebrows lowered, warning the aides to back off—not that he was afraid of criticism, but he, better than anyone in the room, understood how deeply troubled his friend was, and he saw that the time had come to protect him. He knew that the almost boyish enthusiasm with which the President had greeted the plan was in a reality a measure of his deep despair, a signal that the adrenaline was racing—that the President was ready to grasp at anything in a final frantic effort to save the woman he loved.

Driven by his anxiety, Sutherland returned to the wall map. Its rows of blinking lights, now programmed to indicate SAC's conventional bomber air bases, stared down on him. The plan was a long shot. He knew it and the general knew it. It was the longest shot they'd ever played together, but now it was the only one they had to play. Besides, their luck had held so far. Maybe it would keep on holding. Maybe.

EIGHTEEN

In Vietnam at age thirty-four, Si Johnson, a reticent, slightly built New Englander, hadn't been the top navigator in the 501 Bombardment Group, but he had been among the best. When he came home from Nam, nobody was surprised when he was made navigator in *Ebony I*, the lead B-52 in the Seventeenth Conventional Bomb Wing, based at Freeth Field in Alaska.

Lately in his spare time he had taken to playing tennis, but without professional coaching the joy of the game was eluding him. Like most things he had tried since returning from Southeast Asia, he was about to give it up after three or four months. His room at home, where he spent his leave with his divorced and aging mother, looked like a warehouse of brand-new sports and hobby equipment scattered amid a photo gallery of old girl friends. His mother had thoroughly disapproved of them all, and in time they had all been discarded or had left. A few of them had left sooner than most when they discovered that instead of being a flyer and an adventurer full of war stories (which they publicly abhorred and silently enjoyed), Si Johnson away from his job was in fact a recluse. The only reason he had attracted them in the first place was that he'd impressed them as being the most thoughtful and best-mannered man on the base.

Because he was so quiet and reserved, it had always been difficult for anyone to tell when Si was unhappy. People usually thought he was just habitually shy.

On the evening of September 22, his tennis game was going particularly badly; in fact, it was hardly going at all. He had double-faulted all his services in the first game, and his returns were plopping impotently into the net. He blamed the neon lights which had recently been installed in the indoor court in downtown Freeth. But his ebullient partner and neighbor, Len Tresser, an accountant, wasn't so sure. During a break before the third game, Tresser enthusiastically began analyzing the situation. He loved to work on failures; it gave him the same satisfaction as balancing ill-kept ledgers.

"You seem to be hesitating a lot, Si—just as you're about to hit the ball."

Si, who at five five was dwarfed by the taller Tresser, said nothing; he just shrugged momentarily and sat down on the bench, rewinding the elastic grip on his new Slazenger.

"What I mean, Si, is you—well, you're pulling back all the time instead of going right in to meet the ball. Know what I mean?"

Had Tresser been more perceptive, he would have noticed that Si either didn't want his mistakes pointed out or wasn't listening. But he pressed on eagerly, determined to correct his opponent's errors. He began demonstrating what he called his Ken Rosewall forehand. "You have to go to the ball, Si—like this—see? Step into it." By way of demonstration, Tresser, his back towards Si, stepped forward in an exaggerated motion, his left foot leading. He swung low at an imaginary ball. "See—left foot first, racket already back, watch the ball, watch the ball—watch the ball—follow—through!"

Si was looking down at the handle of his racket. Tresser babbled on, reveling in the sound of his own voice. "Backhand, now. Right foot forward—unless you're a southpaw, of course—ha!—on the ball of the foot—watch the ball, watch the ball—follow—through! It's amazing the number of people who fail to follow through. They do everything else right, but they boo-boo on the follow-through. They think it's all finished on impact. Shoot—that's only half the game."

Si raised his head. For some reason he did not understand, his right arm and leg began trembling. He looked up blankly. "Pardon?"

Tresser turned around. "I said you've got to follow through."

"Oh."

"You see, Si, I've been watching you. To put it quite frankly, old son, your game has no ketchup on it. Right?"

"Ketchup?"

"Right. No zing—no pizazz."

Tresser at last saw that none of this was sinking in. "Dullsville!" he said, dropping his arms down and twirling about like a demented baboon. His shadow passed in front of Johnson, who looked up, reacting to the change in light.

"It's your eyes," Tresser went on cheerfully.

"No!" said Johnson with uncharacteristic finality. "No, it's these lights. It's not me."

"No, it's your eyes," repeated Tresser. "You're not watching the ball close enough. I think—hey, what's wrong with your arm? It's shaking like a scared rabbit."

"What? Oh, nothing, just sitting on a nerve I guess." Si halfheartedly got up from the bench and made his way tiredly to the base line. "You ready?" he asked.

"Sure am. Fit as a fiddle."

It was Tresser's service. There was a sharp twack as the ball sped through the air, kicked up the line dust in Si's court, and neatly passed him.

"Fifteen–love!" yelled Tresser, thrilled by his performance. He moved across to the backhand court, anxious to ace Si again.

By the time he got back to barracks at Freeth at about nine-thirty that night, Si Johnson was resolved to try a new sport, not because he had been soundly thrashed—he didn't care whether he lost or won—but because the game was starting to bore him. Maybe he would try squash. Some of the other guys in the wing had said that you got the feel of squash much quicker and that for the same amount of time you could keep much fitter. The question of fitness, indeed the idea of sports in general, wouldn't have mattered to Johnson except that next month the whole wing would have to undergo the detailed yearly physical. Burke, the captain of *Ebony I* and leader of the wing, had said he would have any man who was overweight grounded until he lost the additional poundage. It wasn't that Si Johnson liked flying so much that grounding would have added to his general apathy, but at least he was occupied while he was in the air.

As he showered, Johnson let the water pound on the back of his neck to relieve the headache that he believed the new lights at the court had given him. His leg was still shaking, but the trembling in his arm had largely subsided. He glanced at his watch. It was 9:40. At around a quarter to ten Stokely, the front gunner in *Ebony I,* would come with the jeep to collect him and the rest of the three-plane Ebony group and take them to the officers' mess for the surprise birthday party that the nine-plane wing was about to spring on Noel Burke. At forty, Burke was considered almost a grandfather by the younger members of the Seventeenth.

Si didn't want to go to the party. He'd given up parties. He had nothing against the captain, but the drinks made him sick now and the talk was boring. He'd heard it all before: the same jokes, usually about prostitutes and homosexuals, in that order, and the tale of near escapes, in bedrooms and in bombers. And of course they still talked about Vietnam. They had loved Vietnam.

No matter what the protesting veterans in Washington said, the air force had loved Vietnam. It was easy enough to understand; you never had to see a face you killed, as the ground forces did. Most of the time you just dropped the load on some beautiful lettuce green and rust red papier-mâché map with all the hills in fascinating relief and all the people invisible. You just . . .

The pounding in his head got worse, spreading until it was a band of pain clamped to his temples. He turned the hot water off and the cold on full. While the rest of his body shivered from the shock the pain reluctantly withdrew, retreating low into his neck, where it continued to stab him but where it was more tolerable. He would mention the headaches to the doctor at the medical. Perhaps a flight would do him good. It was the fall, the sudden change in humidity, not the new lights, that was causing the pain. A more rarefied atmosphere might do him some good.

As he reluctantly pulled on a pair of long black woolen socks his mother had knitted him for the coming Alaskan winter, the jeep screamed to a stop and Stokely's footsteps pounded outside the door. Simultaneously he heard the penetrating blast of the emergency takeoff alarm. Automatically he got up, opened the khaki green locker, and reached in for his flying suit.

"Party's off, Si." It was Stokely, framed by the doorway and practically exploding with excitement.

"Why?" asked Johnson, torn between relief that the celebration would not take place and apprehension about whatever it was that had preempted it.

"We're up tonight—that's why. Wild black yonder."

Si zipped down the elasticized legs. "Mideast?" he asked.

"What—no, no. Nothing like that. It's this frappin' great fire that's scarin' the pants off of everybody. Something to do with a rescue. We're gonna have some fun. Some egg time at last—just in time. All this quiet was gettin' on my nerves."

Johnson carefully closed his locker and spun the combination lock drum.

"Bombs?"

"Yes, sir. Grade B—conventional, but eggs all the same. You're gonna get a chance to show that new boy how good you are, eh? Bang! Right on target. Christ, it'll be like Nam."

Outside, Johnson saw that the jeep was being driven by Peters, the recently arrived replacement radar operator for *Ebony I*. Si turned to Stokely. "Sure it isn't just a practice emergency run?"

"No, Daddy, this is for real. They're setting up special briefing boards in the ops room."

Peters nodded to Si with some deference. Fresh out of training school, he was still in awe of the Vietnam veterans. "Evening, sir."

"Huh—oh, hi."

Stokely put his arm around Si, and as the jeep started off down towards base center, he called over to Peters, "Hey, kid, it's your lucky night. You're flying with the *crème de la crème*. Right, Si?"

Si ignored him. The jeep pulled up at another hut, collected the electronics warfare officer for the lead bomber, and then went on to the briefing hall, into which men were filing as quietly as the swishing flying suits would allow them. The electronics expert remarked to Si. "Hey, I was there when the message came through. Capt'n Burke says the President himself asked for us. Reckon only the conventional wing can handle it."

"Naturally," added Stokely in a jocular mood. "We're fast *and* sure—right, guys?"

"Right," answered Peters, who was reveling in the easy camaraderie. It was already making him feel right at home. Si Johnson said nothing. His right arm and leg were starting to tremble again, and the veins on the right side of his head felt tight and swollen. He resolved to exercise more to work whatever it was out of his system.

Twelve hundred miles to the south and five hundred miles southeast of the firespill, the moon's rays slipped through a break in the gathering stratus cloud over southern British Columbia and turned the surface of Harrison Lake from black to silver. In the hotel built around the hot springs on the south shore, guests were preparing for bed, though not necessarily for sleep.

Luxuriating in the deep, autumn-colored carpet and admiring herself in the gilded full-length mirror, Fran Lambrecker sprayed herself liberally with Chanel cologne, not caring whether it dampened the transparent red negligee that swept and clung about her. Indulging her rich-girl fantasies, she moved her head this way and that, opening and pouting her red lips in what she imagined would be alluring and provocative poses for some future lover. She could have done with less perfume, but Morgan liked the smell; he said it turned him on. Everything, it seemed, turned Morgan on, so much so that she was growing a little tired of his indiscriminate lust. He hung around her every waking moment like a stray dog around a bitch in heat, as if he had to fulfill a quota before he'd consider the money for the hotel well spent. But she put up with it. He wasn't a bad sort, she thought. Maybe he did drink too much, but at least he never took himself too seriously, and in bed he was inventive in a clumsy sort of way. And whatever else, he loved fun.

She rarely thought of her husband these days. The three months they had been apart had finally convinced her that she wouldn't see him anymore. She didn't hate him—probably she never really had—but she had resented him. She had been constantly angry with him for his refusal to socialize, to "go out on the town" as she called it. After two years of marriage she had felt like a prisoner, with the sameness of each housebound day dragging on interminably. Now she knew she'd married too early—if she was ever meant to marry at all. Fran's idea of a full life was to be always "doing different things," which mostly seemed to mean to be sleeping with different men, as Lambrecker had suspected and Morgan was about to discover.

At the memory of her early romance with Lambrecker, her mouth twisted with disgust. She had been another woman then. She guessed it had all had something to do with the uniform; she had always found men in uniform attractive. Even Morgan, whose beer belly hung over his belt like a distended wine sack, looked nice in his "walking out" greens.

She looked out the window at the broad, moonlit lake, and to the west among the tall, dark pines she could see a long spiral of vapor escaping from the bubbling hot springs. It reminded her of a country song she had heard—something about love vanishing like steam from a cup of coffee. For her attraction for her husband had long gone. Once she had thought he was really romantic, but since then she had felt nothing, not even the last time he came home on leave. She was honest enough to hold herself largely responsible for what had happened to them. She had read in some women's magazine that when couples finally reached the point of breaking up, they often discovered that despite all the problems, they really felt more for each other than they had believed. Fran knew that this wasn't the case with them. Not with her, anyway. She had decided that she would tell him when he returned—but not to his face. He would go wild if she did that. Instead she would write him a letter. She hated writing letters, but she would keep it simple. Maybe it would be best to sign off "Love, Fran"—something nice, she thought.

Morgan had difficulty getting through the door, loaded down as he was with bottles of ginger ale, collins mix, and a king-sized bag of crushed ice in his determined effort to beat the cost of room service.

"My God!" Fran laughed. "What have you got?"

When he saw that Fran had changed into the negligee he had insisted on buying her from the hotel boutique, Morgan's eyes bulged. "Geez," he said, and began putting the bottles down with such haste that he dropped the ice.

"You're a gorilla," she protested gaily as he dragged her off the soft stool onto the deep shag. He went into a crouch position, then, grunting and letting his arms hang apelike, he proceeded to scratch his armpit in the manner of a baboon.

She laughed aloud and threw her nightdress open. "Come on," she said.

As he fumbled for the dresser light, she was happy that she did not feel at all guilty about what she was doing. She was enjoying it. She wished Lambrecker would stay away forever.

She put her arms around Morgan's neck as he closed his eyes and buried his head in the rug, already starting to grunt. But Fran's eyes stayed open in the darkness, and fear began to grow cold about her. She realized that all this time, ever since he had slammed the door three months ago, she had been acting as if

Lambrecker were dead. Even when she had planned the final note to him a little while ago, she had composed it as if he would simply read it and everything between them would stop, just like that. But suddenly she remembered that the submarine was on its way back. What would he do when he found out—when he came home? He would probably threaten to kill her. He might smash into her with his fist . . .

With an effort, she closed her eyes and pulled hard at Morgan.

NINETEEN

The roar of the bombers was deafening, each of the seventy-two Pratt and Whitney engines screaming in the darkness, gathering its twenty thousand pounds of thrust, as the nine B-52's formed themselves into the three cells designated Ebony, Gold, and Purple, of three planes each, which together made up the wave.

One by one the bombers began "crabbing it," sliding down the runway with their wheels turned at an angle into the crosswind. Quickly gathering speed, they thundered down the tarmac, each one rising into the night in a shattering crescendo that shook every window on the base.

Once airborne, Noel Burke, the aircraft commander of the lead bomber, *Ebony I,* and so commander of the wave, looked about him at the various pinpoints of the bombers' takeoff lights to check the formation. The bomber to his left, number two of his cell, still had Southeast Asian combat markings—a khaki camouflage pattern on top and its belly painted pitch black to terrify civilian populations during daylight raids. It was a change, thought Burke, to be on a mission of mercy.

It was 2200 hours Pacific Time, and Si Johnson computed that the wave, traveling at six hundred miles per hour one thousand feet above the sea, ready for low bombing, would arrive at the sub site in thirty-seven minutes, at 2238, give or take a few minutes for possible change in wind speed due to the buildup of the southbound Arctic front. And they would also have to allow a minute or two for picking up Cape Bingham on the northern tip of Chichagof Island, their initial point of reference, or IP, before turning southwards towards the fire. There he, as radar navigator, would start his stopwatch and the bombing run would begin. He scanned his calculations again, in the faint hope that somewhere they could pick up a few extra minutes, even seconds. But the figures told him the same as before. At the most they would have an eleven-minute margin between the time they arrived and the end of the sub's power and air.

Burke looked around to check the clusters of extender bombs on the aircrafts' wings. With their eight-foot-long "hosepipes" sticking out in front, housing the delayed fuses for the high explosives, these bombs were too long for the main bays, which each carried eighty-four five-hundred-pound contact bombs. In all, each hundred-and-fifty-seven-foot-long B-52 in the wave could carry more bombs than fifteen of the B-17's used in World War Two. In the old days, the President would have had to dispatch a hundred and thirty-five planes—nine squadrons of heavy bombers—to do the same job as these nine.

Burke tried to see whether the fine wires from the wings which would pull out the safety pins from the outside bombs were set properly, but he could not tell. Each plane carried forty thousand gallons of kerosene in its long wings, so the wingspan was in effect a hundred-and-eighty-five-foot fuel bladder. He would have to trust that the ground crew had done their job properly and that there would be no hung bombs left swinging under all that fuel after he pushed the release button.

Unlike the contact bombs housed in the main bays, the extender bombs on the wings were set to explode above and below the water. Normally he would be carrying rockets on the wings as well, but their nuclear heads were considered useless for the present purposes. Despite the absence of the nuclear tips, Burke viewed the mission as an excellent combat drill for his crews.

Besides himself, the crew of *Ebony I* consisted of Beddoes, the copilot on his right; Si Johnson, the radar navigator, cramped in the cubbyhole of the lower deck together with Peters, the new navigator; the electronics warfare officer, tucked aft of the two navigators; and finally Stokely, who occupied the "M" model's nose turret with its four .50 machine guns. The "M" model was a modification of the "H" model that used to house a .20 machine gun in the rear turret, remotely controlled by the gunner in the nose. In the earlier models, the gun had had only a maximum vertical and horizontal angle of sixty degrees. But Stokely reckoned that the position of the guns wasn't that important. This was a nice, peaceable mission, and he and the E.W. officer, whose talents wouldn't be needed either, looked forward to watching the others do all the work.

The really busy members of the crew would be Burke, the copilot, Peters, and most of all Si Johnson, who as radar navigator would be responsible for the accuracy of the bomb run. Burke had flown with Johnson in Vietnam. He thought of the time they had been forced to eject. At least there wouldn't be any surface-to-air missiles on this mission. Now the only enemy was the thirty-seven minutes separating them from the submarine.

The plane on his right yawed a little. He switched on the cell intercom. "Let's keep it tight, fellas. Bernie, you're wandering."

"Right. I've got it, A.C."

Burke grinned at his copilot. "Got what, Bernie—the shakes? Come on now, pull her in."

"Roger."

Burke felt his own plane lurch and slip to the left. "Stokely, what the hell are you doing? Most of the other guys are green, but you're supposed to know the drill. Keep your guns straight ahead. Man, you must have 'em at some angle. Feels like we've got an extra flap down there."

"Sorry, Chief. My trigger finger's itchy."

"Doesn't matter; we're on combat drill. Let's do it right."

Stokely's voice was cheerful. "You're the boss."

"So get that turret in line with the plane and stop swiveling it. You can bump us around some other time."

"Roger." Stokely brought his guns in line with the bomber's heading.

"Captain!" Si Johnson cut in from the black, instrument-crowded deck below.

"What is it, Si?"

"There's something funny on the screen—blips in formation."

Burke instinctively glanced ahead into the darkness. "Formation? Aircraft?"

Si looked at the sweep again. Each time the arm turned around, more dots appeared. Peters leaned worriedly towards the screen. "Looks like the measles."

Si Johnson had never seen anything like it. "Not big enough for planes. I've double-checked all reports, domestic and foreign, and they say the area should be clear. But there's hundreds—thousands—of 'em, all bunched together. It's massive. No recognizable pattern."

Burke switched in to the others on the intercell radio. Soon *Ebony II* was calling the lead bomber. "Same pattern here, Captain."

"Ebony Three to Ebony One. We've got it too."

He spoke quickly to the two cells behind him. "Gold and Purple, is it on your screens?"

"Gold leader to Ebony One. Affirmative, Captain."

"Purple leader to Ebony One. Affirmative."

There was a pause as Burke searched his memory. The only thing he could recall remotely like it was the loads of tinfoil flakes they'd dropped in World War Two to confound German radar crews; but this obstruction was moving horizontally, not falling. His voice was calm, but his copilot thought he detected a note of anxiety in it. He spoke now to the whole wave. "All right, anybody got any ideas? Anybody? How about you new boys? Peters?"

The young navigator shrugged at Si Johnson and looked back embarrassedly at the E.W. officer for help. The latter held up his hands, at a loss. Peters answered reluctantly, "No ideas down here, Captain."

The approaching Arctic front was a dark canopy over them, so Burke did not even have the slight benefit of moonlight. Beyond his cockpit all was completely dark. He looked at his air speed indicator. "How fast is it closing, Si?"

"Moving slow, sir. About thirty miles per hour. But we'll hit it—around ten minutes from now."

Burke looked at the clock amid the mass of dials before him. It was now nearly 2203.

On the lower deck, Si Johnson's left hand clenched on a metal calculator until his knuckles whitened. Suddenly he was drenched in cold sweat. He leaned stiffly back against his seat; his right leg and arm were beginning to shake uncontrollably. Peters switched off his intercom, reached over, and touched him on the arm. "Hey, sir—Si, you okay?"

As if he had just become aware of where he was, Johnson turned his head sharply towards the navigator. "What? Get your hands off me, goddamn it! I'm okay—just a little indigestion. Goddamn junk they give us."

Peters apologized and turned his intercom back on. He believed what Johnson had told him. But had he known enough Vietnam veterans, he would almost certainly have recognized the symptoms of flashback. In any case, he was new to *Ebony I* and he wasn't about to say anything to anyone, particularly now. The captain was back on the intercom. "Si, give me an altitude to clear this, whatever it is."

Johnson found it difficult to focus on his radar set. He spoke slowly. "Three—"

"Three what, for Christ's sake?"

"Thousand—three thousand feet."

Stokely interrupted in a tone of happy relief. "That's no problem. In Nam we dropped our eggs from thirty thousand. That right, Si boy?"

There was no immediate answer as Johnson, switching off his intercom, leaned back on the seat, terrified. He felt trapped in the black hole of the lower deck, the instruments pressing in around him like malevolent eyes in the night. But even in his fear he managed to shoot a warning glance at Peters. Cowed, the newcomer stayed silent.

Above them in the cockpit, Burke again checked the clock and altimeter. "No way," he said. "We can't risk going another thousand. That would put us smack into that cloud. We're going to have a hard enough time seeing anything below as it is. Si, how's that sub's DF signal?"

Peters looked over at Si and was surprised again by the change in him. Now he appeared to be the calm veteran Peters had heard about. "We're right on it, Captain, but it's weaker'n grandma's tea. They're losing power all the time. Could cease transmission any second."

Burke, knowing that at this speed a minute off course would cost him at least ten miles, was quick to respond. "That settles it. We've got to stay on course. Can't afford evasive action." He paused, then said as coolly as he could, "We'll have to go right through 'em."

Si watched the radar sweep again. The screen was no longer speckled with dots but covered with a glowing sheet, so thick and widespread were the oncoming blips. Stokely burst in, his voice raw. "It's the moon. I bet it's the goddamn moon showing up on the screen."

Burke, holding the steering yoke more firmly than usual as they passed over slight turbulence, snapped at the gunner, "Stokely, will you shut up? It's not the moon, you hayseed. Christ, you'd have us over China by now."

The electronics warfare officer, who immediately thought in terms of MIGs and surface-to-air missiles, cut in worriedly. "They're awful thick, Cap'n. Chickenshit or not, we only need a few to hit us in the right place."

Aware that he might have alarmed the wave with his reprimand to Stokely, Burke spoke encouragingly to the whole cell, particularly to the new boys. "Hell, Ebony, we've had bigger stuff than this thrown at us."

Hart, the radar navigator in *Ebony II,* felt his throat going dry. "I—I wasn't in Nam, sir."

"Well I was, son. Don't worry. Hang in there—you're doing a good job. Just you keep an eye on Si over here. He'll lead the bomb run. Can do it in his sleep."

Hart's answer was stoic and quite unconvincing. "I'm not worried, sir."

"Good. Now, Ebony gunners, listen carefully. We're not carrying rockets, so we've got nothing we can blast ahead to clear a gap for us except the .50s. Your job'll be to blow a hole through whatever it is so the wave can keep going. Just concentrate on your own sectors and don't stray into another guy's. It's all up to you. I want a nice big circle of nothing right in front of my nose. Got it?"

"Ebony Two. Got it, A.C."

"Ebony Three. Roger, Captain."

For an instant, as he cocked the four .50 cannons, Stokely wished that he was aboard the early model B-52's, tucked away in the tail.

Now Burke was talking to the whole wave. "I want all cells to stay tight together. Remember, we haven't time to fool around regrouping. The looser we are, the less concentrated our bombing'll be near the sub and the greater our chances of being hit by whatever's coming at us. Gold and Purple leaders, if anything happens to us, carry on with the bomb run. Use Cape Bingham as your initial point, make the turn south, and take the sub's position as your offset aiming point."

"Gold A.C. to Ebony leader. Got it."

"Purple A.C. to Ebony leader. Will do."

Sarah Kyle had simply been informed by Esquimalt Naval Command that the *Swordfish* was experiencing some "difficulty," but that "remedial action" was under way. It did not occur to her to ask for more information. She didn't want to know. Instead, despite the lateness of the Indian summer night, she changed from her nightgown into her gardening clothes—chocolate corduroys, floppy beige sweater, and runners—switched on the backyard floodlight, and made her way out into the garden. Amid the sweet-smelling roses every noise was familiar, every perfume immediately identifiable, and she felt less afraid of the darkness beyond the light than of the unknown which might be visited upon her by sketchy and speculative TV and radio reports about the rescue.

The bombers were less than thirty minutes from Cape Bingham as she began to prune the visible part of the rampant Van Vliet rosebush which in James's absence had entwined itself about the porch, trailing off along the leeward side of the house where the thorny tentacles below the small, white pink blossoms laid claim to every projection and irregularity in the cedar surface. When James came home, she would ask him to prune it fully. Next, she moved to the Nocturne rose bed, giving it special attention in an effort to keep alive as many blossoms as possible, for these were his favorites.

Less than a quarter of a mile away, in a condominium suite with an uninterrupted view of the Kyles' house, Philip Limet, ex-commander of the *Swordfish,* who was still recovering from his near-fatal heart attack of three months before, became aware of a pungent, burning odor trailing from the kitchen. Alice Limet hadn't been watching the warming milk very carefully, and before she could turn off the gas it had boiled up, frothing wildly onto the stove. Alice, who had seen the figure moving about in the Kyles' backyard and who had just been able to identify her neighbor through the field binoculars she always kept handy, was in a quandary. She was trying to make up her mind as to whether she should ring Mrs. Kyle and tell her what one of the junior officers visiting from the Canadian Forces Esquimalt Base had told Philip a half hour earlier.

During the twenty years of their marriage—even before they had been engaged—she had always wanted to know where her husband was. It was a trait she had inherited from her mother, another navy wife. Of course the navy hadn't always told her, especially during the Korean War, but given the choice, she had always preferred to know the danger he was in rather than sit night after day waiting for the call that wives dread. But Alice knew that not all service wives felt like that.

She had never been close to the Kyles, despite their physical proximity. They had met rarely and rather formally at that. Perhaps, she thought, Mrs. Kyle was one of those funny types who really do believe that no news is good news. But perhaps she wasn't like that; perhaps she would like to know. The decision whether or not to ring Sarah Kyle was absorbing all her concentration. It was so hard to tell.

"Do you think I should?" It was ten years since she had been in London, but her cockney accent still came back when she was worried.

Philip sat reading the latest on the extent of the firespill under banner headlines in the Victoria *Times*. He didn't want anything to do with it. "Please yourself. I don't know what women think about these things."

"Then you think I shouldn't?" called Alice, sacrificing her nightly capuccino so that Philip could have the salvaged milk.

Limet turned the page. There were no new details about the fire other than its approximate composition and size, which the newspaper estimated was already approaching thirty thousand square miles. "Oh, I don't know. Perhaps you'd better leave it to H.Q. to tell her what they're trying to do."

Alice's opinion of H.Q. came through as a scornful "Huh!" from the kitchen. She whipped, rather than stirred, the coffee. "H.Q.? Informing her at this time of night? Are you serious? They won't tell her anything till the morning, ducky. Till the morning. I'm surprised they don't shut down the radar and everything at the weekends." She looked up from the coffee. "I'll never forget that time my dad was on that boat, remember?—that escort convoy to Archangel."

"Archangel?"

"That's what I said. In Russia. Well, they never told us a thing. Next morning Mum read that a whole convoy had been lost on that route. We thought he was gone, we truly did. And H.Q. didn't say a thing."

Limet put down his paper in a flurry of frustration. "I've told you, Alice, it was probably for security reasons. Just like this plane business. I expect they're keeping it quiet because it's something to do with the Americans being involved. There's nothing in the papers except a few aerial photos."

Alice was still thinking about the convoy to Archangel. "Security! The papers had it all in next morning. And how about our feelings? Don't talk to me about security. H.Q. don't care. If it wasn't for that nice young man coming around to visit you this evening, we wouldn't have heard about those planes. I'll bet Mrs. Kyle hasn't been told."

Limet frowned. "That 'nice young man,' as you call him, had no business telling me anything. He probably thinks I'll thank him for it. I won't. He's decided to act as his own classification officer."

"I noticed you didn't stop him!"

Philip Limet gave up and returned to his paper. "All right. Ring her if you like."

Alice almost dropped the phone in her eagerness to dial.

"Hello." The voice sounded strained and forlorn.

"Oh, Mrs. Kyle?"

"Yes."

"It's Mrs. Limet here—Philip Limet's wife."

Sarah Kyle began to object, but her caller was so full of sympathy, so concerned, so understanding that she never heard Sarah's all-but-frantic plea to stop. For a moment Sarah thought of putting the phone down, but habit held her victim to politeness, and while she didn't want to hear anything, once she had heard part of the rescue plan, she felt compelled to know all about it so that she could not deceive herself as to the full measure of danger.

When she put down the receiver, the silence in the house overwhelmed her, and she began to cry. After a time she went out again, into the garden.

TWENTY

The *Swordfish* lay motionless sixty feet below the surface. Except for the control room light, the only illumination came from the emergency battle lanterns. The temperature was now 124 degrees Fahrenheit.

Every piece of metal was glistening with moisture. The men on watch sat inert beneath the dim red light, minds dulled and heads made heavy by the constant humidity from the evaporation of water in the bilges.

In their effort to conserve what strength remained, the rest of the men lay strewn throughout the sub as if struck down by some quick and deadly virus. The silent, electrically driven engines kept radiating more heat into the wet, still air. And the batteries, like the men, were now all but completely exhausted; the danger of a cell reversal which would knock out all the batteries and perhaps cause fire was growing by the minute. If this happened they would no longer be able to transmit the DF signal, weak as it was, or receive further instructions about the rescue attempt.

In the near darkness the small sick bay clock, half-hidden amid the angular silhouettes of medicine cabinets, clicked over. Kyle, sitting by the Vice-President's bunk, lifted his head slowly to note the time. It was 2206. At the far forward end of the bay, beyond the silent shapes of the men who lay in fever in the other four bunks, Kyle could see a hump that was Evers, strapped down and heavily sedated. Kyle was feeling weak now, though not as much as most of the crew, who, unlike him, had not had a chance to get a change of air on the bridge during the rescue of the Vice-President. True, the air supply had been largely replenished, but the difference between breathing it topside and in the putrid reek below decks was the difference between feeling nearly exhausted and exhausted. The difference at least enabled Kyle to speak coherently with the Vice-President of the United States.

Since being lowered down the after hatch, the Vice-President had said nothing, and for a few minutes Richards, the sick bay attendant, thought that the convective heat exhaustion would kill her. Like everyone aboard, she had developed the classic symptoms, but to a much worse degree because of her exposure to the radiant heat of the firespill and the severe burns on one side of her face and arm, which flushed her skin to an even deeper red than that of the crew. In dramatic contrast to the stupor evidenced in her glazed eyes, her heartbeat had jumped way above seventy-four beats a minute as the adrenaline raced to the brain, increasing the activity of the sweat glands for cooling and contracting the muscles and causing her skin to go momentarily cold and clammy as her breathing increased. Richards was convinced that the Vice-President was teetering on the verge of shock. When she had been brought aboard he had immediately given her fifty milligrams of Demerol for the pain and tried to cool her with wet packs. Since then, he had periodically been giving her tomato juice, the best he could do after the salt had run out. But now, after caring for Evers as well, he was unable to carry on, and was slumped on the deck.

Kyle sluggishly lifted the battle lantern from the deck, took another can of juice, pulled the tab off, and held it to the Vice-President's lips, straining his eyes to see that he did not spill it. Not knowing where she was for a while, she continued to sip like someone having just emerged into the night from a general anesthetic. As she looked around the sick bay, Kyle could see her awareness gradually growing until her eyes, illuminated by the lantern's dim light, began to focus on nearby objects in the compartment, first the squatting bulk of the chemical cabinet, then the shroudlike shape of a crumpled blanket on the floor, and finally, in the middle distance, sitting motionless like an old black-and-white negative, an elderly, fatherly-looking man with a cap.

"The sub?" she said hoarsely.

The cap nodded.

To Kyle she looked like a child, still streaked here and there, despite Richards's efforts, with oil, as if she had been plucked from play too near a condemned rig. She made him feel infinitely old but somehow strangely privileged, for in her tired hazel eyes there was trust more than alarm; a calmness which belied the rapid pumping of her heart and spoke more of the acceptance of adversity than of anger or despair. It was the look of the brave. For a moment it made him unreasonably happy. He thought that perhaps they could make it after all.

After a few more minutes, Elaine spoke to him again in the growing gloom of the dying lantern. "Are we . . . going home?"

He was on the point of saying yes and smiling, but he knew instinctively, as Harry had, that here was a person who would deal best with the truth. "I hope so," he said. "They're sending in planes."

"Helicopters?"

"No. It's still too black for them up there." He raised his head skywards. "We're still under the fire." The lantern flickered, and momentarily she disappeared from his vision. The darkness made it easier to explain the risks. "We're low on power. We can't make it alone." The lantern flickered again, and Richards's fast and labored breathing came out of the darkness like the straining of wind through a long reed. Before Elaine could ask any more questions, Kyle went on, his heart pounding with the urgency of a steady, rhythmic drum. "Your air force are sending in bombers. They're—"

Richards could be heard retching.

"You okay, Richards?"

There was a roar as the toilet flushed. One of the men in the bunks began to cough uncontrollably.

"Richards?"

"I'm okay."

Kyle knew that he wasn't, but there was nothing he

could do to help him or the man coughing—or any of them. For a moment he felt dizzy and put his hand out to steady himself as the sub heaved in a roll. He felt Elaine's hand grip his shoulder. It was the grip of a child. "Thanks," he said, and patted her arm. The thought came to him that she could be president someday—probably would be president. She was no doubt a brilliant woman, yet here he was treating her as he did his married daughter—like a girl who had never grown up. He knew that she commanded men like him, thousands of them, but still he could not shake the conviction that beneath her grand and proper title there was an irrepressible innocence, which for him was far more impressive than her position, what she had done or what she was likely to do. He had seen it in her pictures, and it seemed to him a very unpolitical thing.

"The bombers?"

Her question started him from the reverie that had followed on the dizziness. "Yes. They're going to bomb the fire. Blow a space out ahead of us so we can surface. Then we can run and recharge our batteries. If it works, they'll try to bomb the whole fire out later."

"How will they know where we are?" Elaine's nose was assailed by the rancid smell of perspiration from the bodies in the sick bay. Kyle wiped his forehead. The temperature was 129 degrees. "We're sending out a DF signal," he said, halting for breath and starting to feel dizzy again. "That'll tell them where we are."

Elaine could still see the coal black sky which had enveloped the fishing boat. "It'll have to be visual bombing, won't it? They'll have to fly low. A few bombs off course and they could blow us—"

"They're flying low," cut in Kyle in an effort to reassure the Vice-President, "and we'll fire marker flares through the smoke if they want. That'll pinpoint us for them."

Kyle heard a deep groan and the slap of leather. It was Evers trying to roll over. Kyle strained his eyes into the darkness. He felt a heavy weight of guilt descend upon him. He was responsible for the man's condition. At the very least, he was the cause of prolonging his agony and that of the other eighty-two men aboard *Swordfish*. If he had ignored the Vice-President, Evers would have been home by now, receiving proper attention.

Elaine put her arm over her eyes to shield them from the weak light which seemed to pierce her like the blinding glare of a torture chamber. "How many are there?" she asked.

"Nine," he said. "Nine B-52's."

"You said they'll carpet bomb."

"Yes."

"How fast are they traveling?"

"Six hundred miles an hour. That's one thing in our favor." Kyle knew that at that speed the timing of the drop would be critical; a few seconds either way would shift the entire bomb load a half mile off target. If the bombs were too close to the sub, they would damage her; but if they were dropped too early or too late, the fire would re-cover the break before the sub could get there. He said nothing of this to the Vice-President.

Elaine felt her heart racing. "I hope they're using small bombs," she added weakly, trying to make light of it. But Kyle took her seriously. "No, small bombs wouldn't be powerful enough to blast out a break; they would only stir the fire up a little. They'll be using high-explosive blockbusters to make sure we have a large enough area to surface and recharge before the fire creeps back in."

Elaine was silent, and Kyle saw the pain misting her eyes. "Well," he added, smiling as best he could, "it's better than sending in A-bombs, I guess. They'd kill—well," he added quickly, "those pilots know what they're doing, Vice-President."

She managed a faint smile. "Call me Elaine."

Kyle returned the smile. "Those pilots know what they're doing, Elaine." He paused. "They'll give us that fire break."

The captain's mention of the fire break took her back to the fishing boat—to the Secret Servicemen—to

Washington. She was thinking of Walter now, of whether she would ever see him again—of him having to make the terrible decision to risk the Canadians. She thought of all the people involved—of all the trouble she had—

"Harry!" she said. "My God, where's Harry?"

Kyle's head inclined slowly in the gloom, like that of an anguished confessor. "He's dead—lost his balance. Looked as if he were trying to throw something overboard. It was too late. I'm—"

Elaine turned her head away from Kyle. As her shoulders began to convulse, Kyle reached over, touched her arm, and turned off the battle lantern.

The passageway was longer than Kyle had remembered it. After asking one of the less exhausted sailors to watch over the Vice-President, he half-stumbled forward, towards the control room. His heart felt as if it were about to explode from his chest, and the distorting veil of perspiration made it even more difficult for him to see in the leaden light cast by the fast-expiring lanterns. The long, bending shadows distorted his vision so that it seemed as if he were lost in some twisting subterranean tunnel.

Lambrecker and his followers were now indistinguishable from everyone else on the *Swordfish,* felled by the killing heat and humidity. They lay still and wan, incapable of even a whimper of rebellion. Ramsey had blacked out several times and was panting rapidly, like a stricken animal in its last moments. All they were interested in now was surviving. Kyle, sick and dizzy as he felt, had decided to press charges against the mutineers. He was not unmoved by their present condition, but he knew that if their energy had not been dissipated by this steaming oven Lambrecker would still be dangerous. No matter that Lambrecker had acted well in bringing the Vice-President aboard; he had tried to seize command of a ship. No captain in the Canadian Navy—or any other navy—would be in his right mind not to press for a court-martial.

But for the moment the mutineers were no threat; besides, unless the bombers arrived and the *Swordfish* had a chance to surface, the problem of a court-martial was purely hypothetical.

Passing the officers' shower, Kyle heard a voice in the darkness murmur, "Happy now, Captain?"

Another joined in. "Probably give 'im a medal for it."

Kyle smiled to himself and leaned against a bulkhead to rest. He was happy to hear the remarks from the disgruntled sailors, for he recalled an old service maxim from the Arctic convoys: "So long as they're bitching, you have a chance. When they stop, you're in Dutch." He hoped a few more would still have enough energy to bitch. He walked resolutely forward and pushed back the cloth curtain of the control room as if it were a heavy sliding steel door.

Inside, the stench of sweat was so heavy it almost made Kyle gag. He was feeling so weak he could barely talk, and his voice seemed no more than a whisper to O'Brien, although the first officer wasn't sure whether it was the captain's voice or his hearing which had been affected. He strained to hear Kyle slowly repeat, "How's the DF signal?"

Sitting on the deck beneath the firing console, O'Brien rested his head against the periscope, gasping like a fish out of water, trying to summon the strength to reply. "We'll have to cease . . ."

"Sick report?"

"Fourteen down—exhaustion."

The clock's minute hand shot forward to 2212. Kyle, sweat lathering his face, looked around the control room in slow motion. He estimated that within the next thirty minutes almost half the crew would be completely prostrate with the heat, incapable of any movement beyond merely breathing and staying alive. And if the planes didn't arrive before 2240, he knew that most of them would be dead; and through the acid imbalance that would send them into violent spasms those few alive would find it almost impossible to operate the sub, let alone operate it with the necessary speed. Perhaps a few exceptionally strong ones and those who had had a chance to go topside during the rescue could do the job, but even they had a limit in this heat.

He began to think about the decisions he'd made in the past twenty-four hours, wondering if anything could have been done faster or better. Now the mutiny seemed far off in his memory, as if it had happened years ago. He wondered if he could somehow have forestalled the mutineers' resistance. He had understood their fear. It occurred to him that he should have had them in the control room with him, where the sense of responsibility might have contained their anger and turned it instead to good account. But then he dismissed the idea, unable to picture Lambrecker not taking advantage of any situation.

"The Vice-President?" said O'Brien.

Kyle stared dumbly at him. The first officer repeated his question, adding, "How is she?"

The captain moved his lips, but there was no sound.

It was several seconds before O'Brien spoke again. "Think she'll make it?"

Kyle coughed to moisten his throat. "She'll make it. Strong girl."

"Her friend—falling off. Does she—?"

Kyle nodded.

The radio operator, shuffling out from his communications cave, broke in. "Captain?" His voice sounded intolerably loud to the others in Control. As the captain turned towards him, the operator saw that his face was the color of damp chalk. "Sir, the last of our emergency running power is draining fast."

Kyle sipped tepid water from a tin cup by his side. "Can't do anything about it, Sparks—got to keep receiving that DF signal so we know when they're overhead."

"Yes, sir."

"How much longer will the power last?"

"Twelve minutes—maximum."

It was now 2216 plus 50 seconds. They would be out

of subsurface running power at 2229—2230 at the latest.

With considerable effort, Kyle managed a smile. "Well, let's hope it's enough, eh, sailor?"

Sparks didn't answer. He moved listlessly back into the blackness of the radio room, where a frantic cluster of tiny red lights flicked on and off like trapped insects.

Kyle looked up as if trying to see through to the sky in defiance of the metal and burning sea between.

The sick bay buzzer sounded. It was Richards. All that Kyle could make out was that the Vice-President was passing into delirium. He dragged himself up and began the long journey back down the passageway.

In the cockpit of Ebony Leader it was now 2217, twenty-one minutes before E.T.A. with the sub.

Unseen at first by the fliers as it approached the roaring Stratofortresses from the southwest, the quiet mass on the radar screen soon appeared like snowflakes streaming toward the windshield of a speeding car. The gunners pulled their triggers and the night exploded in a cacophony of sound and tracer lines as the first birds hit the bombers in a hail of smashing bone.

None of the men had ever seen so many. *Ebony I*'s copilot shouted into the intercom, trying to make himself heard over the sound of the multiple collisions and the deep, choking fire of the heavy machine guns. Within seconds the windshields of the planes were bloody. *Ebony III,* running into a particularly thick concentration half a mile to the right of Burke's plane, started to go down after a minute and a half, five of its eight engines clogged tight with dead gulls. At a thousand feet, unable to climb higher and too low to jettison its thirty thousand pounds of bombs without endangering the aircraft behind it, its captain had no choice but to give the order to eject and swing the plane out of the wave. By now the bomber was losing altitude fast and was three hundred feet above the water. The captain and copilot ejected out of the top hatch. The remainder of the crew were automatically ejected downwards, but needing at least four hundred feet for their chutes to open, they were killed on impact with the sea.

As he watched the pilot's and copilot's chutes opening, Burke was giving the position to Canadian Air-Sea Rescue and to the NORAD base on Vancouver Island. His purpose was twofold: to arrange the immediate rescue of the men in the water and to have a Voodoo fighter wing sent out to disperse the birds by sonic boom lest they bring down civilian aircraft in their path over the mainland.

Crewless, *Ebony III* struck the water with her left wing and cartwheeled for two miles, her bombs lighting the night sky in a giant fireworks display. The pilot and copilot were killed by the shock waves as they floated gently down beneath their burning parachutes.

While the bombs from the crashed plane were exploding, Si Johnson in *Ebony I* sat rigidly in his seat, his hands tightly grasping its metal sides like a man in the throes of electrocution. As more birds struck and the firing increased, he brought his hands up to cover his ears. For the moment Peters did not notice, for in an effort to block out the fear of his first real action, the navigator was busying himself by calculating and checking the wave's position, shutting everything else out of his mind.

Si Johnson was back in Vietnam. In the flashback he saw himself during a bombing mission over Hué, crouching over the visual bombsight and listening to Burke through the din of cannon and surface-to-air missile fire, which he could not see from the claustrophobic blackness of his tiny cubicle. He could hear Burke starting the countdown: "125 seconds to go . . . 75 TG . . . 60 TG," and himself, coolly advising Burke, "Hold it, steady . . . steady, Captain . . . one degree right . . . that's good, hold it . . . a point to the right . . . that's beautiful, Chief . . . hold her steady." Then, as a Russian-built SAM streaked towards them and the electronics warfare officer began his countermeasures, Johnson could hear the tail gunner screaming, "For

Christ's sake drop 'em Si—drop 'em—let's get the hell—" and himself calmly following procedure, taking over the count: "10 . . . 9 . . . 8 . . . 7 . . ." just before the missile clipped the tail, tearing out the kingpin, ripping open the rear gunner's canopy like the cap off a bottle, and sending the plane into a wild spin. As objects flashed past, sucked out by the slipstream, and his flying suit started flapping furiously about him, he heard the gunner screaming again, "Why . . . why the hell didn't you drop 'em? . . . you stupid bastard!" The next instant Johnson had ejected with the rest of the forward crew. When the army chopper picked them up, the gunner's body was found headless. All Si Johnson could hear for weeks afterwards was "Why . . . why the hell didn't you drop 'em? . . . you stupid bastard!"

Peters, summoning up his courage, was shaking Johnson. "Sir? Si—for Christ's sake!" Si leaned back, his face streaked with sweat. The cannon fire was subsiding as they passed through the bird concentration. "Hey, Si—you were jabbering somethin' awful. You okay?"

Si looked about him. "What? Yeah—sure, sure I'm okay—Jesus!" He rose forward in his seat. "You didn't have the intercom on, did you?"

Peters had had his hand on the mouthpiece. "No, but by Christ you oughta see about that." Peters kept staring at Johnson. "Or I will."

Si started to object, but the youngster seemed suddenly to have grown older, so he said, "Okay—okay, I will. Never bothered me before." Peters's eyes were unrelenting. "Well," said Johnson, "not on a mission, I mean. Sometimes at night . . . Okay, I'll see about it. I wouldn't risk the plane."

Peters relaxed, smiled, and yelled above the roar of the engines, "All right, Si. I believe you." He slapped the veteran on the shoulder, as if in recognizing the radar navigator's problem he had overcome his previous awe of him.

The damage reports were soon coming in from the wave. Burke was asking whether anyone else had gone down.

"Gold Leader to Ebony Leader. Jerry Tucker—L84."

"Survivors?"

"Not a chance."

Tucker had been one of Burke's closest pals. "God-damn it," he said. "Anyone else?"

"Purple Leader here, Ebony One. Cell intact but I'm having difficulty with my right number two engine. I'm feathering it now. Think our Vernier deflectors are covered with muck. At any rate, we're having some trouble with maneuverability. Apart from that, worst damage seems to be electron booster for the radar. Temperature's way up. Forward cooling vent must be clogged with guts."

Burke crossed *Purple I* off his chart. "Right, Purple One. Return to base. Your problems might just be starting. Jettison bombs as soon as you can."

"Roger, Ebony Leader. See you boys at Freeth."

The injured bomber peeled out of formation, and the six remaining bombers closed up to fill the gaps while the crews continued the long prebomb check. Now and then, birds trailing the main flock would smack into a plane and startle a gunner into firing a burst or two. This kept the men on edge. Si came in on *Ebony*'s intercom. "Captain, the sub's DF signal is fading fast."

"How far to target area?"

"About a hundred and seventy miles. With this new head wind, we'll reach their area in around . . . seventeen minutes. New E.T.A. 2238 plus fifty-five seconds."

"Give me E.T.A. for initial point of reference."

"Allowing for head wind . . . E.T.A. Cape Bingham eleven minutes thirty seconds."

Aboard *Ebony I* it was now 2221. Knowing that 2249 was the most optimistic estimate of the limit of the sub's endurance, Burke cursed the advancing Arctic front for pushing them back almost a minute—nearly ten miles at their speed. He looked anxiously at his airspeed indicator. Once they turned south from Cape Bingham they should have the Arctic storm under their tails.

"All right. Send the sub our new E.T.A. with instructions to fire flares at one-minute intervals, starting at E.T.A. minus five minutes. He can fire those from subsurface without electric power. And pray like hell we don't hit any more birds."

TWENTY-ONE

Elaine's head twisted from side to side in the tired orange light, throwing her hair over her face in a grotesque mask that was black and wet.

Now and then the mask would stop its demented rhythm to stare into the near blackness—only to see another face mocking its every movement. Richards tried to comfort her, but he could not stand up for more than a few seconds at a time without losing his balance. Several times she called out for Walter, begging him to forgive her. The rest of her raving was unintelligible to Richards and barely audible. She thrashed the air with her arms as if trying to break out of the choking web that was stopping her breathing. As Kyle entered the sick bay, her head jerked from side to side while her back arched spasmodically. Gradually the movement in her body subsided and she lay very still. Kyle touched her arm gently. Her skin was again damp and clammy. The battle lantern held by Richards died to a faint glow.

Kyle carefully moved the oily hair back from her cheeks. The face had lost its captivating smile, but the hazel eyes, though glazed, were still game and fiery with life. Not yet out of her delirium, the Vice-President of the United States looked dazed, like a child waking slowly in a foreign place. Several minutes passed before she saw the fuzzy outline of someone sitting by her in the darkness of the cramped space. "Walter," she said. "Walter—hold me."

Kyle placed his hand on her forehead. It was cold.

Then the attack subsided as suddenly as it had begun,

and she slept. Kyle could hear her breathing rapidly. It did not seem possible that anyone's heart could beat so fast after such a drop in temperature. Then he realized that he was hearing the quick thumping of his own heart.

Within minutes Elaine was conscious, still dopey but surprisingly composed. Kyle had seen the same look before, as a malaria-ridden patient lay becalmed after the draining night fire of fever had passed sullenly into the dawn.

The Vice-President looked around into the night, her eyes following the feeble beam of the flashlight that had replaced the dead lantern. She saw the dim shapes which only a little while before had terrified her—the cabinet, the sink, and the mocking mirror which had been a demented woman.

Slowly she recognized Kyle, then Richards, hunched by the door. She felt a cool cloth on her forehead and reached for it, but there was no strength in her arm and it fell dangling beneath the bunk. Kyle offered her a paper cup half-full of tepid water. Pushing the pillow further under her, he raised her head to a drinking position. Her throat felt bruised and cramped as she swallowed hard. She let her head slide down the pillow again, fleeing the dizziness that lay in wait for her the moment she tried to lift her body. In the edge of the flashlight's beam, she glimpsed a blurred photograph that Kyle had taken from his wallet. It was of a woman in her fifties, with graying hair and a smile which even in the poor light reflected cheerful composure. It was the kind of smile Clara Sutherland wore—a smile of unselfishness. Elaine lifted her hand weakly towards the photograph. "Your wife?" she murmured faintly, trying to take her mind off the waves of nausea which lapped tentatively about her and threatened to overwhelm her at any moment.

"Yes," answered Kyle.

"What time—"

Kyle inclined his wrist towards her. She stared at the watch but could not read the faintly luminescent dial, which appeared nothing more than a green smudge on the darkness.

"2224—ten-twenty-four," said Kyle.

"The bombers—?" she asked, seeking as much information as she could while her mind was clear. Already she was starting to hallucinate; the outlines of Kyle's face were shifting into the features of Walter Sutherland.

"They'll be here," he said.

She began vomiting, bringing up red-streaked bile.

Feeling the nausea sweeping over her, flooding her abdomen with a hot, panic-driven flush, her mind tried to take hold of something, anything, that would anchor her consciousness and quiet the whirling dizziness that was engulfing her and sucking her down into a world of fevered shadows, twisted shapes, and nightmarish confusions of sound. She could feel Walter's hand holding hers as he led her over the steaming, treacle lava and down to the cool, turquoise-swept shores. She thought of the calm green lagoons lying safely beyond, of the steady thunder of the surf casting its frothy nets over Kauai's coral strands, of the gently bending palms in the soft trade wind, of cotton-ball dabs of cumulus lazily drifting above the emerald fronds and out over the endless undulating blue.

Then the nausea swept her away in a savage wave, tearing her from his grasp and flinging her helpless and crumpled into a burning red sea. She no longer knew who or where she was. Kyle put his other hand across her body and took her far wrist, but the spasms were so severe that they shook him, and finally he had to let all his weight press down on her to prevent her from falling off the bunk.

He heard a moan in the darkness from one of the sailors in the passageway, which like the sick bay was now filled with prostrate bodies. Kyle realized that if they could not surface soon, the Vice-President of the United States and many of his crew would be dead. The human system simply could not tolerate body temperatures of 104 to 105 degrees Fahrenheit for very long.

He did not know how long he had been holding her down. It was possible that he, too, had passed out for some seconds at least. All he could remember was dreaming of Sarah and the kids. He was not sure of anything else, for the dream was constantly distorted; Sarah and Elaine seemed to be one, and yet somehow different, two reflections in a pool which in the trembling of the surface had momentarily merged into each other. But both had been smiling, and Sarah had been happier than he could ever remember. She was working in the rose garden, and then one of the roses, a vermilion-colored flower, was Elaine smiling. Sarah picked up the rose that someone had cut and left on the ground and placed it in her favorite spun-silver vase. While she stood admiring it, the rose blossomed even more, becoming more and more beautiful, and the water she poured into the vase overflowed. Kyle felt the water running down his cheek and awoke as the perspiration ran in tiny streams off his neck and face.

The fever attack again subsided, leaving Elaine gasping for breath. Kyle glanced at his watch. It was 2226. He asked Richards to watch over her as best he could. "If she starts up again," he said, "call me." He did not know what more he could do.

Although it had been only a dream, in the approaching delirium of his own fever he could not shake the feeling that Elaine and Sarah were somehow intimately connected. Though he and the Vice-President had exchanged only a few words, he felt that she could be his own daughter. Before he left the sick bay for the long trek up to the control room, he and Richards tried to tie her down, but they lacked the strength.

Dragging himself forward by sheer will, James Kyle promised a nonexistent companion that when he got back to Sarah—if he got back—he would send Elaine Horton his finest rose. She was a fine girl. A truly fine girl.

By the time he reached the control room and lowered himself to the base of the periscope column, the time was 2228. The phone buzzed. O'Brien laboriously lifted it off the cradle, dropping it on the deck and shattering the plastic earpiece. Even so, he could hear the man at the other end. O'Brien mumbled, "Yes? . . . Yes, I'll tell him." He slid to the floor against the slippery wet bulkhead. "Evers is dead."

Kyle didn't bother to look up. "When?"

"About five minutes ago. Just after you left."

Kyle mopped his neck, then let the sodden rag fall in a heap on the deck. His head was now bent forward, resting on his arms and knees. He sucked in a gulp of the fetid air. "We're just about dead on power. We'll have to go up and run for our lives on the diesel—as long as we can—if we stay—we stay down any longer without air conditioning, the heat'll finish us."

O'Brien frowned dubiously. "But the fire?"

"I know, I know. First we'll blow a hole ahead of us," Kyle was forced to rest before going on. "Then once we're up, maybe we can use the remaining torpedoes to keep the fire off us till the planes arrive. Won't give us much time,"—he paused again—"but it's better than staying here."

While Hogarth helped one of the planesmen to the controls, Kyle, wavering and having some difficulty focusing, used the periscope column to pull himself up. "Bring the forward torpedo room to the action state." To O'Brien, the slow cracked voice sounded like a judge's, passing sentence of death. Then the small telex receiver chattered in the radio room.

A few seconds later a figure half-stumbled out of the semidarkness into the control room, crashing into the captain and pushing him back roughly against the attack scope supports. The sailor took no time to apologize. "Sir—message. Air fleet. They're approaching." He shoved a message into the captain's hands. Hogarth let out a croak meant to be a cheer, slapping the planesman on the back. "Jesus Christ! It's the cavalry!"

The message read:

X COMAIRRES TO COMSUB SWORDFISH X ETA 2238 PLUS 55 X FIRE FLARES ONE MINUTE INTERVALS BEGIN 2233 PLUS 55 PST X COMAIR SENDS X

Kyle grinned triumphantly at O'Brien. "Thank God. We're going home." The radio operator started to say something, but Kyle called as loudly as he could, "Prepare to surface!" His voice was so feeble that he had to repeat the order, and the effort brought on another flurry of vertigo. He grasped the long steel column.

Hogarth by the intercom called the other compartments for reports. They were slow to respond. The captain switched on the PA system, stumbled forward and grabbed the mike, almost falling as he did so. "Now hear—now hear this. Aircraft approaching. Get off your butts."

Despite the crew's torpor, the last reports were in within seconds and Hogarth confirmed, "Ready to surface."

"Surface," ordered Kyle.

"Aye aye, sir," acknowledged Hogarth happily, instructing the auxiliaryman, "Blow one, two, four, six, seven tanks," while Kyle told O'Brien to ready the flares at the forward and aft ejectors, then turned to the radio operator.

"Watch the DF signal. Let me know the moment they're above us."

"Yes, Captain."

It was 2230 plus 15 seconds. As the submarine began its ascent, O'Brien ordered that a test flare be fired. The flare shot out from the forward ejector and opened at three thousand feet, bursting in an apple green shower of sparks. It could not be seen by any of the bombers, which were delayed slightly by the increased headwinds of the Arctic front.

Clara Sutherland handed her husband the black bow tie. She wanted to put it on for him, but these days even to be that close almost embarrassed him. Whenever she came near him, to brush off a piece of lint or to check his jacket, he felt that he should somehow acknowledge her presence with a smile, a nod—some small gesture of affection; but the more he felt this way, the angrier he became at her, as if she were deliberately being nice to him to force a response.

Worried about Elaine, the President found it difficult to concentrate on the prepared speech, short as it was, which he would have to give in reply to the sheik of Amar's toast. He glanced at his watch. By now the bombers would be nearing the submarine.

Clara looked her sophisticated best in a long cobalt blue gown patterned with small silver white fern leaves that caught the light as she moved. She opened the paua shell jewelry case that the New Zealand prime minister had given them in happier days, took out a small diamond necklace, and began to put it around her neck. Then she stopped, looking across at Walter. It was like seeing a stranger. Fatigue had aged him, etching deep lines in his face, and bitter anguish seemed to have dulled the color of his eyes. She doubted whether he could put on his public face tonight no matter how important the sheik's oil was to the United States.

Clara brought the necklace down from her throat. "Walter," she called softly.

His lips were moving as he practiced his speech in front of the mirror. Behind his reflection, she could see their separate beds. "Walter?"

"Yes?" It was the same impatient tone that he sometimes used with junior aides.

"Could you—could you do this up for me please?"

He walked over and drew the necklace quickly about her throat. Feeling the diamond chain slide up over her breast and rest coolly on her skin, Clara closed her eyes and knew that if she did not say something, she would start to feel sorry for herself again. "Do you think you should go ahead with it?—the ball, I mean? They can't expect you—"

"They have every right to expect me there. It's the sheik's last night here. He was good enough not to object to the late hour."

"I should think he wouldn't," said Clara protectively. "I really think it's inconsiderate of him to expect you to attend after—"

"Clara," began Sutherland in an exasperated voice, "I know it's ridiculous toasting people after midnight, but you know that we've done it before and we'll do it again. It comes with the job. And you know I wouldn't be doing it if it weren't so damn important. We need the oil, that's all there is to it." He pulled on his jacket. "If I didn't show up, Congress would have my head—let alone the caterers. Anyway, I'll sleep after," he said, knowing he would not sleep a minute until he knew that Elaine was safe and on her way home. There was a silence before he added, "But God knows I'll feel a hypocrite."

Clara reached behind to help him with the clip. Their fingers touched, and for a moment she felt that he was holding her hand. "There," he said, as the clasp slipped into place, and walked away.

For a moment Clara said nothing, but then, convinced she was being self-indulgent to feel hurt, she determined to change the subject.

"Why?"

"What?" he said.

"Why will you feel a hypocrite?"

"Oh, I'll be toasting the son of a bitch when I'm still cursing him for having threatened us with more oil embargoes."

There was a tap at the door.

"In."

Henricks entered, nodded at the First Lady, and handed Sutherland a cable. Sutherland brightened visibly as he scanned the message. "I want to know the second you learn anything. Don't worry about the ball."

"Yes, sir."

As Henricks withdrew, the President turned to his wife and with more than usual attention ushered her graciously out of the room before him.

"What is it?" she asked.

"The bombers. They'll be over the sub in less than ten minutes."

Clara smiled. "That's good news."

Their eyes met, not with love but still with affection. "Yes," he said, "yes, it is," and softly closed the bedroom door.

TWENTY-TWO

When the bombers began to penetrate the black oil smoke, it was Si Johnson in the lead plane who was once again the first to see the dots speckling the radar screen. For an instant, panic squeezed at his stomach. Then he checked himself and informed the captain almost casually, "A.C., there's another batch closing."

"As many as before?"

"No, but they're still thick—and flying faster. Coming in on the left forward quarter. We'll hit them over or around the target area—but not head-on."

"Aren't we lucky!" said Stokely.

Burke switched to intercell radio. "Ebony Leader to Gold and Purple. We'll have to blow another hole through this new lot quickly. Same as before. Maintain the bombing formation. Gunners, you're side-on to them this time, so watch your sixty-degree sweep, and for God's sake don't hit anyone else. We'll stick to the original plan for the bomb run. I'll start the To-Go count at a hundred and thirty seconds before estimated release time. Subject to flare verification of sub's position, count will continue using sub as offset aiming point. I'll release bombs at the end of my radar nav's fifteen-second count and on his direction. This will give the sub one point five miles' safety distance and a bombed-clear area of three by one miles to surface in and recharge its batteries. Remember, don't do anything till after we verify the sub's flare position relative to our position. We'll be visual bombing, so you'll drop your loads the moment you hear my 'pickle' drop signal. Any earlier—repeat, any earlier and you'll hit the sub. Got it?"

The other two cells acknowledged the message. Burke asked Si, "You got that, radar nav? We drop on your call and your call only."

Si answered nervously, "Yeah, I got it—fifteen-second count."

"Affirmative."

At 2232, as the bombers swept towards Cape Bingham, parts of the fire were already visible through the night sky and the curtain of black smoke that now extended for four hundred miles from north to south. At 2232 plus 7 seconds, the bombers swung round from southeast to south in a line that would pass directly over the cape and to the center of the fire, fifty to sixty miles beyond.

At 2232 plus 21 seconds, Peters notified Si Johnson that the final countdown of latitude and longitude to target had begun. "Navigator to radar nav. Final GPI. Counters are good."

"Roger."

Peters glanced at his indicators. "We're one mile off track, pilot. Make twenty degrees S turn to left."

Burke's voice was unhurried. "Roger, navigator. Taking twenty-degree S turn left."

Checking that the aircraft-to-bomb-site director system was working, Burke added, "FCI is centered. Stand by for initial point call."

Peters had the cape centered on his scope. "IP—now, crew."

Si grabbed his stopwatch, wiped the sweat from his hand, and held his thumb over the stop button as Burke chanted, "Stand by, timing crew. Ready . . . ready . . . ready . . . hack!" Si depressed the button as Peters called the captain, "Watches running. Time to release six minutes, fifty seconds."

"Captain to nav. Understand. Six minutes fifty seconds."

Si watched the cross hairs flicking, changing position on his scope. "Cross hairs going out to target area."

Burke, waiting for the birds to hit, announced calmly, "Sixty seconds gone." He had no sooner spoken than there was a thud on the fuselage. Si reported,

"Target area direct at 176 degrees, 56 miles. Reported sub position as offset aiming point is at 176 degrees, 54.4 miles."

Peters, knowing that at this speed three seconds would account for half a mile, was busily verifying that the sub would be at least one and a half miles away from the first bomb that would fall during the thirty-second, three-mile-long release period. "That checks. Offset at 176 degrees, 54.4 miles."

As they approached the sub's position, they could see the flames leaping two to three hundred feet up from the sea towards them. "Holy Toledo!" said Stokely. "The whole fucking sea's on fire."

Burke's voice snapped over the intercom. "Shut up, gunner!"

Two or three more birds thudded against the plane as Si reported, "Looks good direct. Offset coming in."

At 2234 plus 6 seconds, the cannons opened up again, filling the air with tracer as the main mass of birds began to strike the wave. As the bodies began to smack into the fuselage again, cold sweat ran down inside Si's flying suit. His voice was strained as he struggled desperately to keep calm. "Radar nav to pilot. I'm in-bomb now, pilot. Center the FCI."

"Roger. FCI centered."

Next Si spoke to Peters. "Disconnect release circuits."

"Release circuits disconnected."

The noise was like thousands of claws scratching and tearing at the fuselage as pieces of ripped metal flapped wildly in the slipstream. Si could hear again the torn wings and tail flapping over Hué, his voice intoning the same deadly litany. "Connected light on . . . 'on' light on . . ."

Peters's voice came in from far away. "Bomb door control valve lights?" Si could hear the gunner over Hué. But just as his eyes started to go out of focus, he caught sight of the instruments dancing frantically before him.

For the first time, Peters's voice had a ring of frightened urgency, repeating, "Bomb door control valve lights?"

"Off!" answered Si.

Almost over the target area, with the birds still hammering into the wave like a phalanx of antiaircraft missiles, the copilot's voice came in on the intercom. "Where the hell's that flare?"

Hogarth called off the depth. "Forty-five feet . . . forty feet . . . thirty-five feet . . ." Kyle stared above him. It was 2236. At thirty feet, Sparks advised him, "They're three minutes from us, Captain."

"Very good. Mr. O'Brien, fire another flare."

"Fire green flare," repeated O'Brien, his voice carrying to the aft ejector room.

"Green flare away!"

The flare erupted from the sub, streaked toward the surface, burst through the burning slick, and exploded in a green star-shower at two thousand feet.

Unable to see anything beyond the bloodied windshield, Burke strained to look through the side panels, announcing, "To Go—driving 130 seconds."

Peters checked the ground speed. "Doppler looks good." Burke began the initial count, which would be taken up by Si Johnson at 0 minus 15. "125 To Go . . . 75 TG . . . 60 TG . . . 50 TG . . . I see the flare. Copilot, check relative position."

"Roger. Relative position checks out. Resume your count."

"30 TG . . . 20 TG . . . FCI centered."

Peters raised his voice as the cannonade suddenly increased. The plane took a dozen or so more hits in such quick succession that it seemed any more impacts would penetrate the fuselage. Already one engine was out.

As he said, "Bomb doors coming open," Peters was watching the myriad dials before him, praying that none of the air ducts would be fouled up and cause overheating malfunctions. So intent was he that he failed to notice the glazed look on Si's face. Nor did he notice that Si, crouched over the visual bombsight ready to take the final count, was shaking violently, his hands clamped rigid to the side controls of his seat.

As Si took up the count, "15 seconds . . . 14 . . . 13 . . . ," he could no longer hear birds striking the aircraft, but only antiaircraft fire exploding all around him and the voice of the gunner screaming, "Drop 'em, Si—drop 'em—let's get the hell—" and instead of the cross hairs intersecting over the blood red ocean below him, all he could see was the gunner's headless body. His voice began to slur, " 'leven . . . ten . . . nie . . ."

Burke didn't worry. He madc a mental note to have the intercom overhauled, and then with the conditioned reflex of over a hundred missions, he flipped up the safety cover from the bomb release. He could barely hear Si.

"Eigh . . . sev—"

The plane shuddered violently, buffeted by the strong fire winds. Burke gripped the yoke with all his strength and lost the count. He would have to depend on Si. But all Si Johnson could hear was the gunner screaming, "Drop 'em, Si, drop 'em!" and so he called, "Bombs away!" Burke pressed the release button. "Roger," he acknowledged. "Pickle! Pickle! Pickle!"

The moment they heard the first "pickle" of his drop signal, the other six captains simultaneously released their loads.

It was only as the long black sticks of explosive began falling in unison towards the sea that Peters, glancing at his stopwatch, realized what had happened. "Jesus Christ!" he yelled, turning on Si. "You didn't finish the count! You dropped them too early! You stupid bastard—you dropped them too early—you didn't finish—Jesus Christ!"

Si didn't hear him. All he could hear were the gunners still firing—over Hué. Now the missile would not hit them . . .

As the first of the bombs burst around her, the *Swordfish*'s pressure hull imploded. Within three seconds, tons of boiling white water cascaded through massive punctures fore and aft as the crew, working as fast as their weakened condition would allow, tried to close the three-hundred-pound watertight doors. In the engine room, amid a twisted tangle of ripping steel and the screaming of ruptured steam pipes, two men struggled to dislodge a floating mattress that had prevented the compartment's forward door from being sealed, but with a long, hollow roar, a torrent from the after end surged through and swept them forward like driftwood. As the bombs kept falling in crisscrossing chains of explosions, the submarine plunged, rose, shivered violently, and broke in two, its skin still buckling as it disappeared in a black shroud of dieseline.

From the air, all the pilots could see through the smoke were the multiple blushes of explosions followed by towering spumes of oil and water shooting skywards, interspersed with long, red fingers of flame.

Gradually, as the bombers turned away and disappeared into the far darkness, the sound of their engines was swallowed by a more distant roar. Sections of the firespill were already creeping back like pariah dogs to the carcass, and a burning lifejacket marked H.M.C.S. *Swordfish,* along with billions of particles of oil, was snatched from the sea and sucked skywards by one of the wind storms, generated by the fierce heat of the spill that ripped across its molten surface. The life jacket soon fell back to the sea, but the tiny oil particles continued on their southward journey, driven hard by the Arctic front that had failed to extinguish the fire.

TWENTY-THREE

Henricks received the message just as the President rose before the glittering assembly of distinguished guests.

Sutherland took up the sparkling glass of amber catawba juice—the sheik, being a Moslem, naturally drank no alcohol—and smiled graciously at his guest and briefly at the Arab leader's entourage. He coughed slightly. "Your Excellency," he began, "on behalf of the people of the United States I would like to welcome you to our country. I know that you studied here in your university days and are no stranger to our customs—or, I might add, to our problems. Your earlier association with us is, I'm sure, a . . ."

The speech was the usual official address, full of sugary platitudes and punctuated by polite, intermittent applause, ending in a toast to the visiting head of state. Sutherland found it much easier than usual, for in spite of his worries he had been relieved to discover, during the brief, pretoast chatter, that he liked the sheik. It was a pleasant change from the usual diplomatic pretension, which he would have found particularly trying this evening. He was pleased now that he had insisted on keeping the long-planned engagement.

Nearby, Henricks had hesitated long enough. He tapped the President on the shoulder and passed him the cable. The sheik, immaculately bearded and resplendent in flowing white gown and gold-braided burnous, rose to respond to his American host. "Mr. President, distinguished guests . . ."

Sutherland heard nothing the sheik said. Clara

turned to him as he finished reading the cable and took his hand. It was icy. Still smiling courteously at the sheik, she moved her other hand across her lap and cupped it about her husband's. The sheik continued his speech, pausing now and then to smile at the President and the First Lady. Finally he stopped and looked down at the President, whose gaze was lost upon the rows of indistinguishable faces that crowded the ballroom. The sheik's eyes darted towards Clara, who smiled back, wondering just what the cable had said. She reached for her glass with one hand and squeezed the President's unresponsive fingers with the other, desperately cueing him to rise. There were a few embarrassed coughs from the audience. Henricks stepped forward into television range. "The toast, Mr. President."

Sutherland's eyes met his blankly in a fog of nonrecognition. Henricks was close to panic; this had the makings of an international incident. He knew for sure that that bitch from United Press was here. After what seemed to Henricks an interminable silence, the President rose slowly and clinked glasses, robotlike, with the sheik. Jean Roche, meanwhile, had hurriedly convinced the TV director to focus on the guests in the far corner of the room.

Immediately after protocol had been satisfied, the President stood up again. Placing both hands on the table's edge and holding on with all his strength, he began in an almost inaudible voice, "Ladies and gentlemen. I have a very grave announcement. I have just received a message informing me—"

Henricks pushed forward and placed a hand over the microphone. "Mr. President."

Sutherland turned slowly. "Yes?"

Henricks lowered his voice. "The Canadians haven't been notified as yet."

By this time the audience was alive with the murmur of speculation. The President continued to look at Henricks. The aide added quickly, "We should call a press conference, Mr. President—in half an hour—an hour. Ottawa will have been informed by then. We should make a joint announcement. There were over eighty Canadians."

"Killed?"

"Yes, Mr. President."

Sutherland nodded slowly, then left the table. Clara quickly followed. At the same time, following Jean Roche's instructions, waiters streamed out of the kitchen and rushed to refill glasses.

Inside the gloomy study there was silence. Henricks withdrew. Beyond the window overlooking the lawn, the red and blue lights still flashed and a policeman's voice could be heard nasally echoing from a bullhorn.

Clara sat down beside the President. "I love you," she said. "I'm so sorry, Walter."

"I know," he said and went to the window to be alone.

After making love, Fran Lambrecker flicked on the TV to watch the late show, went back to bed, started to munch the potato chips Morgan had brought along with the mix, and began drinking her second martini, having disposed of the olive in decadent Roman style, sucking it down into her mouth like a spider swallowing a trapped fly. Morgan was soaking in the bath, accompanied by a tall gin and tonic.

After the news flash that all hands aboard the sub had been lost, Fran put her glass down and sat still for a long time against the plush headboard, idly picking at her teeth. She felt she should cry, but she could not. She had never been the crying type. She knew the proper thing to do, the decent thing to do, was to cry, to pack up immediately, to go back to Victoria, to dress in black, to arrange a service, and to stop seeing Morgan for a while. But the truth was that her deepest emotion on hearing the news account was a vague sense of loss—like having been unexpectedly informed that a onetime friend who'd stopped writing for no apparent reason had died some weeks before.

Suddenly she called out, "Morgan!"

There was no sound. She yelled out again, "Morgan!" adding in a low tone, "you pig."

There was a splashing like that of a startled seal, and soon Morgan, still dripping, a towel round his stomach, shuffled to the door.

"Yeah, Fran—what's up?"

"Turn off the TV."

He shrugged and moved over to the TV, trying to kick the long, tripping towel away from his toes.

"Yeah?" he said, ready for the next order. She looked over at him. "How did you ever become an officer?"

Morgan grinned. "Personality, I guess."

Her laugh was half sneer. "Come here," she said. As he reached her, she put her right arm about his shoulder and pushed her left fist slowly into his groin.

"Jesus Christ," he said, "not again?"

She looked at him fiercely. "Why—can't you do it, wittle man?"

"Well we just . . . sure, I guess—"

"Come on," she commanded, and flung the blanket aside. After a time, when they began moving together, she closed her eyes and pulled at him. "Come on!"

She knew it was wrong. Everyone would say it wasn't normal. But she didn't care and she wasn't going to pretend. She was going to be herself. What she felt was an enormous and quite overwhelming sense of relief.

The Tlingit village was no more. Unable to find a boat or to attract Sitka's attention through the dense smoke that had blown ahead and enveloped them on the east coast of Kruzof Island, the Indian band had burned to death on the southern perimeter of Mud Bay.

Nothing could stop the fire's advance, not even the dynamite charges bravely thrown from the armada of small boats or tossed by pilots further up the sound as they made their final runs out.

The mass of burning oil had slid through the maze of green islands, setting them ablaze, and was now closing in on the town of Sitka.

From the north, the red black spill had moved

quickly on the tide down through Neva Strait and Sukoi Inlet, meeting and slowing in the wider waters of Krestof Sound, pushing on through Mud Bay, picking up speed in Hayward Strait, and slowing again as it flowed into the northern reaches of Sitka Sound, spreading out as one arm in the spill's pincer movement against Sitka. From the southeast, the fire's southern flank had sealed off the passage between Kruzof and Baranof islands, blocking the only other entrance to the sound.

Most terrifying of all to the last of the evacuees waiting for the helicopters to return was the speed with which the flames leapt onto the Bieli Rocks and the other small islands dotted across the sound. The fire flowed up to them, licked tentatively at their shores for a second, then swallowed them as if they had never been there.

By now most of the four thousand people of Sitka had been evacuated during the frantic air shuttle to Petersburg, ninety-three miles eastwards on Mitkof Island, and to large evacuation centers on Wrangell Island and Hyder on the mainland.

The last ones out silently watched as the two arms of the fire joined in common invasion. Even above the noise of the aircraft, the evacuees could hear the chain reaction of explosions from the clustered fishing boats in Crescent Bay as they disintegrated like so many toy models in the bright orange blanket that was now racing across the mouth of Indian River, leaping ashore, and spreading rapidly through the summer-dried timber. Soon the onion dome of St. Michael's was engulfed in the flames which danced hundreds of feet into the air from the ruins of the nave as if in obscene celebration. Along the streets, power cables that had been kept alive to provide light for the last evacuees writhed across the road, sparking and jumping amongst the debris, while burst water pipes sprayed impotently.

Within an hour the fire, fanned by its own wind system, had completely gutted the city, covering the charred but still-burning skeletons of buildings with a cloud reeking of oil fumes, burned fish from the crumpled cannery, and the heavy, sweet stink that floated up from the ashes of the pulp mill.

And still the fire kept burning, moving now towards the steep, timbered slopes behind the charred ruins of the town, riding on the stiffening north wind.

Traveling at around fifty miles per hour at five to seven thousand feet, the warm air, laden with billions of fine oil particles driven skywards by the firespill, had taken sixteen hours—till past midnight—to reach the cold front that now lay across the dark blur of Vancouver Island. As the warm air began to cool and moisture rapidly condensed about the nuclei of oil particles, Sarah was still sitting alone in the kitchen. The phone, which she had not replaced properly on the cradle, was giving out the dull, persistent burr of the dial tone, its mechanical droning insectlike in the silent bungalow.

A gust of wind howled through the close-leafed rose garden and banged a swing window shut. Instinctively, she got up and locked the window securely. She stood there, not knowing where else to go or what to do. She dimly recalled that the admiral—it had been he who had rung—had said something about sending someone out first thing in the morning to arrange things and to give her a hand. She had no idea how they thought they could help her. Several more gusts tore into the garden, shaking the bushes with such ferocity that Sarah's attention was finally arrested by the sound. She moved slowly to the kitchen door and switched on the porch light. It struck her that if the floodlight went out, she wouldn't know how to fix it. There was something you had to unscrew, some wire mesh or shield you had to take off, before you could change the bulb, and she didn't know how to do it.

Soon she could hear the rain drumming on the roof, and panic took hold. She raced out to the covered porch, pulled on her long rubber boots, picked up the pruning shears, and ran towards the garden. They had done this before—rescued the garden together, goading each other in happy competition to save as many flowers as possible before the squall smashed them.

But now, in the garden, she was confused, expecting him to be there, not knowing which bed to attend to first. She started towards the Nocturnes. A strong gust temporarily blinded her with a rush of rain and she slipped and fell heavily on the border.

When she could see again, she reached for a small Nocturne rose, but it was already in tatters, its velvet-soft petals disintegrating even as she held it gently between her fingers. Not only was it tattered almost beyond recognition, but it was as black as the night about her. It was only then that Sarah realized that the rain was black and stank of crude petroleum. She did not understand why, for she could not see the long crimson line advancing southwards through the night. Suddenly she realized that she would never see him again. Standing alone in the storm, she began to sob helplessly at its unfathomable fury.

ABOUT THE AUTHOR

IAN SLATER lives in Vancouver, British Columbia. He has written a number of radio plays for the CBC, magazine articles, and stories, as well as several unproduced screenplays. *Firespill* is his first published book.